SPYFUNK!

....

EDITED BY
MILTON J. DAVIS

MVmedia, LLC
Fayetteville, GA

MVmedia, LLC
PO Box 143052
Fayetteville, GA 30214
www.mvmediaatl.com

Publisher's Note: This is a work of fiction. Names, characters, places, and incidents are a product of the author's imagination. Locales and public names are sometimes used for atmospheric purposes. Any resemblance to actual people, living or dead, or to businesses, companies, events, institutions, or locales is completely coincidental.

Cover Art by Sean Hill
Cover Design by Uraeus
Book Layout ©2017 BookDesignTemplates.com

Ordering Information:
Quantity sales. Special discounts are available on quantity purchases by corporations, associations, and others. For details, contact the "Special Sales Department" at the address above.

Spyfunk!/ Various Authors. -- 1st ed.
ISBN No.: 979-8-9857336-0-0

contents

To The Black Dispatches

Spy School

John F. Allen

If Oxford Jameson had his way, he'd have wooed her, determined what she knew, double-tapped her, and been done with it.

However, his assignment was to retrieve and copy the data, destroy the original, and do so without incident—*if possible*. This would prove to be a much more complicated mission because the Brits decided to send one of their top MI6 agents to the party.

This particular agent graduated at the top of her class at HMS Raleigh and had worked several years in British Intelligence, according to her dossier. Aisha Zewde was a standout in the MI6, with dozens of successful missions to her credit.

She was known within the international espionage community as the Secretary—named for the rare, and beautiful, African bird of prey.

As he walked through the throng of partygoers—a Cuban Cohiba in hand—he picked out ambassadors, foreign dignitaries, world leaders, and at least a dozen people at the top of the Interpol red list.

Jameson grabbed a cocktail glass of cognac from the serving tray of an elderly waiter as he brushed past him. He scanned the expansive ballroom in the palatial residence owned by their host, Bartok Varga.

Varga was a Hungarian national who was the suspected leader of the Shadow Legion, an international cabal dedicated to influencing foreign governments and manipulating world events. He had intel which he intended to use for manipulation of foreign energy markets and political influence. This could disrupt the balance of power across Europe and parts of Asia and was something the US could not allow to happen.

If MI6 had one of their agents there, it only made sense that the intel he'd been tasked with retrieving contained something the SIS wanted kept to themselves. The Crown obviously had similar objectives as the US, as they were cooperating nations. But some of their dealings with other European nations weren't meant to be shared, even with allies. In this instance, whoever gained access to the intel first would share redacted intelligence with the other.

Zewde made her way up a large marble staircase; he followed. She made her way through the crowd, champagne flute in hand, and headed toward a balcony off the second-floor promenade.

Jameson studied her as she sauntered past the sparse attendees along the walkway to stand alone on the large mezzanine.

The flawless ebony skin on her back glistened in the moonlight. She wore a blue, backless, sapphire satin gown which accentuated every curve of her backside. Her hair was a series of tight, jet-black Bantu knots. Silver stiletto sandals gave her about an even six feet in height. A stunning diamond necklace hung around her long neck with a matching bracelet on her wrist. The Brits were selling her cover story as an African diamond heiress to the hilt.

She was elegant, regal, and absolutely gorgeous. The aroma of expensive perfume mingled with the salt water–tinged air, from the waves which crashed against the jagged rocks below them. The ample balcony of the spacious palatial structure built into a cliff overlooked the Mediterranean Sea.

"If I picked you out of this crowd so easily, Varga's security detail certainly will, sooner or later," Oxford said as he stepped up beside her.

She smirked as she avoided looking in his direction.

* * *

Zewde noticed the American as soon as he entered the residence.

He was tall with a fresh crew cut, a neatly trimmed moustache, and an impeccably tailored black tuxedo. His hazel eyes contrasted brightly against his onyx complexion. According to the intelligence report she had read on him; he was the top agent out of Langley.

Oxford Jameson was a former US Navy SEAL, cut his teeth as an FBI agent before he switched organizations and landed with the CIA as an analyst. A sudden change in his status and he seemed to disappear for five years. Shortly after, he popped up on the international espionage community radar as a field operative.

Jameson was extremely charming and handsome. He had an athletic build with a refined but rugged look. His reputation as a ladies' man was well known throughout the intelligence community, especially amongst the female operatives.

She figured that he would attempt to seduce her and extract any information he could, all the while unsuspecting that she would actually be seducing him. If she had her way, she would bed him and dead him. All for queen and country, of course.

Zewde noticed the elderly server she got her champagne from roaming the promenade. He wore spectacles and carried a serving tray of assorted cocktail glasses, champagne flutes, and hors d'oeuvres. He appeared to be in his mid to late sixties and reminded her of Desmond Tutu.

"You Americans are so bloody arrogant. Your reputation precedes you, Mr. O'Kono, or should I say Agent Oxford Jameson. What's the saying your country has about *the pot* and *the kettle?*"

A shallow grin crept across Jameson's face. "Touché, Mrs. Erika Pennington, billionaire diamond heiress, or should I say Agent Aisha Zewde."

Zewde gave Jameson a brief sidelong glance. Her body language was graceful and guarded.

"So, now that informal introductions have been made, I suppose we've reached the precipice of our mutual due diligence and now find ourselves at odds with one another," Zewde said.

Jameson snickered, "A very astute observation, Ms. Zewde. However, I don't see us being at odds with each other at all."

Zewde turned and faced him with an incredulous glare. "And exactly what the bloody hell is that supposed to mean, Jameson?"

Jameson took a pull from his cognac before he took a drag from his cigar and set them both on the balcony rail. He took a step toward her, wrapped his arms around her, and kissed her passionately, "While we've been having this enlightening and entertaining tete-a-tete, I've been uploading Varga's bank statements, personal ledgers, shipping manifests, and a lot more." He pulled a small device with a flashing green light from his jacket breast pocket.

Zewde placed her right hand on his chest as she pursed her lips and sighed. "Perhaps MI6 underestimated the CIA and I underestimated you."

She splashed the contents of her champagne flute into Jameson's face, tossed the glass over the balcony, and aimed a vertical punch toward his solar plexus. He barely misdirected her aim to just beneath his right pectoral to avoid the effects of her strike. Jameson was taken off-guard for a split second, which was long enough for Zewde to grab the device from his hand.

"Or perhaps we had anticipated the US obtaining access to the data first only for us to take it from you," Zewde taunted.

Zewde and Jameson stood several feet apart, both in fighting stances, muscles coiled like springs and a determined look in their eyes. Zewde had slid the device into her clutch bag, secured the wrist strap, and held it in her left hand in a defensive manner.

Zewde chuckled. "You Americans talk too much. Now I have the data and you have to report back to your handlers empty-handed."

"Is that so." Jameson smirked as he held his left arm forward and used his right thumb and forefinger to squeeze the sides of his gold Longines watch.

Two small barbs shot out of Jameson's watch toward Zewde. She managed to catch them with her clutch. The projectiles were charged with enough electricity to stun an average adult male, she assumed. Jameson pressed his attack and grabbed her left wrist with his right hand in an attempt to wrestle the clutch bag from her.

Zewde took the opportunity to raise her left knee toward his groin, which he shifted his body to avoid. She grabbed the wrist of the hand that held hers and turned her body 180 degrees. Zewde used her ample buttocks to ram Jameson and dipped down to throw him over her back.

* * *

Jameson found himself going over the balcony handrail but managed to grab ahold of the concrete bottom rail with his left hand to avoid plummeting to his death from the three-hundred-foot drop down to the jagged, sea-soaked rocks below.

He watched as Zewde leaned over the handrail with a smirk.

"How's it hanging, Mr. Jameson? Well, guess I'll be going now. Feel free to drop in," she said.

Jameson smirked. "Sure, but aren't you forgetting something?"

He held the device in his right hand; the light was then a steady green. He quickly slid it into his outside jacket pocket.

Zewde reached over to grab his wrist, but he had let go of the bottom rail and seemed to disappear into the darkness below.

She looked around and saw that the other guests were preoccupied, so she ripped her gown away and kicked off her sandals. Zewde pressed the largest diamond in her necklace, and in seconds, a black nanotech bodysuit covered her from head to toe. It was sleek and extremely non-reflective in the moon's glow, perfect for stealth. She reached into the clutch bag, pulled out a small set of night-vision goggles.

Zewde put on the googles, took a small pistol from the clutch bag, and attached it to the nanotech belt on her bodysuit. She detached the wrist strap from her clutch bag and stretched it out to a length of about five feet. Zewde attached the bag to her belt, and it morphed into a black utility pouch.

She picked up her right sandal, attached the strap to the sole, and wrapped it around the balcony handrail. Zewde pulled it taut, held on to the strap, and leapt over the side of the rail.

She landed on another mezzanine below, which led to a pitch-black room. Zewde donned her night-vision goggles which cut through the darkness as she crept slowly and scanned the room.

In an instant, someone she assumed to be Jameson grabbed her from behind. She wrestled in his grasp, but he had the advantage for the moment.

Loud footsteps and shouting came from outside of the room's doors before a half dozen figures in black military fatigues entered the room. Each one was armed with an AK-47 rifle aimed at them.

Before either could react, a shimmer flashed across their eyes and transformed the pitch-black room where Zewde, Jameson, and an unknown man stood.

Jameson released Zewde as she crumpled to the floor. Four blurry, holographic images of people hung against the far wall from them.

"What the bloody hell, Jameson? Is this more of your American subterfuge?" Zewde demanded as she rose to her feet and removed her goggles.

Jameson turned his head and stared his rival down with a hard, sidelong glance, "Me? This looks more like some of your MI6 hijinks to me."

One of the holographs spoke. "We are not working on the behalf of MI6 or the CIA, but both organizations are well represented here."

The blurred holographs coalesced into sharp images of three men and one woman. Zewde looked over at Jameson with a raised eyebrow, which he returned in kind.

Zewde recognized the director of MI6, Helen Northington, whose pleasant expression, in her experience, belied her true feelings as always. She also identified Jideofor Awuzie, director of the National Intelligence Agency, the Nigerian intelligence Organization, and Harlan Jacobs, director of the CIA.

The third image from the left spoke. "I'm sure you are familiar with the directors of your respective organizations, as well as Mr. Awuzie. My name is Director Elijah Bishop of the Global Espionage Network of Elite Supernatural Intelligence and Surveillance—*also known as* GENESIS."

Bishop appeared as a middle-aged Black man with an olive complexion, coal-black hair slicked back on his head, and a pencil-thin moustache. His features were pleasant, but his eyes held a predatory look, like a snake preparing to strike.

"Okay, so, now that we've established who everyone is, where are we and why are we here?" Jameson asked.

"Agent Jameson, you aren't in any particular position to exhibit any bravado here," Director Jacobs asserted, his ruddy-complexioned face resembling a pig.

Jameson smirked and said, "With all due respect, I'm the one who's holding the intel," as he pulled the device from his jacket pocket.

Jacobs chuckled. "Son, you ain't got dick!"

Jameson began to counter but was stopped short by Zewde smugly averring, "That's because while the American playboy was randy for a shag, I copied his data-drive intel and erased it afterward."

Zewde reached into her clasp bag and produced a tube of lipstick, which was actually a sophisticated thumb drive.

Director Northington stared at her field operative and shook her head with weary disgust. "I'm afraid the intel you retrieved was compromised, Agent Zewde."

Zewde failed to hide her astonished expression, "But, ma'am…"

Director Northington flashed her a stern frown. Her porcelain skin tensed, and her ice-blue eyes narrowed, "Not another word, Agent Zewde. We shall address this further once you've returned to SIS."

"Yes, ma'am," Zewde said, crestfallen.

"Each of you were given an assignment to retrieve information from Hungarian nationalist Bartok Varga. He is the target of a high-profile Interpol operation, which GENESIS has been involved in for almost two years. We devised a holographic training scenario to assess your actions in the field. Five months ago, you were unknowingly ensconced from your residences and placed in a holographic virtual-reality simulation. Since that time, we've been observing you," Bishop said.

Director Jacobs frowned. "Agent Jameson and Agent Zewde were given dossiers on each other in order to test their actions in the field. Their proclivities and predilections for bravado, diving headfirst into the unknown, lack of planning and sexual manipulation notwithstanding. Attributes which, despite being made popular in Hollywood spy films, do not produce results in the *real world*."

Awuzie spoke next. "Unbeknownst to you *show-boaters*, the NIA had our operative infiltrate the premises well in advance of your arrivals. He had a deep cover, which he had spent months developing, and disguised himself to be easily ignored."

Awuzie's bald head reflected the light from wherever he was, as did his thin-framed eyeglasses. His dark brown eyes were large and matched his skin complexion. Awuzie appeared to be in his late fifties, with a thin face and handsome features.

Jameson and Zewde both turned to the other figure standing next to them in the room. They looked at each other and then to the holographs. "The old waiter," they said in unison.

Awuzie and Bishop smirked, while Jacobs and Northington sneered.

The elderly waiter straightened his posture and began carefully removing the prosthetic facial applications, gray-haired wig, and glasses. When he finished, he appeared as a nondescript, average-looking Nigerian man in his late twenties.

"Yes, Agent Kwento Adebayo is our top recruit and was hand-selected to this assignment by President Buhari himself," Awuzie said.

Adebayo nodded humbly at the NIA director.

"Once Agent Adebayo had secured his cover identity, he assessed the residence and immediately identified Jameson and Zewde as undercover agents. He came into brief contact with Jameson and switched devices," Bishop said.

Jameson frowned in silence as he caught a glance at Zewde's crestfallen face out of his peripheral vision.

"While you two were hem-hawing around playing footsie, Adebayo was executing *real* espionage," Jacobs said.

"Agents Jameson and Zewde, while your fighting and survival skills make you formidable agents, the lack of subtlety and subterfuge makes you poor candidates for further intelligence assignments at this time. For now, you are to report back to your respective organizations' headquarters immediately for remedial training. You're being taken out of the field until further notice."

Jameson and Zewde stood rigid in silence before they responded affirmatively to the disembodied faces and left the room through an open portal.

Adebayo took up the rear.

"Not you, Mr. Adebayo," Director Bishop said.

Adebayo stopped and returned to the center of the room and stood at attention. "Yes, sir."

"Your actions in the field were exemplary, Agent," Awuzie said. "The NIA is very pleased. And, though they do not know it, our country is indebted to you."

"I am grateful," Adebayo replied. "But sir, may I ask what's next?"

Awuzie pursed his lips. "I will allow Director Bishop to explain." The NIA leader's image shimmered and disappeared, as did those of Jacobs and Northington.

Bishop smirked. "Agent Adebayo, you will report to GENESIS HQ at oh six hundred hours tomorrow for extensive training. A briefing packet has been sent to your secure communications portal. Please read it thoroughly once you've returned to your hotel."

"Yes, sir," Adebayo replied as he turned to leave.

"Oh, and one more thing. Congratulations, Mr. Adebayo; welcome to Spy School!"

She Loves How He Glows

Eugen Bacon

It's a night of black flies, soft-bodied and bioluminescent, dancing their lights in a hunt or a woo. They're not the dead, no mark of a djinn branded on their foreheads. These ones walk in plain daylight. Some of them are green-leafed, pregnant with a shimmering mould. The rest are glistening with morning dew, silhouettes of bodies, holes where hearts should be.

But they all have cerulean eyes. Where they appear, birds refuse to sing, and fall from the sky. Fish float belly-up in the river. The undead stagger and prowl in leaves and dew, to and from the city of lights, to, fro, as village men and women worry their naps into nightmares until the staggerers stop prowling. Instead, they dig and step into graves scattered with fermented yams and false beer made from bush beans, not the mopane berries.

Chief Ade put the tokens inside dig-outs. Now she calls out a name,

> watches as the
> unbranded burst into
> flames, lit by—
> what was it?
> cerulean eyes.

Chief Ade wonders if Weightman has anything to do with this, since she refused his hand—sure, she's widowed eons now, but *him*? If he were an animal, Weightman would be a hyena. Cunning, greedy, a pack animal. She'd never know how to navigate life with such a man. He's an excitement machine who commands adulation. Many a village woman would leap at the chance—isn't he a ruler of the city of lights? See how it glows.

But it's a city that sends out mischief, instigated by aliens who visited, splashed it with luminescence. No one saw the visitation. The exaggeration of the intruders' lustre and tallness is a myth, greater or lesser reliant on who's telling it.

...twinkled like shooting stars—
...loftier than the oldest baobabs—

It's possible that Weightman *did* cut a deal with some foreign government. His city shimmers with lights no village has seen. If a pact were struck, what Weightman got out of it Chief Ade is yet to comprehend. As far as she knows, he made a deal with the devil, one she's not inclined to follow suit for her village of Kitale.

Sometimes she feels abandoned. She wishes her daughters were here in the village. Tele, the nurse, is working at a university hospital in Tongi town. Celestina, the case worker, is with the UN in a refugee camp up north in Safura for villagers fleeing the undead.

Having accomplished her magic that rids the village from unwelcome intruders, Chief Ade is not searching for truth on her way home from the river.

But the flies are restless, fast forward, slow backward, splicing the forest here, there just so. She sees in them lost children, all strays. In fact, six of them drop to the ground and claim their human form. She's at ease; they're too young to be emissaries. They are wet to their heads with the water's mud. They flee her approach, vanish behind a shrub, and then another.

Each journey begins with a step, and what she feels as she treads after the children is not going or returning. It's simply enlightenment. Hers is a promise to the gods of the trees, the goddesses of the rivers, that each child will be okay at dawn, shushed from the angry buzz of glows in a hunt or a woo

that's not funny,
may be dangerous,
and never sacred.

The forest is bigger inside than it looks at the elbows
where it starts. It pipes and whistles, blows its nose. It
points to a space, a souvenir from the centuries, and in it is
a yeti. Chief Ade blinks and the yeti is gone, just shapes
and shapes of twilight that look down with scars, owl song,
and spent acorns.

Finally, the children step out from behind a whistling
thorn tree. Quintuplets. They're spike-haired ragamuffins,
nudging at each other—who'll approach first? She peers for
the sixth. She can see the lovegrass on his head, the child
not so well hidden. He finally peels from a bush. He's a
pot-bellied toddler—well, he looks like one. She suspects
he's five to ten. He has the river blindness and looks like a
missing key.

He approaches as if with eyes. He gropes in the air but
knows exactly how and where to reach her. Her heart sug-
ars with love for the cheeky imp, and the rest now taking
turns to touch her hem.

She speaks softly to them, and then hums. Hers is a
mother's voice reminiscing about egg yolks and chicks,
nothing remaining but an omelette. She remembers when
she was a child how she looked everyone in the eye, so curious, like this one, the toddler, who can't look but can
touch. She wants to turn away, slip away, but it's impossible in the glow of his interest that swallows her restraint.
Never has longing been so bright,
so tangible she can
trace it with her finger
to forever yours
in response to
cherry ripeness.

With her dead husband—he was a kind man she
couldn't save with herbs and chants, her dear leopard,

keen-minded, fearless and free—and without her daughters, free and grown to chase professions, her life has been lonely. She needs something, someone...

She looks at the boy. This child can help her make the transition. After all, he's picked her. She can unpick him any time.

The children topple in glee down the dusty road where the forest thins and gives in to a scatter of huts, some of burnt-brick walls and corrugated iron roofs, others of mud and thatch. Closer to the village, they slow and lag behind, all the way to her boma, what's left of home: an enclosure with her two cows, three goats, seven chickens, and now six children.

Already she can see hut doors opening, lanterns flickering. Curiosity lurching her way with sufficient intent. She leaves the news for the village gossips. Mish-mashed rumours, distorted, twisted inside out. They are stories about her widowhood, stories about her daughters—the first educated women to leave the village. Myths and legends on the source of her magic. They trusted her late husband because he was a man, one of them. Chief Ade? Not so much. They don't know how to contain her difference, living alone and sending girls to school. But the village welcomes her magic, is curious about it. They can't wait to get a fingernail into her life. Understandably, after all, she's their chief.

She feels waylaid, attacks on her widowhood from within, without. The morning will come with its rituals:

How are the cows? a villager will poke their head into the boma and ask.

The cows are well, she'll answer. *How are the goats?*

One is carrying a child, thank gods, the villager will say.

Tell us about your visitors, someone will finally venture.

She has no answer for them. *A gift from the forest—the goddess of the trees still giving.*

Ebo, they will accept her explanation. She's the chief.

Some visitors don't arrive for news carried in the hollow words of a greeting. They're scavengers, visiting daily, bringing along a calabash to carry leftovers home. For this very reason, Chief Ade has a potful of crushed pomegranate seeds. She sun-dries them, bakes them in hot ashes, finally pounds them. Mixed with water, they form a good paste that cooks into a meal, plenteous for leftovers. Sporadically she brings out mopane beer, but this is rare. Mostly, her special ferment might come out when a villager is bereaved or going through a difficulty—like the mother of thirteen mouths, whose husband was thinking to leave.

#

Days, then weeks pass with her new children. They chase after her to the river. She goes to find inner peace but also to inspect her borders. As the children splash about, Chief Ade harvests quiet, disquiet in forgotten speech swallowed in the halfway river that will never feel an animated stream's touch—just visits from the village gossips who talk about solitude, fear, curses, and witchcraft, even though there's nothing to start a rumour about. Knowing magic is not a wrongdoing, and it protects the village from the undead ones with cerulean eyes.

At night when all lanterns are out and the hut is closed to the full moon, Chief Ade can still pick out the little one. He's lightly snoring on a kudu skin closest to the warming embers of the three hearthstones. She smiles. Wonders at how she didn't know she needed him until she saw him. Her language is now empty, no personality or experience. What's the message in its dialect, undancing in its gaps?

As with every mother, she has a favourite. He's the big-eyed toddler, not so much the quintuplets, not even Tele or Celestina. He's haired with weeping lovegrass—that's what his hair feels like. It attaches itself to everything, mostly her clothes of tempered bark. It's hair that falls, regrows. Full of fibre yet smooth. The child is the colour of wet sand. His

name is Gogodi, he finally says in a croak. Her heart over-
flows.

Today, he won't play with the rest, just clings to her
skirts.

#

She steams yams and casavas in fresh banana leaves for
her children. Stirs a pot of pigeon or groundnut sauce,
serves it with pickle from the mopane berry. The gossips
are still talking. She ignores them when she can. She's done
this to great effect, the ignoring, but it's impossible to continue when something is picking off her brood.

It started with the quintuplets a fortnight ago. They grew
pot-bellied, then seriously ill. The first one nearly died—
Chief Ade had already put ash on her head—when he recovered. But the rest are vomiting and passing wet stool.
She grinds ginger and cloves, mixes the concoction with
honey, a crush of black baobab bark. She mutters a spell to
the gods of the trees, the goddesses of the river, who bring
fertility and health:

cold fog no frogs
pump and stretch
senews whole

a drop of sorghum
wine to sunned earth
ripple, ripple
perfectus agreenos

seventy heartbeats
of forgotten remembered
puff your throat

sacrifice appeasement
cold fog
no frogs
posticus tibialis.

And the children recover.

But the sickness has worsened the gossip. Villagers talk in such detail, embellished or not, and it's talk filled with fear. Some villagers boycott to sleep under their burnt-brick houses, preferring mud huts under a thatched roof where "a bad eye cannot reach."

#

Complex patterns signify inarticulable longing only eyes can speak. Chief Ade never walks the past without switching off tomorrow's name. She practices speaking the nameless in front of a calabash's mirror—it's filled with magic water. But her tongue is knitted with a moment that is now. She touches Gogodi's forehead.

He's boiling. The child has refused to respond to her magic. This time she believes the ash on her head, as she did for her husband moments before he died. It's only a matter of time. She accepts the morning with its rituals, even though villagers greet from afar, mistrusting the boy she's carrying and the burnt brick.

How are the chickens? Someone pokes their head through the gate.

Still laying, she answers. *How is your daughter-in-law's newborn?*

Finally suckling. But he still needs a fingertip and honey to get his mouth going.

Chief Ade has educated the women on the hazards of birthing at home, but they are still fearful of the hospital. She encourages them to go to the clinic for health advice on their toddlers. It falls on deaf ears.

Aya, what do you think our ancestors did without clinics?

Will you return the children to the forest? someone finally asks. They look fearfully at Gogodi cradled on the chief's back. *The gods are calling for that one.*

She has no answer at first, then surprises herself with an epiphany. *I'll visit my daughter, the nurse in Tongi.*

Ebo! They fall away.
The hospital will take your blood!
Even if you're not the one who is sick!

#

Chief Ade sends a runner to the UN camp in Safura. The young man returns as a passenger in a truck taking bags of sorghum to Tongi, to return from the city with antibiotics and bandages for Safura. The driver, an older man in a khaki suit, helps the chief into the cabin, doesn't insist on a seatbelt, but Chief Ade wears it.

In her arms Gogodi trembles in chills. First, they drop the quintuplets—boisterous in the semi-trailer—at the UN camp for Celestina to look after for a while. Celestina frowns but accepts the children.

Now Chief Ade nods with the truck along the dusty road, until they reach tarmac, when she finally sleeps.

#

She's a ghost, spilling from a calabash and into a cheek.
She's a spectre, brimming from the sun and into the wind.
She's a year, lonely as a book savoured by phantom eyes.
She's a memory, hunting the fragrance of something lost, a
pleasure forgotten. She's a seed, unimagined in a garden
that whistles songs of plague.

> *she's a distance,*
> *and it opens*
> *to a wake.*

#

I'm hungry, says Gogodi weakly from the white sheets of a hospital bed.

Chief Ade falls into Tele's arms and weeps—it's taken the boy a week to recover. It wasn't worms, or malaria, not even a virus. What they found in his stomach was a bright blob of light that irradiated the operating theatre.

I am hungry too, says Chief Ade to her son when she can finally speak. *Let us get you something to eat.*

You can eat your stubbornness, Mama, Tele hisses at her when they're out of shot from the boy's ears.

Where is the stubbornness? asks Chief Ade.

Don't you think the boy is a spy from the city of lights?

If he were, then the sickness is a reminder that he's rejected his mission, as did the quintuplets, says Chief Ade.

Knowing this, would you have taken him in?

Yes, says Chief Ade. *Yes,* more firmly. Nurture, for Chief Ade, supersedes preservation. Always.

It's all lucid to the chief now. Weightman has been at it again. First the undead, now kiddie spies. He'll not stop anytime soon, and she's not sure it's just about heart matters or something more toxic. Enchantment can mask as a tree—somewhere in the forest is an inhabited whistling thorn tree. She'll know it's inhabited because it's the only one that ants will refuse to climb. She'll destroy it, burn it with magic to its roots.

And, with the obliteration, the city of lights will lose its hold on her children. If Weightman keeps at it, she contemplates, she might consider the quiver tree. Send a message in a magicked arrow. To deter or execute? She's not sure yet.

But first she must take the truck on its return with supplies from the town, collect the others at the UN camp and take all her children home. She'll try but is not sure she'll convince the villagers to once more sleep in their burnt-brick houses.

Gogodi is devouring a coconut-and-banana muffin, though he's never seen one in his life before. The blob of light is gone. Yet the boy shimmers. His eyes flutter, then open—awe in them at his first sight of her. He reaches for her cheek, his hand warm and sure. The river blindness was no more than the poison of a killing mission.

She hands him a vanilla milkshake whose tetra-pack car-
ton has the face of a lost child or cat,
> she looks
> at her son…
> from the
> city of lights,
> oh, she loves
> how he glows.

Not For Nothing
A Mad Skillz Story

Jeff Carroll

"Just because President Obama has reassigned us to domestic duties doesn't mean we are going to rekindle some old flame." Skillz looked straight into Nakeyah's eyes. She flashed the smile she had the day he first fell in love with her. Her dimples were deep into her full cheeks as she tried to shake off his words.

"Marion, I'm not trying to pressure you into doing something you don't want to do. I'm just happy your back safely so you can spend some time with Jazmen. Skyping gets boring and she's had to see her father on a screen for over six years."

Skillz grinned himself. Nakeyah was as slick as he remembered. "Well, I'm just saying so things don't get all confused up in here. 'Cause I see you coming here looking so dressed up and fine." He looked down at her thick legs and the smooth skin of her calves, and felt his focus of attention start to shift. Nakeyah was his first love. She was a sexy-ass sister and her brain was as big as her behind.

"I was starting to think you didn't notice."

"Nakeyah, I would have to be wearing Stevie Wonder glasses not to see you."

"Marion," Nakeyah moaned.

"Okay, you can ease back on that *Marion* softness. You have moved on and all we are just co-parents now. You're with Winston now and I'm married to the government."

"So, you're installing security systems here now?" Jazmen looked up from her spaghetti. She sat between her parents, but they talked like she wasn't there.

"Yes, baby. I have been relocated stateside and will be working on securing domestic properties now." Skillz kept his eyes steady and his voice even. It broke his heart, having to lie to his daughter in person. All his years of using verbal manipulation to resist interrogation, and he felt like he was going to crack from the pressure of talking to his daughter.

"You put cameras in dolls so they can catch bad babysitters, or do you put cameras in grocery stores so you can catch bad guys?" Jazmen's voice should be used for interrogation. He could cut his time in half with his daughter asking the questions. Who could lie to her?

"Something like that. I do bigger projects like office buildings and government facilities. The criminals I catch are much more dangerous than a drug addict wearing a ski mask."

Skillz was in his zone now. He felt natural, mixing the truth with fiction. Sitting in his new favorite restaurant Amy Ruth's on 116th Street was as natural as the back alleys of Afghanistan. Carl, the owner, was happy to grant a war vet a private table. Carl loved to tell customers how he used to work with Reverend Sharpton before he opened the restaurant. Skillz suspected the table he was given would be where Carl reserved for activists and politicians like Reverend Sharpton. The table had a privacy to it, and Skillz felt free to make up any story he wanted out of the earshot of any other soul-food customers.

"You and Mommy can get back together now." Jazmen smiled at her parents like this was the first time she had seen them together. "Mommy's boyfriend Winston got arrested and he won't be coming back for a long time."

"Jazmen, please. Didn't I tell you not to say anything." Nakeyah smiled at herself, having had her business put out. "I thought we had a deal. I'm going to take those earrings back now since you want to start snitching."

"So, Skinnyman is in jail. I should have guessed something was up when you agreed to meet with me so easy." Skillz turned to his daughter. "That wasn't snitching, baby. You mother didn't want to tell me because when I left for the service, she left me for Skinnyman Winston. She thinks I'm going to hold it against her."

"I was young, Marion. You know how things were back then, and Winston wasn't like he is now." Nakeyah took a sip of her lemonade.

"Look you don't have to explain to me. I understand you are good. You work for the city now. In the law library. That's good." Skillz put his hand on Nakeyah's shoulder. "Yes, times were different. You had a young child and you thought Skinnyman was a good choice because he had money. I ain't mad at you, because you always let me talk to my daughter, and that's the relationship that's most important. Feel me." Skillz paused. Nakeyah was now tearing up and slowly nodded. "It also explains why you came up in here looking like you're going to a club. Now, that's back in the day. You looking like you're in a hip-hop music video." Skillz felt a little emotion in his chest as he thought about the nineties.

"Jazmen, what you need to know is you have two parents who love you. See, when I graduated from high school, I was working at a drug store, and I thought I was going to become a pharmacist. When your mother got pregnant, reality hit and I couldn't provide for you as a wannabe pharmacist. So, I manned up and joined the army. It was 2002 and the war was all anyone was talking about. There was so much death back then, people thought going to the army was a death sentence. You mother did what she thought was best and got her a guy making money. Who knew her choices were between an assistant pharmacist and a street pharmacist." Skillz smiled and laughed in his cool way. His laughs were so rare that Nakeyah even laughed.

"Yeah, baby girl, things were different back then."

Skillz looked out of the window again. Harlem was a lot different than it was before 9/11. It was more diverse. There were more Asians and white people. Before he left, the only Muslims in Harlem were Black Muslims, and all they did was sell newspapers and delicious bean pies. Now there were people from the Middle East, Arab, Kurdish, and Palestinians. Just looking out of the window, it felt like a United Nations village.

Even with Skillz' trained eye and his years of experience in Afghanistan, he still couldn't tell the difference between all of the people. All of the people looked the same to him, especially the men. He only described the people in his reports as tall or short or fat or thin. He stole glances even now and then out of the window as he continued his lie about his domestic security system assignment.

He paused his conversation for a moment, thinking he saw a man from his past. The man was across the street one second, and when Skillz looked again, he was gone. He excused himself and picked up conversation again. He saw another man drive by in a SUV who seemed like he was looking straight at him. This was uncomfortable. It must be his nerves. Even a Middle Eastern man pushing a refrigerator on a cart looked suspicious.

"What's wrong, Daddy?"

"Ah, nothing. I know I'm here in America, but sometimes my mind still thinks I'm in a war zone."

Then he saw a sniper barrel pointing at him. It was sticking out of a hole in the big box the tall Middle Eastern man was pushing. Mind trick or not, this was nothing he was ready to dismiss. He looked at his daughter, and her head was perfectly lined up between him and the gun.

"Jazmen, is that your earring on the floor?" Skillz said as he pointed down.

As Jazmen looked down, Nakeyah leaned over as well. "What earring?" Nakeyah asked.

"Over there." Skillz bent over to point farther on the floor in no particular direction.

Just as Nakeyah squatted down, Skillz pushed down on her back. Seconds after, they were all on the floor and below the window as bullets flew through it. The sniper bullets made no noise, but as the large window took hits, it started to shatter. The sounds of the falling glass caused the other customers to run for cover.

Skillz motioned to his daughter and baby mamma to stay under the table. He then crawled to the end of the room divider. There he saw Carl pointing to the bathroom.

"Hurry," screamed Carl as he hid behind the thick bar. Bullets flew over the counter, shooting bottles and chipping away at the wood. Customers were scrambling out of the front dining room. A couple of them got hit in the back and fell to the floor. Carl pushed a red button at the end of the counter, which made the sprinklers come on.

The spray from the water gave Skillz enough cover for him to get Nakeyah and Jazmen out of the back. As soon as Skillz saw the alleyway, he held his arm out and his hand straight. Nakeyah and Jazmen stayed inside the doorway. They watched as Skillz approached two men dressed in black holding guns.

Skillz moved in quick. They were both Middle Eastern guys and looked just like the guys shooting up the restaurant. They were standing on different sides of his black government-issued Escalade. He chopped the first guy in the neck before the other man noticed. When the first guy hit the ground, the second guy turned to see what happened, and Skillz caught him in the back of the head with a hard blow and twisted it around until it cracked.

The blow was only strong enough to get the guy's attention. This second guy was a lot bigger than the first guy, so Skillz quickly hit him with another two-piece combination of body blows. This brought the big guy to his knees. Skillz grabbed the guy by the back of his head and slammed the guy's face into his knee. The guy dropped his gun and Skillz slammed him into the truck. The guy was still moving. The guy reached for Skillz's hands. Skillz pulled the guy to the ground by his arms. He then flipped over on the back of the big guy, still holding his arms, and used his weight to bend the big arms back, popping them out of their sockets. The big guy screamed as he brought his head down.

Skillz motioned for Nakeyah and Jazmen, but they both were standing, still marveling at Skillz' lethal hands. He waved again, and they snapped out of their trance, ran out of the building, and jumped into the truck. Just as Nakeyah pulled her leg in and closed the door, more Middle Eastern guys stepped out at the end of the alley. The released a barrage of bullets. Jazmen screamed and put her head under the seat. As she looked up, she noticed the bullets bouncing off of the windows.

"Hold on," Skillz said as he slammed the truck into D2. The lower gear made the truck a two-ton ramming weapon. He drove the truck down the alley, straight at the men. The big SUV clipped a dumpster and hit a couple of rubber garbage cans before it flew out of the alley.

Skillz sped the truck north on Lenox Avenue, aka Malcolm X Boulevard. He was crossing 118th Street when more bullets started hitting his truck. He looked back and two cars were speeding after him. He swerved the truck between car after car, trying not to hit pedestrians. As he reached 125th Street, the light was just turning red, and he hooked a right turn. Cars were just pulling into the intersection, and Skillz couldn't avoid hitting a cab. As he backed the truck up, another car hit him in the back, breaking the rear windshield.

"Come on," Skillz said as he looked at the approaching cars. They would be on him in only a few seconds. As shots hit the side windows, traffic on the busy street slowed and became easier to navigate. Skillz made haste and quickly made his way east on 125th Street.

"Go, Daddy," Jazmen yelled as she held on to the door handles.

He turned at 5th Avenue, but the cars were still behind him. He turned onto the 138th Street overpass and onto the Major Deegan. North on the Deegan was always crowded, but when it was a Yankees game, the highway was a parking lot. Good for Skillz the Yankees had an away game.

Unfortunately, cars were able to weave through the high-way traffic easier than Skillz's big SUV, and before Skillz, was ready one of the cars rammed him in the back. With the back windows shattered, the bullets were able to shoot into Skillz' truck. Skillz swerved the truck into the chasing car, giving himself a little space.

"Nakeyah." Skillz looked over the back seat while steering the truck into a clear lane. "Look under the seat and hand me the black case. Feel on the floor for the latch."

Nakeyah turned her body to look under the seat. She braced herself so she could find the latch.

"When you find it, let me know."

"Okay." Once she found the latch she pulled out the case. It was a big black metal case which fit under the seat so well, if Skillz hadn't told her she would have never noticed it.

"Got it."

"Push the numbers 51925."

Nakeyah kept her head from jumping up when the case popped open. Inside the case were four guns neatly placed in perfectly shaped black foam cut-outs. Jazmen reached for one of guns and Nakeyah pushed her hand away.

"Wow, I expected to see screwdrivers and wires."

Skillz looked out of the window and he saw the exit for the Cross Bronx Expressway a mile away. "Hand me the forty-five."

"Which one is that?"

"The big one." Skillz swerved the truck as one of the cars chasing him pulled around, passing cars on the outside lane shoulder. The car bumped and scraped against the concrete divider as it weaseled its way to the side of Skillz. The guy in the passenger seat shot out the driver's-side window.

Skillz ducked as bullets flew into his truck. He reached between the front seats, and Nakeyah handed him his .45. Skillz quickly returned fire. He waited for the car to fully get beside him, and then he hit his brakes hard. Then, with the car in front of him, he hit the gas hard and rammed the car. His big SUV muscled the smaller car so hard, it slid into the concrete divider. Due to the speed the car was going, it immediately flipped over the divider, into a sanitation truck in the southbound lane.

The loud collision made Jazmen stick her head up out of the back seat just in time to see the car flip in the air. She imagined how it felt as the little car was tossed in the air by the heavy truck like fumbled football. The car bounced on it rear bumper, then again on its side before sliding into the Manhattan River. She screamed as the car made a splash as into the water.

Skillz swerved the banged-up truck into the right lane. The sign for the Cross Bronx Expressway was about a quarter mile ahead.

"Jazmen, get down," he commanded.

Just then, the other car hit the back tire of Skillz' truck, causing the truck to spin a full circle and slam into the right-side wall. The second car pulled past Skillz' SUV and stepped out of the car. The two guys sprayed Skillz' truck as they slowly walked toward it.

Skillz struggled with his truck. The impact of the wall caused the truck to shut off. Bullets flew into the battered bulletproof windows and scraped-up side panels. Skillz held his head down and turned the key. The truck's engine turned over once and stopped. He propped his gun against the gas pedal and turned the key once more as glass fell on his head. The tough, reliable truck jumped forward as it started. Skillz took the metal case and held it up to the window. Bullets shot into the case, but it did its job, blocking the bullets.

Skillz grabbed his gun, shifted the truck into drive, and whipped it around. Skillz stuck his gun out of the corner of the window as the truck turned around. He drove straight for the guys, hitting their car as he drove back into the flow of traffic. His truck was banged up quite a bit, but even with the back wheel wobbling, he was able to get it moving.

The guys wasted no time. They were in their car, trying to cut Skillz off. Now their car was able to trade bumps with Skillz' wounded truck as it tried to run Skillz into the wall. The car ground against the bigger SUV. The guy in the passenger seat tried to shoot over the hood of the car, but the constant collisions made it hard for him to get off a good shot. The driver focused so much on the goal of running the truck off the road that when he pushed the SUV onto the shoulder, he never noticed that it was an exit lane.

Skillz made a hard turn up the exit ramp, causing the car to lose control and crash into the metal railing.

"Okay, is everybody alright?"

"Yes." Nakeyah sat up in the passenger seat. She brushed glass off the dashboard, then looked around to see if there were any other cars chasing them. She saw Jazmen doing the same thing.

Skillz turned off at Jerome Avenue and pulled into a building that said *Sugar Shack* on it. The build looked old, run-down, and worn out. The truck was smoking and sputtering as he brought it to a halt around the back of the building. He took out his cell phone and typed a number, and what looked like a plain wall front began to rise. The door rose fast, and Skillz drove his truck in quickly.

"Okay, what was that?" Nakeyah asked right away. She had barely gotten Jazmen out of the truck before she started her questioning.

Skillz was over in the corner of the dark room, turning the lights on and opening up a cabinet. The cabinet held a variety of guns, long sniper rifles, and grenades inside. There were two laptops, a pair of small binoculars, and some other gadgets.

"Marion," Nakeyah said as she walked toward him. Jazmen ran ahead of her mother. "What is all of this? Where are we?"

Skillz took off his dinner jacket and put on a black bulletproof vest. He put two handguns in holsters, one under each of his shoulders.

"Daddy, why do you have all these guns?"

Skillz lifted a long sniper rifle off its hooks and grabbed a box of bullets. He threw the rifle over his shoulder and was reaching for his grenades when Nakeyah stopped him.

"Marion, what the fuck? Answer us." She got in his face, preventing him from continuing to load up on weapons.

"Nakeyah, please." Nakeyah wiped a spot of blood from the corner of Skillz' mouth.

"These men tried to kill us. This is America. This ain't Baghdad." Skillz took off his rifle and laid it on counter. He moved Nakeyah to the side and put two grenades in his pockets.

"So, what are doing with all of these guns? Are you a terrorist? What, your security systems aren't good enough?"

Skillz opened a closet and put on a black leather baseball jacket as he walked over to a large tarp covering something equally large; whatever it was, it was as big as his SUV.

Jazmen followed close behind him. "Where are you going, Daddy? The bad guys are already dead."

Skillz flipped one side of the tarp up and revealed the front of the hood of another black Escalade. He turned to his little daughter.

"Jazmen, those men were just hit men. They work for someone else. Whoever came after me, I mean us, will try again. They will keep trying until I'm dead."

"Why do they want to kill you? Did you put in the security system wrong?"

Skillz leaned over and put his hand on her shoulder. This

was not the time for him to tell his daughter. She was too young, and telling her something confidential would make her a liability.

"I don't know why they are after me. But all I can tell you is it's not because of a security system."

"Your father isn't going to tell. He's just like Winston or Tirani whatever his name is. He's probably some drug dealer or working for one." Nakeyah pulled Jazmen away from Skillz. "He's lying. Just take us home."

Skillz grabbed Jazmen, and the little girl was in a tug-of-war between her parents.

"Listen. I ain't no drug dealer."

"So, what are you? Huh?" Nakeyah tugged a little harder and pulled Jazmen out of Skillz' grasp. Skillz stood there, frozen.

Skillz took a deep breath and caught up to them. "I can't tell you."

"Please."

Skillz walked in front of them, cutting them off. "I can't tell you what I do. I don't want to lie to you, but its classified."

"My ass. Classified. Think of something better. I know somebody who's caught up in the drug world. Marion, I just spent five years with a man who acted like he was a rap artist but was a nothing but a drug dealer. I don't want to be around a drug dealer because of what just happened to us. We could have gotten killed. Bullets can't tell the difference between you, me, or our daughter. So, whatever you do in the drug world, I don't want your drama around us."

As Nakeyah pushed Skillz to the side, he stood his ground, causing Nakeyah to walk around him. Skillz turned and grabbed her arm.

"Nakeyah." Skillz paused. He had never expected to have to say what he was about, but after what Nakeyah had just gone through, it was worth changing his strategy. "Okay, okay, you made your case. What I'm going to tell you is something I am not supposed to tell you. I am only telling you this because I don't want to live a lie. I want you to know who I really am."

"Well, who are you? Is your name even Marion?"

"Nakeyah, listen."

"Mommy, calm down."

"I was never a security-systems installer in Afghanistan. I was a special ops soldier. I was recently assigned to New York as a domestic agent. I work for the department of STRESS, the Street Tactical Rule Enforcement Secret Service."

"Daddy, are you a spy like 007?"

"I'm more like Jason Bourne. I'm a Mobile Agent of Defense and Destruction. We are called MADD."

"So, what do you do?" Nakeyah's voice was now at a normal, calmer level.

"MADD agents are authorized to use the tactics used in the Middle East to protect the United States."

"Where are we, in your Bat-cave or something?" Nakeyah asked.

"This is my black house. *Black* meaning not on the map, like *blacked out*. It's similar to a safe house, but this is not a hideout. We cannot stay here. This place is not equipped for you. I will take you to your house. Whoever is trying to kill me does not know where we are."

"What are you going to do?"

Skillz walked back to his other truck and finished flipping off the tarp. He hit the key, and with a chirp, the doors unlocked.

"Nakeyah, these men just tried to kill my daughter and her mother. I don't need some executive kill order to deal with these guys. This is not for nothing; this is personal."

The Interview

Keith Gaston

Three a.m.

Lying on the cot, eyes open, Cinnamon stared up at nothing, hoping to penetrate its emptiness, but the totality of the dark defied her every effort to see through its black veil. It didn't help, being locked up in a room not much bigger than a janitorial storage closet. It made her claustrophobic, like being laid to rest inside a closed coffin.

"Might as well be in one, I suppose," she said, filling the emptiness with her voice.

All that awaited her outside the darkness of the cell was a syringe filled with liquid death. The presiding judge had delivered the sentence swiftly and without emotion: Death—ten counts of first-degree, eight counts of second-degree, and one count of third-degree murder.

All the blame for those homicides didn't fall squarely on Cinnamon's shoulders. Other assassins carried out many of the murders she would die for, killers like herself, remorseless and lethal.

The police and the prosecutor had presented all they needed for the trial to indict her, and damn any other evidence that forced them to seek others involved. Cinnamon could have fought the ruling, tried to tell the judge and jury her side of the story, but she had too much pride for that.

Besides, she figured, *there's more than enough blood on my hands to justify the judgment*. A warranted outcome, and she could live with that. The thing that irritated the assassin about the sentencing was having to be stuck with the third-degree verdict.

When I kill someone, she reflected, *I damn sure do it deliberately.*

Once she was inside prison, her reputation made her equally a target of guards and inmates. After surviving multiple violent incidents, killing some of her attackers and seriously wounding others, the warden had quarantined her, denying the prisoner's legal right to be let out into the yard for sun and exercise each day.

She was well into the tenth day of her latest stint inside solitary confinement when a baton's hard rap struck the metal door on the opposite side. The blow resonated inside the small room like a thunderclap. She had been expecting the intrusion. Each night since being quarantined, the guards felt compelled to hassle her. One of two things always happened: either they banged for an hour on the cell door or hosed her down in the enclosed space. One guard had made the mistake of thinking he could rape her. When she drove her knee into his nuts hard enough for his balls to crawl up his throat, no one else dared come near her.

She lay on her back, staring up toward the ceiling, wondering which torment it would be: constant banging on the door or being hosed down. The door swung open. Corroding decades-old metal hinges shrieked loudly in protest. Artificial light flooded inside from the hallway, asserting itself into the darkness of the small cell.

The hose, then, she grasped; otherwise, there wouldn't have been a need for the guards to enter. She craned her head to the side, craving the light, and was rewarded by pain. She blinked, squeezing her eyelids shut for a few seconds. A soft curse escaped her lips. She had been in darkness too long. When she dared to open her eyes, a shadowy profile of a man stood in the center. His right arm seemed to slowly stretch to an unnatural length as he let his baton slide down his hand into sight.

It seems this guard wanted a little variety tonight, she thought. *This man intends to beat me.*

"You must be new," she said. "Otherwise, you'd know better to come in here alone."

"Who said I was alone, prisoner?" the guard shot back. More figures crowded in behind him, varying in shapes and sizes, their number made up of men and women.

"It's a party, then," she said.

She gradually rose in her cot, letting her bare feet drop over the side to the concrete floor. Counting heads, there were a total of six: four men and two women. The space inside the room would make it impossible for all of them to file inside at once. They would either come one at a time or have her step out into the hallway, where they would have a more significant advantage.

"Woods is back from the hospital, and he—" the one in the doorway said.

"Who?" she asked.

"Woods! The guard you kicked in the balls."

"Oh, him," she said, grinning. "I'm surprised he's still able to walk." She stood up and stretched her muscles.

The rattling of large chains reverberated beyond the doorway. Manacles dangled in the hands of several of the guards. They planned to shackle her as they did their dirty deed.

"You won't be kicking anyone in the balls tonight, bitch," one of the shadowy figures said.

Taking on a fighting stance, she said, "Come in and get me, then."

No one crossed the threshold of the doorway.

She wondered if they would chicken out until the all-too-familiar electronic crackle of a Taser filled her ears. More than one hummed to life.

The guard in the doorway took a tentative step forward and then another. His cohorts filed in behind him, arms extended with their Tasers ahead of them like villagers carrying pitchforks. Crackled energy from the devices they held in their hands reverberated off the walls. The air in the cell was thick with the tang of charged ozone and the sounds of their uncharitable laughter.

After incapacitating her, they dragged their prisoner into what she'd guess was an interrogation room. They secured her to a metal chair bolted into the floor. She could look left and right as well as wriggle her fingers and toes, but that was all she could do. They'd stripped her down to her bra and panties.

The six attackers circled her chair akin to a pack of hungry vultures in one of those old westerns, readying to feast upon the wounded cowboy left for dead in the desert. One of the female guards, an Asian woman, licked her lips; her piercing gray eyes ranged freely up and down the prisoner's body. The baton swayed back and forth in her hand.

The Asian woman stopped her stalking, no more than a foot away from the prisoner. Gripping the baton in both fists, she stroked her right hand slowly up and down the length of the slender metal cylinder. "Oh, the things we're going to do to you tonight," she said with a knowing leer. "I don't know if I should envy you or feel sorry."

"I'm going to kill all of you," the prisoner shouted, trying desperately to break free of her restraints. It wasn't out of fear. What bothered her more than anything was being unable to fight back against her tormentors. She hated being helpless more than being locked up in the darkened room.

All the guards laughed.

The door swung open, silencing the room. The guard she had hurt, Woods, catapulted into the room with a severe limp that he tried desperately, but failed, to cover up. His huge gut hung over his belt. The buttons of his shirt threatened to pop off if he inhaled too hard. His thinning head had a horrible comb-over trying to hide his bald spot. Woods' gaze fell onto the prisoner's.

"Hello, bitch," he said.

"How ya doing, dickless?" she shot back.

He scowled while she smiled.

Woods pointed his beefy finger at her, about to utter his threat, when the lights flickered. It hadn't just been inside the room, either. Through the opened door, the hallway toggled between bright and dark.

"What the fuck?" Woods yelled, awkwardly trying to spin around. He stuck his head out the door and shouted his question again. "What the f—"

He never got to finish. Between the flicking light show, Woods' head exploded in a spray of blood and bone. His body stayed upright, oblivious to its missing head. Screams of fear and confusion filled the room as darkness took hold. When the blinking stopped and the illumination was fully restored, the headless body finally gave in to gravity, falling to the floor in a wet heap.

"Shut the door," the Asian guard demanded.

The prisoner was laughing, now reveling in the madness that seized hold of the guards as they tried to drag Woods' heavy body out of the way of the entrance. They planned to lock the door, barring anyone from entering to save themselves from the same fate as their headless coworker. But they were too late.

Two men, each holding one of Woods' legs, were beginning to drag his corpse out of the way when one of the female guards screamed for dear life. They all looked up in time to see a man clad in all black standing at the entrance with a sound suppressed pistol. Cold eyes stared through the slits of a balaclava, taking in everyone inside the room.

Everything went dark.

Screams erupted again.

Six quick flashes winked in and out of existence.

The room went eerily silent.

When the lights returned, all the guards were flat on their backs with neat dime-sized holes in their foreheads.

The killer stared at the prisoner and spoke, but his words weren't for her. "I've secured the target."

She heard heavily secured doors opening and the heavy padding of approaching feet coming down the corridor. The killer made no effort to release or communicate with her. He casually inspected his pistol to fill his time. Whoever dared to arrange to break into a highly top-security prison and didn't have any qualms about killing guards must seriously want something that only she could offer. She couldn't figure out what she had that made her so important.

Encompassing the doorway was a behemoth of a black man in a dark two-piece suit. He had to duck his neatly trimmed buzz-cut head before stepping inside. When he stood upright, he must have been nearly seven feet tall. His right eye socket was milky white, blind to everything. An ugly scar extended around that same dead eye.

The giant stared down at the prisoner. "Hello," he said in a deep voice that would make James Earl Jones envious. He glanced over a shoulder at the killer. "Free her."

Obediently, the man pushed himself off the wall and pulled a set of keys off one of the dead guards. After releasing the prisoner from her restraints, he returned against the wall near the door. She rubbed at her wrists and stood up from her chair.

She put some distance between herself and the two men. "Who the fuck are you?"

"My name is Boss Jacobs."

Jacobs? She knew the name, though she'd heard he'd gone into hiding years ago after a botched protection job. "They call you the Devil," she said cautiously.

"They do." He nodded. "And you are called Cinnamon."

She couldn't help but notice that Jacobs didn't seem worried about being discovered. Her gaze went to the other man, focused on his pistol. She hated not being armed and felt vulnerable.

"What do you want?" she asked.

He sat in the vacated chair and then crossed his massive legs. "You."

"What?"

He pulled a cigar out of a pocket and lit the foot with a wood match. The distinctive triple cap wrapper leaf identified it as being Cuban. "Leave us," he said, talking to his killer. As soon as the other man had gone, he spoke again. "What can you tell me about Sphinx?"

Cinnamon's lips curled in disgust. "I hate that bitch, for starters." Her eyes raked the room, unwilling to focus on anything. Taking a deep breath to calm herself, she let out a heavy sigh. "She's the reason I'm here now."

"I know," Jacobs said. "But what can you tell me about her?"

"Her name isn't Sphinx."

Boss Jacobs lowered his leg and leaned forward in his chair. He grinned as if pleased by her answer. "Who is she to you?"

"Tease," she replied. "Her real name is Tease." From his composed reaction, she could tell he already had known the answer.

Boss Jacobs got to his feet and shuffled toward the door. "You work for me now. Come."

"Just like that, huh?" Cinnamon threw her arms up into the air. "The guards weren't expecting anyone to break into the prison, but I'm sure as fuck they're ready for anyone breaking out! You act as if we can waltz our asses out without any trouble."

"Precisely my plan," he said, glancing over his shoulder. "I've already paid off anyone of any importance. Even these dead fools had received some compensation. I found out the guard, Woods, had a hard-on for you. I got word that he came in a day before my scheduled arrival so he and his friends here could have some fun with you. That, of course, was not part of my plan. I had to change my timetable. That annoyed me." He waved his hand around, indicating the dead sprawled across the cell. "This is what happens when I'm annoyed."

She looked down at the overweight guard and spat on his corpse. "Fuck you, Woods. Rot in hell."

"If you have the clout to pull this off, why do you need me?"

"You and I share a mutual hatred for Tease," he explained. "I underestimated this woman before and lost an eye because of it. Not ever again! I need someone who knows her tactics, knows the way she thinks, and knows her weaknesses."

"This is an interview, then?" Cinnamon laughed. "All this shit to destroy one person? Talk about obsessive."

"Tease is not one person, not anymore." Boss Jacobs' one good eye narrowed as he stood. "A shadow government agency has recruited her. Now I need an answer. Are you in, or shall I return you to your dark hole?"

"Oh, I'm in, big guy."

"Excellent," he said, crossing the room and ducking beneath the doorway. "The interview, as you called it, is over. Your indoctrination into my organization starts now. Follow me."

"Does this organization of yours have a name?"

"Arsenal," he replied.

Cinnamon trailed closely behind him into the long corridor. "Arsenal? Really? Wow. That certainly is ominous. It sounds like you're readying for war."

Boss Jacobs glowered down at her. "We are."

The End Is the Ecstasy

William J. Jackson

Sanchin Slitherway
2125
Machines toiled for ninety years to rebuild the metropolis the
Germans had inked over two centuries before. Next York on the
hot move. The Slitherway functioned as their main thorough-
fare, resource, bridge, and seawall, a cantankerous aerosteel tube
along a flat connector of buckytubes with rising and descending
plates to control the seething tides. Lights cerise and aqua shone
every twenty meters, highlighting mammoth industrial printers,
arthropodal tower drones welding new plates. In the distance,
the crater of Manhattan had become a horseshoe dome of
seacrete under a perplexity of native trees and those new polyhe-
dral housing units so popular along the flooded Eastern Shore.

A Ducayne Flat '79 Swift passed through, powered by be-
numbed battery jockeys, Jersey's lowest. Swift tracked at over
one hundred and five mph as it scraped a Machine waterproof-
ing the seawall. It pulsed orange, copper, chartreuse as the three
jockeys inside, windows down, screamed victorious. Next York,
right ahead, represented escape.

The Machines didn't expect the Swift.

Fine. Jockeys weren't expecting Bet.

Bet's old-school Afro blew back in the torrential wind. Teeth
bared, profound dark eyes barely visible behind neon yellow
Carver break-lenses. The wind beat his face up good, but it took
this jump flycycle to play catch up. Jockeys were live-fast-die-
young mercs, but they knew when to turn spirit. Bet came up behind the rectangular Swift with its aerodynamic cuts, its pinpoint
taillights, and clicked his teeth. Flycycle pumped an air jet, hop-
ping onto the Swift's minimalist trunk. He gauged forty seconds

to get the box and turn spirit before Next's buffer screen made him a bug on a force windshield.

The jockeys were frothing. The Swift angled left from the weight, narrowly missing the cylindrical wall. But Bet pushed harder. That was his set. Air jet forward plus downward thrust sent him and the cycle into the slit of a rear windshield. Crash. Hologlass pixelated into a scrambled network of webbed lines. The Swift dove. Jockey behind the wheel lost control. Vehicle scraped bottom. Sunshine metallic powder-coated Machines dusted the wall. Flycycle took a nasty swipe left as Bet flew forward. He waited for the artificial ground to meet him. Thank the House for good gear. The Vantablack military jacket, mandarin collar, roving digital ticker tape reading *GET BACK* along the upper back, spit out hundreds of inflated coils.

Instead of crunching bones and wetware on the deck, Bet rolled with something approaching grace. Fingers found the Pulse-12 and inspired the arm to reach out for firing. Bet estimated he needed six shots due to the roll. He let off eight. Pop-bangs to remove what was left of the window. Concussion caps to put battered, foaming-at-the-mouth jockeys one step closer to Lalaland. As the roll ended, his knee struck the edge of a printer. Not a good feel. Knee lacked wetware. *Should have worn the padded jeans.* Bet hopped up, limping, ripping off the impact coils on the move toward the Swift. He reached it, looking down at this slender, compact, ridiculous piece of tech from when the United States was a thing, and kicked glass out of the way. Jockey driver groaned in sleepytime slowmo.

Bet knelt down, reaching between driver and controls, searching, grunting. Soon he felt the box, smooth, slippery, pulled it out, and tucked it into the jacket.

"Sorry, guys. In case you never heard, the House always wins."

Aqua lights began to blink hard. Signal to clear the way. Next York Troubleshooters were on their way, full lethal. Bet hobbled off for the printer. Crawling fast under the legs and cables, looking back for safety, he found the circular access hatch and flipped it up. Blackness and the sound of the Hudson.

He fell into its black-ice hold. Somewhere in the dark, an awaiting skiff would pick up his bio and zoom in.

Mission accomplished.

Stockton Wood, Maryland

Two days' reflection and a hospital stay did the job. Black-Eyed Susan, the sole casino in the region, provided the premier visual. Bet loved the grand window in Game's twelfth-floor office. Huge and bulging, like the bay window in Dad's house growing up over on Lot's Isle. Stone's throw away from here, across from tranquil Stockton Wood. Good times. Simple days.

Maker Street formed a halo around the casino grounds as the setting sun cast a fiery spotlight on the region. A day like this, he could forget half of Lot's was subaquatic. This view, a glass of Bacardi in hand, almost made up for the tenderness in the knee. Life was complacent. The op a success. He turned, raised his shot glass to the statue of a brother in antiquated clothing standing valiantly on the crumbled word MANIFEST.

"Another notch on the belt, Chance." Success felt like closure. Bet could exhale.

Until the door slammed shut.

"Mr. Athanasius Wynne. So glad you decided to show your face after the dumpster fire you left for me in Next." Game, supervisor for Black-Eyed Susan, director of the House, nestled here inside the casino. She clipped across a paneled floor of red oak in seven-inch spiked heels that slithered up elegant high-yellow legs. Game moved the way a lioness prowled, straight back but with the head forward, shoulders hunched, gray eyes piercing Wynne's placid expression for signs of weakness. In her hand, a collection of files from the archives whose beige fade clashed with her form-fit violet dress and gilded silk poncho. A dozen broad platinum bracelets on each arm made windchime melodies. Her hair in ram's horn braids under gold and silver netting.

"It's still Bet, right? Have we stopped using assigned names in House?"

"Mr. Wynne."

"I mean, I wasn't gone for that long, now, was I?" He approached Game's holographic war table. She called it a desk. "Injuries. And the job's click so--"

"Wynne!" She gave him the once-over. Quilted black pullover turtleneck. Personal comm of cold green triangular holo hovering over the left-hand personal avatar. Tailored forest-green slacks. Six silver rings on six fingers. A bit taller. Must be sporting boots, yet still a shade under Game's six-foot-three.

"Fine. I jettisoned. But Troubleshooters were clipping me. No time to bring back one of the mercs or tap a mem." He stared up, Bacardi swirling in the glass.

Game withheld a snarl. "Your op was twofold. Retrieve the box. Bring back one, count them, *one* jockey so we can figure out what new form of Wither Jersey's putting into them these days. The lab boys need samples. The box gets us to our next lead, but right now those mumbling battery boys are killing our people." Files hit the desk. She hugged herself as she sat down. "Sometimes literally. I received word. Fold blanked." Game closed her eyes.

Bet heaved. "Fold? I told you his op was a bad idea." He paced the office, gave the Chance statue another look. "Listen, nobody knows more than me how hard it is to infiltrate Jersey, not to mention the cost. But it can't be a top priority, right? What are we having a co-op with Delaware for then? It's our buffer from Jersey's intel gathering. Can't even recall when I last encountered one of their special Ops anyways. It's all jockeys now."

"That's the problem you're clearly not seeing." She flicked an index finger. The desk emitted a solidified holo of what was known as the tri-state area, though the term seemed to float around a few of the eastern states before the States of America nixed the United part. "Every East Coast Solo is running on some form of illicit commerce to make ends meet. Delaware infiltrates false currency. Pennsylvania operates on alcohol, Jersey uses these simpering, amped-up jockeys to run Wither, Freeline, and God knows what else through the river tolls. They don't really need Ops anymore. Secretive data is sent on a jockey's back, we believe in the form of atomic data placed on the body. Poor little drugged pawns don't even know."

"Okay. So, since Maryland became a Solo, our once-inconspicuous cadre that helped Black people with powers who were victims of the old regime is now working for them. But you don't think dear, sweet Mary is laying fog behind the scenes like the rest, Game?"

Her kill glare returned to meet his irascible gaze. "Ours is not to dissect the hand that feeds us but to keep the outside from dealing a crippling blow. Listen, you know the lore as much as I do. To the rest of the Solo, we're small-time, nothing more than a curious historic town built by Black hands with people who stay to themselves. They don't know us because it works to our advantage. The greatest hero Old United ever had delivered our ancestors from that experimental hellhole up on Hillman Hill, showed us how to use our gifts without the forced traumas. To be discreet. We owe it to the memory of everyone who came before us to keep things together, even as the tide rises and more people tick-tock their agenda closer to nihilism."

Muscular arms folded over the chest. "Uh-huh. Fine. I dropped. There's more to it. Give it to me, then. That box I brought back is important. What's my next move?"

"Not what I was hoping for, but definitely something big. The box held a currency tag of six million in Jersey coin, plus rezoning plans, stock options in four Pharmcons, and *this* as the payee." She altered the holographic map.

Wynne frowned. "The governor's office. Inner Harbor. A yacht party for outside investors, but why…" Truth hit him like a sack of bricks. "They're bribing Baltimore to defect." The arms uncrossed as the severity of the matter surrounded him.

"Governor Lanningdale's lackadaisical political status notwithstanding, you know we can't have it. Without the city's draw, Maryland will be crippled. Unlike Missouri and its Rail City full of brand-name Masks packing mega bomb-level abilities, we've got low-graders like you and me and no standing army. Can't force a stay. This requires finesse."

Wynne walked fast over to a Victorian highback chair and reached for his coat, a gloved jade three-quarter trench with a retractable fade hood. D'Ivoire style. "On it. More politics than espionage, but I'm on it. Need to set a few things in motion en route. You want this hot or cold?"

"I want it to never have happened. Clean sweep. That's why I called you Bet from day one. Twelve years ago, you were over-eager and wet behind the ears." Game eyed the statue. "But I took a chance on you. Don't make me regret it."

"Never that. Send Fold's family a dozen flowers, on me."

Bet went out the door.

Inner Harbor shined auspicious. Baltimore fared better after Mary dropped the United front, priming trade deals with Ireland, Free Texas, the Red Nations. Capital went into clean power, an extensive floating pier, and bathing the area in cool emerald laser lighting. All the old dilemmas were media fog.

Under Rule was built to impress. A luxury yacht, she selfishly held in her frame the sea architecture of a keeled ship, trimaran, and flatbottom, depending on the mood of its owner. At three hundred meters of glistening bronze with new diamond framing, she stunned the city speechless. She made the city a global star. Her presence signaled a second golden age that would further pull Mary up from her weird, laid-back roots. Dignitaries from around the globe flooded the ship to see her modular hull, holographic furniture, eighteenth-century salon gaming room. Crystal chandeliers never ceased to charm.

"...this is why we cannot forget the past. Lincoln sent in the troops to quell Mary. On that day, she lost her Southern heritage, her birthright, and was relegated to mid-Atlantic obscurity. I intend to change that. Our fair city suffered an even harsher urban blight, negligence by state and federal hands. But we are on a faster-than-light trajectory. Let's slip free of one final shackle, shall we?" Governor Bedford Lanningdale uttered the end of his speech from the raised dais at the fore of the gaming room to a packed house. He had physical charm to counter social alienation. Chiseled jawline. Razorblade cheekbones. A thin body but piercing large, penetrating hazel eyes and that foppish black hair kept the governor eternally boyish.

Dignitaries from Scotland, Imperial Russia, Kiiro, a Chiricahua from the Red Nations, and many others applauded as he departed the dais for a seat at the roulette table. "Give it a good spin, Roger. Let the ball of tomorrow roll over the wheel of time until it finds the perfect date."

Svelte Miss Maryland, strobe-light tiara on, fake-giggled, approached to clutch Lanningdale's arm. The governor kept as many models as he disposed of, but for tonight her presence kept all eyes on him, the center of the world.

"A half mil on twelve black, Roger, if you please? Now, who wants to step up and enrich their avatar...or mine?" Lanningdale laughed. His captive audience followed suit.

As Roger spun the halcyon wheel, a man took up the challenge.

"I think I'll take a piece of that action." Bet leaned on the roulette table. He rocked a Shelling black suede longcoat over a five-strapped silk cream dress shirt, military collar. Fingers ringed up. Ears as well. Afro perfect. A holo pin displaying a small, rotating red rose rested on the top shirt button, with a matching pair as cufflinks. He set a stack of chips, stand-ins, for Mary e-cred, down and grinned. "All of it on red five."

Dignitaries and locals gasped. His weigh-in inspired others to place wagers.

Lanningdale pursed his lips. "That is a substantial investment, Mister..."

"Bet. Fancy ship. Mind if I win it?"

Bet scored laughs and Lanningdale's disdain. It fed the grin and helped it grow. Dimples showed out. "Don't do me wrong now, Roj." He tapped Roger on the wrist.

"Mr. Bet. A playful name." Lanningdale sucked teeth.

"Oh, it's more than just a name. It's a way of life."

Wheel slowed as faces leaned ever forward, whispers stifled into anxious silence. Big money on the line attracted eyes. The white ball tripped to a halt. Twenty-four red, six black, nine red...

Twelve. Black.

All those assembled exhaled and filled the air with riotous applause. Lanningdale, lifeless, offered an old royal wave in response. "It would appear you should reconsider your particular lifestyle, Mr. Bet."

Bet shrugged, tweaked an earring. Rubbed a thumb ring. "It's fluid. That was my clock money. I've got options in eco burning a hole in my pocket, though."

"Oh?" Lanningdale raised his hands. Several observing this head-to-head mumbled. Eco stocks weren't cheap by far and were Maryland's not-so-secret cash cow. A little went a long way. "Are you implying a second round might be in order?"

"Only if the stakes clear orbit."

The dignitaries swiped open avatars, brilliant light pyramids holding complex graphics packages and system data feeds. Bet. Eco. There it was. Legit stocks totaling millions. A shadow investor right under their noses. Crowd went wild. Lanningdale performed the same social diagnostic but covertly, the sole registry of it being a twinkle in the left eye.

Bet's earring caught it and did the math. Top speed. Good clothes. Big talk. Think fast. Gadgetry. Bet in a nutshell.

"It would seem you can back up the talk, sir. State your wager."

Bet dropped the grin, picked up a warrior glare. "A third of mine on a number. I lose, you gain, plus another third is broken down across all comers who tap in. Top stocks, automatic foreign investments, instant cred lines. Billions in the bank from the changeover if I'm doing my arithmetic right, yeah?"

Dignitaries used avatars to confirm his conclusion. One point nine four billion spread. Lanningdale needed no external modes to come to the same.

"This is an incredibly steep offer, Mr. Bet. Life or death. But I can see you are serious."

"Scan," Bet said.

"Pardon?"

"You said 'see.' but *scan* would be more accurate."

The governor stared. "The House can't be faulted for keeping security, now, can it?" Lanningdale circled an index finger in the air. Two security men flanked him. Big boys. Stockwell EM impact under sheaths peeking out like silver necklaces. "Now, whatever shall I wager?"

"This yacht!" one of the dignitaries joked.

"Quite funny, but please, this is a true battle of probability. We must take this duel for what it is. A class struggle."

Bet rolled his eyes left to right, considering the phrase. "Old, but I think *species struggle* hits hardest, don't you? I put up stock. I expect this to be equal. What do you got?" Hands fell from the table. Bet loved to throw down gauntlets, especially after studying the field. Telepathic taction. A fancy name for his minor inherited power. Roger's wrist. Roulette runner had a fixed wheel. Typical. Earring tapped a House micro-sat in space, looking for tech and weapons on Lanningdale, a way around the cheat. Results were unexpected but notch.

Lanningdale fumbled. Guests began to notice he wore no avatar patch. Everyone had an avatar. Without it, a person was exposed to the world, secretless, out of touch with Data. Data is paradise.

"Here"—Bet flicked his avatar up—"let me help you, and everybody else can pitch in. Let's see her, Governor Bedford Lanningdale...no...no... Hmm, you're a hard man to find. No. Well, wait. I got you. Is that what I think it is?" He leaned toward the Russian dignitary for an answer.

"Jersey cred?" The Chiricahua dignitary exclaimed. "You have cred with the most crim Solo on the East Coast. The black-market conversion alone would be astronomical."

"Do Americans debate legal status when all of them are illegal?" the dignitary from Kiiro asked.

"Who are you calling American?" a few locals demanded to know.

Lanningdale stiffened. Miss Maryland backed away for X-ray pics in the corner with a paying fan. An upswell of discontent seized the crowd at the roulette table, its energy pulling in more people curious to know what all the fuss was about.

Bet raised a brow. "Thrust, that's hardline, man. But I won't judge you for it. Who cares about Jersey money or if it might be tied to Wither labs, am I right? I keep my nose in Mary's business and only Mary. Now, if you want big stakes, Mr. Governor, well, you and I have them to play with. The action is yours." He soaked the glare in jet fuel and let it burn.

All eyes on the center but not in the way Lanningdale desired. Even he felt the pressure, weight of nations, fingers making adjustments to data margins. Secret wagers going from him to this strange man with the diamond-coated bravado. The governor's eye twinkled. Three more security brutes blocked the door leading out to aft.

"You good?" Bet asked.

"I'm perfect." The twinkle died out.

Bet grimaced. "Then call it."

Lanningdale offered the crowd a weak grin. "Half of my Jersey options. On a win, you get fifty percent of that. The other fifty percent will be divided up among any who tap. Agreed?"

They waited for Bet to respond.

"Up mine to half," he said. Bet made the appropriate updates in the pyramid. Dignitaries tapped like mad; so did a few dozen onlookers, reporters, staff, and one in security. The roulette table became the main event on the yacht's avatar. Everyone ship wide could see it, and the feed spread. Eastern Shore. Maryland. Delaware. Black Market Avatar Zero. New Jersey.

"All eyes on great Baltimore," Lanningdale announced. "It is as if it was fated."

"All eyes on us, Governor," chided Bet. "Don't slip up."

Dignitaries lost their senses. This was an unrivaled bout of gambling. Two men in; one would leave tonight financially ruined, avatar scattered. It would take a decade and more to recover. The perils of secession. Everything made up on the fly, and legal tender is but a technicality. A synthetic control mod asked the crowd to settle down.

Bet laughed, fueled by adrenaline but trying to remain low-key. "I like that. We're getting that good vibe right up front."

"You believe this to be the height of excitement, Mr. Bet?" Lanningdale asked. "Perhaps you are a virgin to more matters than just common sense. Whether it's intercourse or gambling, ecstasy, you see, comes at the end."

"Then lead the way."

"Gentlemen, choose your numbers," Roger announced.

"Nine red," said Lanningdale.

"Six. Black." Bet clicked rings together.

Roger made it happen. A pin dropped at this point would have deafened all ears. The wheel blurred as it went around, controlling fate. Lanningdale crossed his arms. Bet rapped fingers on the table. The wheel seemed sentient, taking longer to slow down, making them sweat it out.

"Genetic," Bet mumbled, eyes on the governor, knowing he heard him.

Lanningdale matched glares.

"Polymer."

The wheel entered slow-motion rotation.

You are messing with fire, a message sent into Bet's avatar, mind to mind.

Entity. Bet responded the same way as the governor.

GOTCHA.

Twelve black. Ten red. Seven black. Twenty-four red.

Stop. Drop. Six in the black.

The dignitary from Imperial Russia pulled off his holoshades and screamed in exhilaration. Hands went up in the air. Calls for drinks all around. The hands of a dozen strangers slapped Bet on the back. As they did, he worked their thoughts. Tips on illegal stocks. Offshore weapons caches. Secret meetings. Juicy news for Game during debriefing. Security wandered off.

Lanningdale stood alone. His one step from domination stretched out into a gap as wide as the universe. Bet shook hands, stole secrets, tipped Roger, and made his way over to the despondent governor.

"Good game. Lots of tension. We gave everybody a hot story to tell when they get back home, huh? You good?" He offered a hand to shake.

Lanningdale accepted it, firm grip. "Of course. I did not go through all I have to lose my sense of self. One deal collapses. Another will arise."

He pulled the governor close to keep their discussion between enemies. "Maybe. Must be hard faking it 'til you make it. A rogue AI escaped from the Canadian Corporate Skirmishes, slinked into an organic protoplasmic form, and living under a completely false identity. Rough. But I see it. Get them before they get you." Bet smiled. He could do friendly with the opposition on occasion.

"You are very well informed. Most citizens care little for what happened fifty years ago."

"I keep my ear to the ground, you know? Never know what I might hear that could prove useful. Speaking of, why did you do it?"

"The wager, you mean?" asked Lanningdale.

"Yeah. Jersey wanted a defection. They're gonna expect one, and when they don't hear of it, I mean…"

"Yes, but you forget that I am but an algorithm in a shell. I can easily jump ship, pun intended. If it comes to that, Mr. Bet. it seems your House has routed mine."

Bet bit his lip. "AI mind. Top line. You got that."

"Good. Then we understand one another. You have gained what you wanted. I cannot afford Baltimore's independence. Now, can you secure a safe departure? Or did you not think that far ahead?"

Bet gave him a sarcastic laugh. "Good one. Maybe I'll see you again someday."

"Perhaps. But how would you know it was me? Now, to the aft door. The nanovirus I put in your bloodstream is fast-acting." He released the shake and held up the palm. Lanningdale. Smiled. Robotic.

Bet backed off. He saw security moving back in, walking speed. He began to perspire. *Dammit! Got too bold.* The Op made for the coat-check room, trying to appear suave. More people got in his path to congratulate him. He had to give fast thanks and move on. He tapped the right earring. Nothing. Not a trace of toxin scanned in his bloodstream. Spirit shot. He grew worried.

Security by the door tightened their position. He knew he couldn't bum rush, but this time, Bet did prepare a backup. He pulled a handkerchief from his pocket, tapped the wet brow dry, then turned on a dime right to the coatroom.

The hostess was a hologram amalgam of influencers from back in the day, her voice sweet as honey.

"Hello," Bet said wearily. "I have a briefcase here under Wynne." He felt brutes breathing down his neck.

The hostess moved into a rotating rack of personal items until she eyed a gleaming platinum case with a stylized curved handle. "Here you go, sir. Enjoy your evening."

"Thank you very much." He turned a pinky ring ninety degrees left and then faced the brutes. "What's going on? You guys looking for a tip?" Hands raised, the ring blinked white.

"We want you to come with us."

"Well, now, I—" Both brutes hit the floor, noses bleeding, instant migraine. Bet shoved one aside and took off. Once he exited the coatroom, he shut down to a standstill. No need to draw attention. Aft door to his right, clean escape. He went out.

But the weather couldn't be cajoled into working with the plan. Pouring rain. Choppy waves. No land in sight. Bet cursed the sky. His fingers were falling asleep. The distance from the door to the end of the ship seemed to lengthen. He fumbled on the avatar controls but eventually thought up the proper code to initiate the sequence.

The door slammed open. Three more brutes, yelling threats. The first one out charged Bet, who turned to face him. They engaged in battle while the briefcase shifted into crescent shapes and bright light holographic windmill forms. Rain splatter. Bet blocked with the case, stepped fast, but still took a right hook to the jaw. He countered using that momentum, spinning into a kick. Not his best, form was off, but it connected to the chin and sent the brute sideways.

On anger alone Bet shoved a knee up into the man's nose just for good measure.

The second brute ran and slipped on the wet deck. Maybe weather was on Bet's side. His fail was the Op's inspiration. As the third reached in his pocket and pulled out a rectangular box that clicked open to transform, Bet summon up what reserves he had left to run. He leaned back and let hydroplaning carry him to the end of the ship. The case had changed over and its battery hummed to life. A barely noticeable seat. Handlebars. Crescent skis. Hard holo holding it together.

Third brute's box became a blackout pistol. Stun capsules, quiet-firing. Doesn't disturb important gatherings. He let off four rounds but the rain and wind swallowed them whole.

Bet jumped over into the torrential dark. The jet-ski case held up despite the flimsy appeal. They struck water, and the force almost made Bet fall off. Fingers were senseless. He had to look down, blinking from the rain to make sure he was indeed holding the bars.

Ice-cold, lips quivering, he looked back. No pursuers, lights out. Bet had only the mean sky and turbulent waters to beat him up now. Toes curled under. Tongue fuzzy. Satellite informed the avatar he had twelve miles to cover to reach land. He put the ski on max and jettisoned. Tonight, he truly lived dangerously, all on the line, and now he might end up another missing person, the second Op the House lost. He huffed. He raged. Anything to stay alive and see Stockton Wood again. But the evening held all the cards.

Place your bets.

El Originario Extraño Del Kalypso Kid

Joe Hilliard

New York Special Daily News, AP Wire, February 28, 1954, Ciudad de México. The Seventh Central American and Caribbean Games are to be held in Mexico City. The games will commence March 5 and run through March 20. Some 1,356 athletes from twelve nations will be competing. Amongst the most anticipated events is the wrestling, with some of the best athletes from around the globe. The Jamaican team looks extremely promising, led by young talent Dante Davis. The participants are arriving this week by planes, trains, and automobiles. One intrepid fellow from Chiapas even seems to have come via llama.

* * *

"What do you think of Mexico City, Kid?" Coach Rudy leaned over to look out the window of the DC-3, pushing back against Dante's broad shoulders. He could barely see the city below.

"Looks like any other city to me. Just bigger." Dante rubbed his pale amber eyes and squinted. "Have you seen our schedule?"

"We start against the Cubans. Como siempre, as they say." Dante cocked a quizzical eyebrow at Coach. "Like always, Kid. Like always. Me thought you were going to practice the lingo before we got here."

Dante shrugged and leaned back in the seat. "What for? We won't be here long. I know their names. That's all I need to know." He leaned over to check the sheaf of notes on Coach's lap. "Is it Garcia to go first? He's a good grappler."

"But you can take him."

Dante crossed his hands behind his head. "I always do."

* * *

Inspector Gustavo Ximenez of the Special Investigation Bureau pored over the Aeropuerto Central report detailing the luggage and personal items of the Jamaican contingency. One collection jumped out: 50 singlets; 60 jockstraps; 25 jackets, unlettered; 10 jackets, lettered with names; 1 Soviet-made Zorki 3 camera; 7 rolls 35mm film. What were the Jamaicans doing with that camera? He expected that from the Venezuelans. Or the Cubans. Demanded it, even. It was part of the game. But the Jamaicans? This was a novel twist. He went down the checklist of the Jamaican contingent: athletes, officials, trainers, crossing off names. Who was connected with these items? Nothing in the notes. The government officials kept their starched-collar shirts separate from the athlete riffraff, como todos las países. He sighed and flipped through the photos. There, the bag with the camera, black with the Jamaican flag embossed on it. Underneath the Olympic wrestling logo, and stenciled in white all capitals—*COACH R. RUDY.*

With a sigh, el inspector picked up his telephone. The games had begun. On several fronts.

* * *

Garcia sighed and ran his fingers though his coarse black hair. The federales had left him and all the Cubans alone at the aeropuerto. He had noticed them swarming around, but their contingent had come through with nary a jaundiced eye. That was what Garcia needed. Stay hidden in plain sight. Win a medal. Complete the mission. Castro had been clear when they had last met before Garcia embarked on the flight.

"Our Soviet comrades are watching us. They don't believe we are capable." Castro had spat on the floor of the small farmhouse they had met in. "They don't think we are worth supporting. They think…they think we will sell out to los Estados Unidos."

64

Garcia had stiffened. "Surely, they know better than that."

"Bah! They think of me as American as baseball. But if we can show them we mean business…"

"Just get me access to the target."

Castro had clapped Garcia on the back. "¡Excelente! I knew you were our man in Havana. The station agent is expecting you." He had pulled a cigar out of his jacket. "Just one more item."

"¿Sí, señor?"

"Bring back a medal. When we are triumphant in Havana, you will be one of our sparkling jewels."

*   *   *

The called Dante Davis the Kid. Barely twenty-two, his baby face made him appear even younger. His afro was close cut on the sides, like the buzzcut popular in the boarding schools he'd been sent to. It made his ears stick out. One of them had already taken enough punishment to start marking him. Cauliflower ear. His tall, slim build reminded some people of the American Woody Strode. He smiled easily and often, as long as he wasn't in the ring. In the ring, the Kid was all business.

That's the way Coach liked it. That's the way Jamaica liked it.

*   *   *

The crowd roared as the Jamaican wrestlers entered the arena. The Cubans were not popular there in Mexico City. *Arrogant*, the crowd murmured. And if they weren't pantalones elegantes como their leader Batista, then they were communists. Their shared language only made the insults rain down harder on the Cubans. And the cheers much louder for the Jamaicans.

Garcia grimaced and sucked his teeth. He had no love lost for Dante Davis and the rest of the Jamaican team. While in the same weight class, Dante wore his weight in his height and muscles, but the stocky Garcia wore his in his broad shoulders and thick, bulging legs. Worse, Garcia had to admit, the chiseled features of the Jamaican cut a nicer line than his squat face. If he could have got away with it, Garcia would have spit on the mat. But protocol. As Castro said, play the game when you have to. Cheat when you must.

Today was not a cheat day, but he was sick and tired of losing to the Kid. There had to be a way.

* * *

The Kid pushed up off the mat. Garcia rolled onto his side. With a quick feint and a slide of his arm, the Kid had avoided the grasp of Garcia and flipped him neatly onto his back. Pinned. It was like the Kid was a mind-reader. Garcia pounded his fist on the mat before he got up. He could hear the dismay from his corner. He'd hear about the outburst later. But right now, he did not care. He was sick and tired of losing to the Kid. He knew the local station agent would be reporting back to Castro as well.

The Kid strode off the mat to his corner. As he approached, a man in a rumpled suit was accosting Coach. Much shorter than Coach, he pulled Coach down to speak into his ear. But even twenty feet away, Dante could see Coach's face stiffen.

From his vantage point, Garcia also saw the exchange. His brain quickly processed the face, an inspector out of the local espionage division. Interesting. What could be happening with the Jamaican team?

* * *

Guachichullca sat behind his desk, smoking a thick Cuban cigar. It was good to have the games in Mexico City. Make the crowds want some real lucha libre, some real wrestling in the squared ring, not that weak grappling in small circles. And perhaps the chance to recruit some new talent to the promotion. If he could get a medalist to stay in Mexico. Take on el Caballero Blanco. Then the promo would really explode. Or maybe get one of those Cubans to stay. A new rudo that would really bring in the dinero. He templed his fingers in front of him on the desk.

The cigar was good. Perhaps the contact that brought them would be even better.

"The governor requests your appearance, Señor Guachichullca." Or perhaps not.

* * *

El Inspector Ximenez sat outside the temporary office of the governor in the Plaza del Azul Hotel. The governor had taken over an entire floor. A hatchet-faced guard greeted el inspector at the elevator and marched him to the suite. The guard knocked imperiously.

"¡Entre!"

Governor Rafael Villa Macho of the State of Mexico was not impressive in and of himself. But the political machine behind him was. El Inspector gave it all the deference due it. He bowed slightly as he came in and then cursed inwardly for doing so. The governor deigned not to notice, barely motioning at a chair.

"Sientate, Inspector. It is good that you could come so fast. ¡Muy pronto!" The governor laughed. El Inspector ran his fingers through his thinning hair. As though he had any choice in the matter. "Tell me. Digame."

"At your order, we have arrested the coach of the Jamaican wrestling team for espionage. Suspected communist agitation. Also at your order, we have not made a statement to the press. They do not know he has been taken into custody, although the man from the *New York Special* suspects."

"Good, good. Nothing must come out yet."

"It will soon enough. Someone will notice. Someone will talk."

"But not too soon. He is after all, completely innocent of the charges. The evidence was planted."

El Inspector burned holes in the Governor with his eyes. "The investigation has not..."

"The investigation is a sham, Inspector. Surely, you were informed?" Surely, he was not.

"¿Pero, por qué?

"To throw the scent off the real spies. El asesino. Lull him into making a mistake."

"You know who the spy is?"

"The assassin. And his target." The governor mopped his brow exaggeratedly. "Fortunately, we discovered it just in time." He waved his arm around the suite. "And sacrifices were made to ensure my safety."

"Indeed, Governor. And the spy…"

"The assassin, Inspector! The assassin! Yes, the Cuban wrestler, Garcia. Although we cannot prove it yet."

"What is it you want from my department?"

"Naturally, for you to keep completely silent. Por supuesto."

"Por supuesto." El Inspector sighed.

* * *

Guachichullca pushed his fedora back on his head. he stamped out the Cuban cigar in the brass ashtray in the Plaza del Azul Hotel lobby. It had lost its flavor. No sabor. He stroked his moustache.

He had to get to the Hippodrome. He needed to make some calls. Muy pronto. Looking up, he saw an inspector he had dealt with before heading out, and a wrestler he wanted to know heading in. As he stood to leave, a hand grabbed him by the shoulder.

* * *

The hatchet-faced guard ushered Dante into the Plaza del Azul suite. He had seen the man behind the desk in the papers. The governor of the State of Mexico. He began speaking even as Dante sat. "What do you know about lucha libre, Kid?"

Dante swallowed. What did this have to do with Coach? "Nothing. Not much. It's ring wrestling. Like Gorgeous George and all that."

"What do you know about communists in Cuba?"

"What? Nothing. I barely know any Cubans. Definitely no communists."

"Just Garcia. You're chummy with him."

Dante smirked. "Chummy? I've fought him. A few times. I've beat him. Every time."

"Yes. In many places. Caracas. Lima. Even Havana. And at every location"—the governor slammed his hands down on the desk—"dead anti-communists. Dead enemies of the Soviet state!"

"I don't…"

"No. You don't. We need to know why. You and Garcia are the only common links." He steepled his fingers and stared at Dante. "You and Garcia. So, ¿quién es? Who is it?"

"Not me."

"Prove it." The hatchet-faced guard now ushered in a strange little man with a singularly thin, sharp mustache. "So, I ask you again, what do you know about lucha libre?"

"I know how to wrestle."

The other man bowed slightly at the waist. "Allow me to in-troduce myself, Señor Dante Davis. I am Señor Guachichullca. I handle a promotion here in la Ciudad. It's not much"—the gov-ernor snorted at this—"but it pays my bills."

"And that's where you come in." The governor leaned for-ward. "We need you to fight Garcia."

Dante shook his head. "I just did."

"In the Hippodrome. Challenge him. To a rematch. ¡Un gran lucha!"

"You're crazy. You're both crazy." Dante stood to leave.

"Your Coach is already in jail. Espionage. Communist sym-pathizer." The governor's voice was barely a whisper.

"It's not true."

"Doesn't matter. He will be convicted. Shamed. You could be too. I just need to pick up the phone."

"Wait! What?"

"Caballeros. Gentleman. Please. Por favor. A minute. Un mo-mentito." Guachichullca raised his hands. "Please. It's already taken care of." He unrolled a beautiful duo-tone red-and-blue from under his arm: *Lucha Libre Profesional! Promoter: J. Guachichullca . Un Gran Velada de Lucha Libe. Tres Combate de Peso Media. El Primer Combate: Lucha Libre Olimpica. El Gran Garcia contra el Kalypso Kid!*

The governor shook his head. "¿Y Garcia? The Cubans? They have already agreed to this?"

"¡Por supuesto! All I had to do was invoke their national pride."

"Ha! You questioned their Cuban manhood?" The governor laughed.

"In every way possible. In several languages." Guachichullca hoped this would be true once he left the suite. The governor was much too impetuous.

The governor swiveled his gaze to Dante. "So?"

Dante sighed. "If it frees Coach." He glanced over the poster again. "Who spells Calypso with a K?" He shook his head. What was he getting himself into? "And why calypso?"

"The music of the islands! Makes you look exotic! Wild!"

Dante raised an eyebrow. "No. Now, look. I'm the only Black guy here as it is. I don't need some African witch doctor put-up. I've seen some of your masked nonsense. No spears. No damned mau-maus get-up. You got that in mind, just toss me in jail with Coach." He went to tear the poster. Guachichullca put his hand softly on top of Dante's.

"Do not worry, my friend. No *from parts unknown* for you. You will be the pride of the islands. Trust me, we can sell that." He laughed. "I can sell anything."

"Then make me the Kalypso King! With two Ks." Dante did not like to raise his voice. He preferred to let his actions do the talking.

Guachichullca laughed and clapped his hands like a little child. "¡Excelente! You make a great luchador already! That will be for your next fight. After you defeat el Gran Garcia."

"What next time?"

"There is always a next time. Siempre."

"It's settled." The governor stood. Guachichullca and Dante followed suit. "Make sure this ends. Tonight. In the Hippo-drome." He strode away, his guards following. As soon as he left the room, Guachichullca sank back in his chair. He patted his pockets, looking for another of those Cuban cigars. *They may be good*, he thought, *but not good enough to put up with this*.

Dante raised an eyebrow. "What the hell does that man have on you?"

"Amigo, you don't even want to know." He bit off the end of the cigar and spat it on the floor, "Man, I wish el Santo was in town this week."

"Who?"

"You'll find out soon enough, Kid."

* * *

Guachichullca waited in the lobby of the Hotel del Luna. Unlike the ostentatious Plaza, the Cubans had chosen much more modest accommodations. El Inspector would not have been pleased with this hotel either. Guachichullca sighed as he sank into one of the leather chairs, his back to the elevators. He hoped the governor's intel had indeed been correct and this plan would succeed. And that it would get the governor off his back once and for all. His operations were much grander than the governor.

He heard the elevator open. A shadow fell on him. Guachichullca looked up. Garcia was a fine wrestling specimen up close. Heavy forearms, almost bursting his suit. The shoulders. That face, though. If there was a luchador that would do better in a máscara, it was Garcia. A maroon one, perhaps. With silver eyeholes. Guachichullca let his mind wander for a moment.

Except that for Garcia, there would be no next time.

"I believe you are waiting for me, Señor Guachichullca."

"If you can get me some more Cuban cigars, then I certainly am."

"¿Perdona?"

Guachichullca waved his hand. "Never mind. Allow an old man his fancies. I have a proposition for you, Señor Garcia. One I think you will like." Guachichullca motioned to a chair opposite, but Garcia set his legs firm and crossed his arms. Yes, he would do well in the ring.

"What do you want?"

"But no, Señor Garcia. What is it you want? Revenge?"

71

"¿Qué?" Garcia turned to walk away. Guachichullca held up a hand.

"I can give you the Kid. Dante Davis. In a packed arena. No holds barred." He handed the poster to Garcia. Garcia barely glanced at it.

"What do you think this matters to me?"

Guachichullca laughed. "Please. All men want revenge. It is in our nature. Especially a man such as you. And on such a grand stage as well." He leaned forward. "Pero, there is algo más. Also muy interesante, I think, to you, Señor Garcia."

"I am listening."

"Good. As this comes at a great price. Greater than you imagine." He lowered his voice. "Governor Villa Macho himself will grace the event."

Garcia stiffened. "And why should this interest me?"

Guachichullca spread his arms. "Perhaps I was mistaken, then." He rose from the chair. "I apologize for taking up your time, Señor Garcia. I bid you adios y vaya con dios. I am sure all of Cuba will be proud of you." He took the poster back from Garcia.

Garcia put his arm out in front of Guachichullca. "Wait."

* * *

Coach looked up from the bare bench, his lanky form covering most of it. His fellow prisoners had left him alone since he had been brought in. Several borrachos were sleeping it off on the floor.

El Inspector led Dante into the pen but did not unlock the holding cell. Coach looked up but did not rise. He slumped further back into the wall, like he would disappear if he could. "What are you doing here, Kid? You'll only get yourself in trouble."

Dante laughed ruefully. "Too late for that, Coach. Way too late."

Coach nodded. "Can't take a Black man nowhere but trouble will follow him."

"It's not like that, Coach. I just got to take care of a few things. Then it will be alright."

"Will it?"

"You know it, Coach. Just hang in."

* * *

Static crackled in the radio. The local cell had proven to be even more disorganized than Garcia had feared. He sighed, and fiddled with the dial, moving deeper into static. How had the Mexican promoter unearthed the target so easily? What else had been detected? Was he working with the inspector he had seen lurking about? Why had the authorities arrested the Jamaican coach? Was it a ruse? Or, more troubling, was there an operation he was unaware of? He shook his head, remembering Caracas two years prior. He had escaped with his cover in tow, but others had not been so lucky. He needed to know if the Soviets had sent someone. But discreetly. How did Guachichullca and his offer fit in? And Dante Davis?

The station agent, a pale young man barely starting to grow a mustache, shrugged off Garcia's glare. Garcia threw the headset down. "Let me know as soon as you have confirmation. The operation has to go forward. I am going to the Hippodrome tonight. Have your people ready."

"Sí, Señor Garcia."

* * *

"Are you really putting the governor at risk?" Dante sat in the Hippodrome locker room, lacing up the unfamiliar tall white boots that Guachichullca had presented to him. Along with a flowing white cape and white and gold striped shorts. It wasn't Gorgeous George, but Dante cut quite the figure. He had been amazed at what Guachichullca had pulled together so quickly.

El Inspector sat down next to Dante on the bench. "No. It won't even be the governor. It's a double."

Dante scrunched his face. "Like an evil twin?"

Guachichullca and el Inspector burst into fierce laughter. "If only that were true," el Inspector sighed. "If so, we would have rid ourselves of that one many years ago. He is the evil twin."

"He has several body doubles he uses to make appearances for him. It's a common-enough trick. Good at a distance." Guachichullca smiled. "We do similar with the luchadores sometimes. When they wear the máscara? ¡Simón!" He and el Inspector laughed again.

"Believe me, the Governor no esta aquí. He's probably in that suite of his, gorging his face and drinking their best wine."

"¡Salud!" The two toasted each other with phantom cervezas. Dante rubbed his temples.

Guachichullca stood. He bade Dante to stand up and gave him the once-over twice. "A few more days, we would have got gold trim for this cape and a braided cord to tie it." He sighed. "You would have been glorious."

Dante raised an eyebrow.

"Trust me. Simply glorious. As glorious as this evening's show will be."

Dante shook his head. The crowd roared. It was showtime.

*　*　*

The station agent stood in the corner. It was risky, but it was the best Garcia could do, even if he looked like a rat-faced spy and not a corner man. No one on the national team could be trusted. They were staunch Batista men. Garcia shook his head. He didn't see other cell members in the crowd, but he hoped the station agent knew what he was doing.

No word had come from Cuba. Garcia was flying blind on the Jamaicans. The Kid had just walked out of the tunnel to greet the crowd. *All capitalist machismo in his white and gold*, lamented Garcia. Like a duck to water, the Kid had taken to this decadent lucha libre. Guachichullca was probably filling his ears with sweet nothings of cold hard cash.

Garcia smiled. No holds barred. This was his time.

* * *

The crowd erupted as the Kalypso Kid made his entrance. Dante threw his arms up high repeatedly as he walked down the aisle into the ring. Each prompt brought a further eruption. Guachichullca had been right; the crowd was starved for this. For him.

As he approached his corner, the announcer's yelling dying away, Dante realized it was vacant. Coach was not there to urge him on. He was still wallowing in a cell. Dante's face fell, grew angry. The crowd near him gasped. Business. The Kalypso Kid meant business.

He glared across the ring at Garcia. Dante knew why he had come there.

* * *

El Inspector y Guachichullca sat close to the faux governor. From a few rows away he could still pass for as Villa Macho, but the ill-fitting suit and unkempt mustache made it obvious when up close. El Inspector shook his head. Hopefully, Garcia would not realize the ruse until it was too late, until he had committed.

Guachichullca leaned over. "Terrible! I could have done better. This is a catastrophe!"

"Let's hope not." El Inspector rose with the crowd. Garcia had already been introduced and had noticed them sitting several rows back. He had feigned indifference, but el Inspector knew. Como un tiburón. With blood in the water. "Otherwise, it will be a very short night."

* * *

Dante caught the faux governor and his entourage out of the corner of his eye. Best not to look their way. The actual planning had been haphazard. Wait for Garcia to make a move. Prevent it. Improvise. Just like wrestling. Anticipate. Don't just react. Feint to make the opposition give itself away. Go for the kill.

Garcia always gave himself away. Dante smiled grimly. And he would again. El Inspector had filled Dante in on the assassinations attributed to Garcia. It stopped now. It stopped tonight.

The bell rang. *Start the fight.*

Garcia came out swinging. No change to his style. Dante swatted away his blows. Suddenly, Garcia went low and swept a leg out, knocking Dante flat onto his back. The crowd roared. New tricks.

Dante grinned in spite of himself. Good. He liked a challenge. Before Garcia could pounce, he pushed up with his legs, from prone to cat-like position. Garcia pulled up, warily. He snarled at Dante.

"Your best won't be good enough hoy, Kid."

Dante kept silent. He swung an open-handed slap that connected hard on Garcia's chest. New tricks. Garcia staggered back, eyes bulging. Taking advantage, Dante rushed in and grabbed Garcia under the arms. He lifted Garcia over his head and tossed him flat to the canvas. The ring swayed under the impact. Dante staggered as well.

Garcia quickly leaped to his feet, glaring. But he remembered the real mission. He was facing the side of the ring where the governor was seated; only Dante stood before him in the ring. The station agent was moving as well. Now to sell it to the crowd. To the Kid.

Garcia screamed as he lunged directly at Dante. Dante squared up his shoulders, hoping to use moment to flip Garcia over and onto his back.

As Garcia hoped, Dante swung low. At the last second, Garcia pivoted. He glanced off Dante's shoulder and into the air. Perfect momentum. Into the ropes, his hand out, flipping himself up and over, propelling himself into the seats. Into the governor.

Dante spun with the blow. In an instant, he realized Garcia's plan. No time to think; Dante hauled himself up onto the top rope. Garcia had knocked over several seats and was at the governor. Dante saw another man approaching the governor with a knife.

And Dante leaped off the top rope into the crowd, crashing down his full weight on Garcia's shoulders. As he went down, Garcia's face caught a chair, splattering blood all over the faux governor's cheap suit. Not taking any chances, Dante rained blows down on the back of Garcia's head.

The faux governor stood up and shrieked, flailing into the station agent as he tried to escape the blood spray. El Inspector knocked the knife from the station agent's hand and quickly handcuffed him.

Dante pulled Garcia up and tossed him back toward the ring. Garcia staggered, eyes clouded with blood. Dante caught him up and pushed him under the bottom rope.

"*Remember, no one must suspect. Or there will be chaos. El Inspector will never get your Coach free,*" Guachichullca had admonished him.

Dante slid under the rope. Garcia had staggered to his feet. Dante grabbed him in a reverse headlock and held fast. Garcia had no choice but to tap out.

Ring the bell. Match over.

* * *

Guachichullca leaned back. One thing he loved was a rapt audience. "El Inspector has gone to alert the governor of our success. But, knowing him, he already has a complete dossier." The glow of the fight still suffused Dante's face. Guachichullca knew to strike when the iron was hot. "You know, I have promotions throughout Mexico. Even on the other side of the border into Arizona and California."

Dante took a drink of water. His eyes glittered. "That's impressive. I've never thought of wrestling as a career."

"Luchador, Kid. It's a little different. And there's more. A lot more. If you're interested."

"More?"

"What happened with Garcia. It's only the tip of the iceberg. We need guys like you that can travel the world. Como Garcia, pero for good. Not evil. We're putting together a network. El Santo. Blue Demon. You will meet them."

"I am not wearing a mask."

"I don't expect you to." Guachichullca laughed. "I have enough of those in the stable already." He pointed at Dante and raised an eyebrow. "I want you. Just like you are now."

"Then I'm the Kalypso King."

"You most certainly are. Deal. Now go learn some Spanish already."

"¡Sí, Señor!"

*　　*　　*

Dante shook Coach's hand and gave him his travel bag. "Make sure no one hid a camera in this one, right?"

Coach smiled wanly. He was haggard from his days in jail. He was ready to go home. Jamaica beckoned. "Are you really staying, Kid?"

"You know it, Coach. I got a job. I got more than a job. And I think I am going to like it here."

"Good luck, then. Just watch your back. It won't be easy."

"It never is. It never is."

Inspiration: Dorrel "Dory" Dixon came from Jamaica to Mexico City for the 1954 Caribbean Games as a weightlifter. Dixon decided Mexico was where we wanted to be, and without the proper paperwork, or even knowing the Spanish language, he hid out with friends he had made. The son of the governor of the State of Mexico met him and hired Dixon to work for his father until his papers were approved. Soon after, he was approached by Salvador Lutteroth, one of the fathers of lucha libre, and his wrestling career began. From there, both under his own name and as the Calypso Kid, he wrestled for close to thirty years in Mexico against some of the biggest names in Mexican wrestling: El Canek, Fishman, the Black Shadow. After retiring, Dixon became a Seventh-day Adventist pastor in Mexico, which he still does to this day. The tradition set by Dory Dixon and other Jamaican and African-American wrestlers continues in Mexico and wherever lucha libre thrives. In Orange and San

Diego Counties, California, there are monthly lucha libre matches held outdoors, in parking lots, in arenas. Mike Cheq can be seen going up against the likes of Lil Cholo and el Mariachi Loco on any given weekend.

Was Dory Dixon a spy? Is Mike Cheq a spy too? ¿Quién sabe? Who knows? Everything is real in lucha libre. You just have to believe.

When the Tide Turns

Tiara Janté

The air is crisp and cool like the steel and titanium skeleton holding me together. As I sit at my desk, observing each person passing by the one-way mirrored partition that separates my lab from the busy hallway of Epogee, I marvel at all that I've accomplished without ever being seen. I wonder if they know who dwells behind these walls? The truth is, most have no clue that I am the mastermind behind the buzz and chatter surrounding this company as of late. Instead, when I encounter them each day on my way into the lab, I'm aware that they never notice the tall, dark woman with the fuzzy, waist-length tentacles dangling from her scalp, wearing the white lab coat, who has never called off. The woman who's poured more of herself into this company than all of them combined. But I didn't do it to be noticed or acknowledged. I did it for my people, and today I will be rewarded in ways more than their awards and recognition could ever yield. So, as I sit here, I can't help but smile as I await the culmination of all of my efforts. Today is a means to an end.

It's been five years since they stole him from me. It's been five long years since they stole the promise of hope and revolution from a world in dire need of the many changes that only he could bring. The only person on earth capable of initiating a technological and evolutionary disruption that would bring the most elite to their knees and the most in need into power was exterminated with less care than vehicles give squirrels on the roadway. Five years ago, to the day, they murdered my lover, the only one with the heart and will to deliver his people and mine from the oppression that plagues us. But he's gone now, and as Earth continues to hurtle through space and time on a course toward its demise, continuing the work that he started to save our people is the only reason I pour into this company at all.

My ancestors arrived on this planet as refugees. My mother was fleeing tyranny from leaders on our home planet, only to be met with similar if not worse circumstances here on earth. If only we had known the young blue world we knew so little about would harbor more prejudice toward us than the tyrants we left behind, due solely to the color of our skin, maybe we would've gone elsewhere. My people are not like the humans with dark skin who preexist us in this world--Black people. No, we are much darker, and everything about us is much larger than the humans who live here. We are giants in a foreign land, but it's our melanin derived from the five suns that heat our planet that the humans in power hate the most.

Initially, we were captured and caged. But, once they discovered our abilities, the ruling elite immediately found a use for us in their societies. They call us the Obsidians, but our actual name is the *Meiyechu*, the people of many suns. Now, here we are, doing our best to navigate a world in which most have no plans to accept us as their own. Despite the seventy-five years we've been here, following human laws and adapting to human social standards, we are only welcome in Black communities, but even *they* know we are not exactly the same. Still, we get along peacefully with most of them, some of us forging interspecies relationships that have resulted in a new hybrid species. I am one of the first who was born of such a relationship.

So, it is for my people that I put on this invisibility cloak and slave away at a corporation that pays me pennies on every dollar they get for my ideas and innovation. Therefore, it's no surprise to me that as I sit here, waiting to meet with the man I vowed to kill five years ago, he hasn't the slightest idea who I am, and that's exactly how I like it.

For the past five years, I've developed the perfect plan of action—one so unsuspecting that the potential for failure is impossible. I positioned myself strategically, expertly implementing the art of stealth, a skill I'd honed through years of arduous training and observation. I dedicated myself to a task so genius that they would never dare to acknowledge the Black hybrid-woman behind it all. But, in this case, it's fine with me.

My lover, Dr. Jonathan Wade, was one of the world's most renowned innovators. He was on the verge of revealing one of the most significant scientific discoveries the world would ever see when he was murdered by one of his closest colleagues, Teffrin Bane. Bane is the CEO of Epogee Enterprises, the world's leader in AI weapons engineering. A little over ten years ago, Jonathan came into possession of a legendary codex believed to have been created by an extraterrestrial source. Years earlier, the codex was uncovered during a secret exhibition of Mayan ruins. Once properly decoded, rumors began to spread about its power to give anyone who possessed it the ability to create life or end it at will. In essence, whoever had it would become a god on earth.

After being bought and traded among the most powerful men in the world, all of who were never able to decipher it, it ended up in the hands of the wealthy leader of a terrorist organization based out of Russia. To ensure the terrorist organization wouldn't initiate World War III, Jonathan hired Bane, his friend, and a former covert operative, to locate and bring him the codex. However, after obtaining the codex, Jonathan was betrayed by Bane, who killed him and everyone on his team who had knowledge of the mission. A year later, Bane launched Epogee Enterprises. What Bane didn't realize, however, was that there was another part to the codex that Jonathan hid, and without it, the part he'd killed for was useless. But, even with the knowledge that the artifact he'd killed for was incomplete, Bane kept that fact to himself while organizing secret missions around the world to locate the other half. That's where I come in.

Shortly after Jonathan's murder, I joined CORE, an underground faction of some of the most skilled operatives in the world. I'll be honest, without Jonathan's name and legacy I would have never gained entry, but the leader of CORE owed Jonathan a favor, and he repaid it by teaching me everything he knew. After working with CORE, I established a new identity and began making plans to infiltrate Epogee. I played my role and did just enough to make the right connections and stand out professionally, with an ultimate goal to become part of Teffrin Bane's inner circle.

When word that Bane had acquired extraterrestrial technology leaked out, he became both a legend and a target, forcing him to keep his public appearances to a minimum—but I had a plan. After years of dedication and strategic planning, I successfully infiltrated Epogee as a junior level lab technician, quickly working my way up to Lead Scientist in the Exo-Planetary Fusions Division (EPFD) where I single-handedly obtained and decoded the second part of the codex. Next, I developed a link to its extraterrestrial power source, creating an invisible beacon of information that I named MAYA. Once activated, MAYA has the power of omnificence. Needless to say, everyone wants a piece of MAYA, but I am the only one who knows how to make it work.

Due to all the press I've received as the first Black hybridwoman to spearhead such a monumental project; it was only a matter of time before the elusive Mr. Bane requested a private demonstration. Bane's security team consists of six physically identical hybrid assassins. While they possess parts of the consciousness of some of the fiercest assassins who ever lived, they are primarily inhuman, and that gives me an edge because machines take commands.

As I await Bane's arrival at my lab, a news report playing on my PC captures my attention.

Artificial intelligence has proven to be the fifth element itself—catapulting the scientific world into an age of limitless potential. The power of artificial intelligence has become so great that when fused with MAYA, a human and alien mixed technology, it has the power to animate non-biological objects, providing them with intelligence and abilities that far surpass our own. As we've merged into a world co-inhabited by both humans and intelligent hybrids, the question of whether hybrids should have rights has become a topic of discussion among legislators. Should non-human entities have the same rights as their human counterparts? Are hybrids

*responsible for their actions in the same way that hu-
mans are? As the law currently stands, all hybrid entities
are still considered machines, and therefore are not ac-
countable for their actions...*

"Ma'am, Mr. Bane has arrived." My assistant's voice sounding through the intercom interrupts the newscast.

"Thank you, Emma. I'll be right out."

As I head toward the laboratory to meet Bane, I can't help
but smile. In a few short years, I've accomplished something ex-
traordinary. Aside from infiltrating Epogee, I've established myself as one of the most admired minds in the scientific
community. None of the fame and notoriety matters much, however. The mission at hand is what's most important to me, and
when it's all said and done, revenge will be mine.

As I power up MAYA, I rehash the mission's logistics in my
head. I must do everything as planned. Bane is led into the lab
just as I enter the final commands into the workstation.

"Good evening, Mr. Bane. It's an honor to meet you finally."

"No, Miss. Grier. The pleasure is all mine. You have proven
to be one of the most valuable additions to the Epogee family.".

I do my best not to visibly cringe at Bane's reference to 'family' as flashbacks of the last time I saw my lover play in my
mind. Sadness begins to filter in as I remember the only person
who ever loved me. Jonathan's for me was so immense that
when I was killed in a car accident, he worked tirelessly to de-
velop a way to bring me back. After years of trial and error, Jonathan resurrected me. However, due to the unorthodox nature of
his experiments, he kept my existence secret.

After successfully capturing and then reinserting the rem-
nants of my consciousness into a hybrid body made to look exactly like my physical one, Jonathan introduced his methods into
the world, and thus the hybrids that co-inhabit the world with
humans today came to be. I was the original, however, and as I
aged, adjustments were made to my physical appearance, the final adjustment completed only months before Jonathan's death,
making me forever thirty years old. During the final adjustment,
Jonathan also inserted the key to the codex inside the deepest

parts of my consciousness, and I later used that information to create MAYA. So, when I say I am the only one who can make MAYA work, I mean it. If I were to cease to exist, MAYA would be rendered useless.

"Please, have a seat, Mr. Bane. The presentation will begin momentarily."

As I prepare to begin the presentation, I notice Bane is staring at me intently.

"You remind me of someone Miss. Grier. In fact, the resemblance is uncanny."

"Really? Who may that be?"

He pauses as if he's choosing his words carefully.

"Your eyes—they remind me of someone close to an old friend of mine. Unfortunately, she passed away some time ago. But enough about that, I'm eager to see your demonstration."

As I watch Bane settle in his seat, a feeling of excitement begins to trickle throughout my core. The moment I've anticipated for what seems like a lifetime has arrived. I quickly key in a few commands at my workstation before turning my gaze to Bane's assassins who return a knowing look. Due to our connectedness as hybrids, I'd sent several commands to divert their loyalty to me.

Next, I focus my attention on the screen in front of me, as images from some of my most difficult memories begin to project onto the screen. My accident, my death, my resurrection, my physical transformation, Jonathan's murder as witnessed and recorded through my eyes, my work at Epogee. I glance at Bane to observe his reaction from time to time as the scenes play out in front of him. However, as he stares at the screen silently, I'm uncertain as to what his reactions mean. It's almost as if he has no reaction, and then I realize that Bane is a sociopath. He cannot feel empathy. He can care less about any of the pain he's caused me and this revelation infuriates me. As the scenes near their end, I begin to walk toward Bane until I am standing directly behind him. Once the scenes finish, light begins to filter throughout the room, but before I can say a word, he speaks.

"I've always known who you are, Miss. Grier. Did you really think you could get something so significant past me—in my own company for that matter?"

I'm at a loss for words. I can feel my temperature rising within my core.

"The problem with artificially intelligent hybrids like you is that you forget your place in this world. You forget that you are more machine than anything, and for that reason, you will always submit to the will of human beings. After I obtained the first codex …."

"You mean stole?" I interjected.

"As I was saying, after I obtained the codex, of course, I realized there was a part missing. I searched everywhere, but I never found it. Then, the answer came to me in a dream. In my dream, I was back in my old friend's lab, on that unfortunate night when sacrifices were made, and my mind's eye forced me to remember something peculiar. In the far corner of a lab, there you were. Admittedly, I initially assumed you were some weird experiment, but look at you now—you're the key to it all. It makes me wonder, though. If you loved Jonathan so much, why did you do nothing as I killed him?"

"I was programming, you bastard! But, I saw everything, and I promise if I were able, I would've ended you where you stood!"

Bane chuckles. He's not taking me seriously at all, and the rage within me is quickly intensifying.

"Anyway, once I realized that the key to the codex is inside of you, I devised a plan to get you on my team. At first, I couldn't find you—but then suddenly, there you were. I sent a signal out that my team created that can remotely control and manipulate all of you machines. In that particular signal and several other subsequent signals that I sent, I embedded instructions that would motivate you to do exactly as I wished."

"You did no such thing! I planned this all! Everything I've accomplished has been because of me, not you!

"You did what I told you to do, like every other machine I command. I admit you're a bit different than the others, but ultimately, you're more machine than anything else, and therefore you have no free will—no matter how much you things like to believe that you do. Humans are at the top of the food chain, and no matter how intelligent we make you, we will always remain superior."

The smirk on his face disgusts me. I want to break his neck. It won't take much effort, but I can't move. Something is preventing me from doing all the things I've planned. I glance at my fellow hybrids for any sign of support, but the expressions on their faces are unreadable. Suddenly, the emergency alert system begins to sound throughout the facility.

Emergency. National security. Please evacuate the building.
Emergency. National security. Please evacuate the building.

"Cuff her!" Bane instructs his security. One of the hybrids handcuff me, and then we all begin to leave the building through the V.I.P. exit. As we exit the building and into the parking lot, hundreds of employees are already outside, staring at something above. I follow their gaze upward, and my eyes land on a massive silver disc nestled above the tallest tower at Epogee. Suddenly, loud buzzing noise sirens from the vessel, and the humans cover their ears while grimacing in pain. But the sound doesn't bother me. After about five minutes, the buzzing stops, and an electronic-sounding command sounds from the ship.

We heard the beacon. We are here for MAYA.
Surrender her peacefully, or you will be destroyed!

I look over at Bane's puzzled expression, and I smile as he returns my gaze. "Now, who exactly is in control, again? I guess you're not at the top of the food chain after all."

Codes and Coda

B.J. Jones

Dakkaran, Marinado, January 5th
"Effective immediately! All cab and livery service vehicles in the city of Dakkaran are suspended. A national emergency is declared!"

A man's voice sounded the announcement from news broadcasts throughout the country of Marinado. Sirens blared. Cell phone alerts went off. Panic and terror ensued. Attentive ears around the country, and then the world, listened in over the first five minutes of the broadcasts.

Amina Ngo steadied herself, then began to speak. "The state alarm has been issued in response to a thwarted terrorist attack in the city of Dakkaran in the state of Zeni, in Marinado. All cab services, including jitney cabs and livery service vehicles, are suspended and all cab licenses are being reviewed. One hundred people have been arrested in a plot to detonate fifty suicide bombs in cabs, in an attempt to shut down the capital and immobilize the country."

Photos of the drivers flashed across screens. It was an international mix of brown faces. All pawns. Not the masterminds.

Dakkaran Presidential Palace, two hours before the declared state emergency
In a high clearance briefing at the Presidential Palace, President Kofi Patori called in his top advisors. Only hours before, he received a call on his secured line from Jeffrey Ben Ivan of Ivan Research Corporation that exposed the plot. It was followed by a text with a link to videos. President Patori showed a series of videos of the plotters to those assembled. One showed three men in a meeting. One very nervously chain-smoked. Another man grinned as he accepted an envelope of US dollars. The third kept his head down so it was hard to see his face, but he wore an

identifiable uniform with a K.D. Cab logo. There was knock at the door and the three men almost jumped to attention.

A short, stocky man entered and, in a voice very higher than expected, stated, "Tuesday by 9 a.m., your crews are to be in place, at their stations. No exceptions."

President Patori and everyone in his meeting recognized the face of the stocky man. He was a commander in the Marinado Navy. Commander Eman Nguvanu was seldom seen except in certain circles. This usurper had made his way up the ranks through skillful alliances.

President Patori, barely holding back his anger, seethed. "Why is it that I must learn of this plot against my capital city, a citywide attack, from Ivan Research Corporation? A global tech firm? With a fleet of dogs! Why must we be a step behind our enemies?"

The Ivan Research Corporation (IRC) was an African-American global tech company. Their clients included governments, non-governmental organizations and wealthy individuals. Unique to IRC was a corps of specially bred and trained dogs, strategically placed around the globe. The network of intelligence personnel and satellite resources, aligned with the dogs' "assessments," allowed IRC to access information in real time. It was an organization that worked with those who moved in shadows and plain sight. IRC was effective and impactful.

"My source at IRC says that Dakkaran was a test! So, now we have shown the world that we are keener than global pawns. Each of you must check your staffs, your down lines! Every agency! Top to bottom! Bottom to top! Purge whatever, WHO-EVER, hints at being wrong! The devil you know and the devil you don't! We will not be fighting from behind!" President Patori's dark face was almost purple with rage. He lifted his index finger into the air in a prophetic point to heaven. His eyes narrowed into slits like a Yoruba mask of his ancestors.

When the city of Dakkaran suddenly suspended all cab services, it was primarily based on intelligence from the Ivan Dogs. A cadre of cabbies was on a suicide mission across the city. Patori thought that the Ivan Dogs hit on the smell of explosives around the city. He figured that the pattern from the smells made it evident that the cabs were linked. He was unaware that the dogs were also the source of most of the audio and video intel. Jeff had intercepted and cracked communications codes that allowed Patori to keep tabs on foes and friends alike.

Accra, Ghana

Back at his office in Accra, Jeff watched earlier events play out on an encrypted screen. President Patori's elite guard broke down doors. The doomed operatives were caught before they ever got into place. Most were killed on the spot. But key leaders were kept alive. In a few hours, they would wish for the mercy of a gunshot.

All remaining terrorists and a few generals were executed after quick trials. Commander Eman Nguvanu fled the country. A month later, his dismembered body was found in a shipping container in Jamaica. One of Nguvanu's ears was missing. It was a signature of some of President Patori's bodyguards to take an ear as proof of life, or as a death trophy in this case.

IRC tied in to all the cameras on the streetlights that President Patori installed. The same K.D. logos were popping up around town. Ivan Dogs were dispatched to a few places that the cabbies frequented. Video showed that men with two or three dark green backpacks entered and exited particular restaurants. The Ivan Dogs got hits on explosives in various restaurants. A location that seemed to hold the mother lode was a former St. Lucian embassy safe house frequented by Commander Nguvanu.

Jeff called his brother Jim. "The decision had to be made in real time. We had to pull the trigger on it twelve hours prior to the plot's execution. We need to find out whose alliances are in that St. Lucian property. We do not want the wrong folks caught up in this net. It's got to get back to the right people in the right ways."

Jim interrupted Jeff. "The bigger picture is that President Patori is more interested in technology and space than many older world leaders. Nigeria and Marinado now have the most formidable space exploration alliance on the Continent. Patori respects having a seat at the table. That is another reason why he couldn't allow terrorists, real or imagined, to thrive in his country. Geopolitical moves have dictated his power base to date. He seems ripe for the United Nations Chairmanship. Good and bad things happen to folks with Ivan Dogs." Jim leaned back in his chair.

Paris, France, two weeks later

The evening was pleasantly cold. Tourists filled the streets during the day, but this evening, this part of town overflowed with locals. Businessmen, politicians, and facilitators seeking discretion peppered inside café tables. Secrets and intercession were the currency.

"I can't seem to get used to the wine, you know. I never used to let my brain get foggy. These days, I almost don't care. But this is such a crazy time that I've gotta be careful. No need putting myself at risk. These fools tryin' to blow up the planet. I'm trying to save it. A few of us are trying to save it, anyway." Jeffrey Ben Ivan smiled more and more as he spoke. He knew he was getting drunk. He didn't care at the moment.

Aliza Nemitts-Alasco sat across the table from Jeff. She ordered a steak. Rare. He ordered seafood. She liked Cuban cigars and preferred dark liquor to wine. But this was a celebration of sorts. So, she ordered the wine. She was quite the connoisseur, since her international finance networks deemed that she be comfortable in a variety of company.

"What brings you to Paris, again?" Aliza asked. She made small talk even though she usually was quite direct. The barter of confidential information was her forte.

Jeff focused his gaze on Aliza's face. "I was a presenter at a seminar. Not much new accomplished. Glad this project is over. I did get to present some new theories based on my research. I'll write it all up soon and publish what I can. Whatever survives the security-clearance edits. After it's redacted, the remainder is pretty simple and can be included in my next book."

"Well, everyone who knows you knows how thorough you are. How utterly meticulous. But you..." Aliza paused and glanced subtly, with just her eyes, around the room.

Aliza was polite and familiar as she motioned to the waiter. "Sinclaire, who is the gentlemen at the bar in the grey Armani? He seems to be interested in my table."

"Madame, I believe that he is a Swiss." The waiter spoke clearly and confidentially close to her face as he handed her a dessert menu as a semi shield to their conversation. Sinclaire was the head waiter at Moreno Gato. The owner, Manuel Elizondo, was Basque, like part of Aliza's family. That connection afforded Aliza certain favors with him and his staff. The patronage of his restaurant by her wealthy friends, and recommendations for executive parties and private catering for their soirees, also secured his loyalty. Elizondo greatly respected the exclusive circles Aliza was in. Aliza affectionately called him Tio.

Aliza nodded towards Jeff. "Swiss."

"Swiss? I would think that he would be less obviously trying to eavesdrop. He is taking this tete-a-tete more seriously than we are. Let's get some dessert, then head out." Jeff laughed.

As Jeff and Aliza walked over to the jazz club, he spotted the Swiss man again. "Maybe he's following us? Let's see what his next move is. I may have to kung fu fight him!" Jeff waved his arms like he had nun chucks. He realized that the wine was having more than its usual effect. Whenever he was in Paris, he drank too much. But now he was becoming a little suspicious of Liza, Tio, and that Swiss guy.

Jeff loved his trips to Paris. The blues and jazz in Paris were American. It was truly still one of the few places that these musicians could earn a good living. In the States, they got to play but were not really paid well or treated as musical royalty. Overseas, the greats got their just due, and the damn good at least got recognition. The folks in Paris knew Black folks' music better than most African Americans. Jeff loved jazz more than math. Codes and coda. But he always said that Music was math.

As they walked from Moreno Gato, Jeff and Aliza ran into Tyler Patterson, an old friend of Jeff's from Georgetown University and the Defense Intelligence Agency (D.I.A). Jeff had been in D.I.A. Special Operations. Tyler was known to train African special ops and militias. Jeff wasn't sure if Aliza knew much about him. He and Tyler had last crossed paths in Dakkaran at a party hosted by President Patori.

Tyler ran over to meet them. "Jeff! Jeff! Hey! Good to see you, man. My brother! Nice to see you, lovely lady." Tyler kissed Aliza on the cheek in a too-familiar way. She seemed very comfortable with him.

Jeff thought, *Something is up with these two. Some history. Good thing I'm not too invested.* He smiled at Tyler, shook his hand, and pulled him close. "Hello, brother! We're going to Paul's Jazz Club. Join us! I am sure we'll be able to get a great table near the band."

The trio crossed the street and entered the club. Paul greeted them personally, showing them to a table. As they sat through the first set, Aliza didn't seem into the music.

"This must be what they call avant-garde or something. It's the 'something' I seem to be missing. Is this experimental or…" She sipped her drink.

"It was a lean-in moment rather than a lean-back moment. We had to listen in to be sure of what was being said by the music, not relax to it. With some music, you've got to pay attention," Jeff explained in his professorial tone.

"Well, then. It's next-level stuff. But tonight, I am not ready to go to the next level. I'm out." Aliza smiled.

"I'll get you a cab," Tyler jumped in. Again, too familiar.

Tyler and Jeff gave each other a thumbs-up as the couple departed. Jeff appreciated the time alone to collect his thoughts. He didn't always know when he and Tyler were working on the same side. The thwarted terror attack in Dakkaran was one time when he was sure of Tyler's alliances. His expertise in training Patori's elite forces helped prevent an all-out descent into hell for Marinado. Jeff had a few more drinks. This time, Cuban rum in a nod to Aliza. He had no idea until months later that the rum cut the potency of the poison from the wine. Jeff looked at his watch. He was ready to get back to the States.

Fort Washington, MD

"Jeff—you up for this, buddy?" Jim looked concerned as he noticed that his brother, who usually outpaced him, was out of breath. He looked his baby brother up and down.

"I'm fine. Just a little winded. Allergies. I seem to have developed allergies again. Probably breathed in some asteroid dust from NASA by mistake." Jeff laughed.

Jeff began to cough. He blew his nose and felt like a lump was in his throat. He shivered but tried to hide it from Jim. He knew that he could hide some things from Jim but knew Jacquelyn was too in tune with him as her twin, not to notice even minor things.

"Let's get back to the office." Jeff sounded a little raspy and out of breath. His breathing was labored. He steadied himself and jogged toward the tree line. Jupiter and Eclipse barked almost in unison as they ran ahead to announce their masters' approach.

Jacquelyn sat at the computer screen, reviewing compiled video. Jacquelyn Ben Ivan was the chief scientist at the IRC. She heard Jeff and Jim enter the room but didn't get up. Jeff came over and kissed the top of her head. Jacquelyn laughed, then turned her chair to face him. She recognized that he was ill. Jeff blinked as if to break her gaze.

"Jacquelyn, aren't your eyes tired from looking at that screen for so long?" Jeff hoped Jacquelyn would consider that she was tired and not really seeing his weakness. But Jacquelyn got up and rubbed his shoulders. He was gaunt. Her touch just confirmed her suspicions that Jeff was ill.

Within a few weeks, Jeff was unable to walk without a cane. He monitored his oxygen levels throughout the day. His oxygen decreased with excursion. A scan at IRC revealed bone marrow damage. He couldn't produce sufficient white blood cells. Jeff had radiation poisoning.

"Jacquelyn, Jim, remember my trip to Paris? I was poisoned there. You know the players. Five Eyes. NASA, the Swiss dude, Tyler, Aliza, Tio— Paul, the Jazz Club owner? I let my guard down. Check all our seals for leaks. Check our alliances. Be really careful. I let my guard down…"

Jeffrey Alonzo Ben Ivan didn't make it to spring.

May 12th

The call came in at an odd hour on Jacquelyn's private line. The voice was familiar but unexpected. Tyler Patterson called to set up a morning meeting with her and Jim. Neither she nor Jim totally trusted Tyler, but there was something in his voice that seemed urgent. She needed to see what he knew about what happened to Jeff.

Tyler Patterson showed up at the IRC global office with coffee and soft pretzels at ten a.m. Morning pretzels were a habit that he and Jeff had acquired from their days in Philly. It was a peace offering.

"I want you both to know that I wracked my brain over what happened to Jeff. That last night in Paris, I did some things that may have seemed confusing at best and selfish at worst. I joined Jeff and Aliza at Paul's club on purpose. I was on my way into Tio Manuel's to scout out a spot for a meeting with a business associate. The other thing that caught my attention that night was a Swiss operative, Steffan Gunner, who was observing them a little too closely. Steffan started out as a good guy, but he became a hired gun for some really bad actors. I also knew that Tio's staff and he could be bought at the right price."

"Why should we trust anything that you have to say?" Jacquelyn looked at Tyler skeptically. "You admit that you're a hired gun. Who knows what motivates you?"

Jim looked at Tyler intently. He knew that Jacquelyn would speak her mind, but he hoped that she held back a few cards in her deck. Right now, he was holding back all of his. He wanted to know as much as possible about his brother's murder. He could not afford to be emotional.

"You may want to believe that I have no loyalties, but that's very far from the truth. I still truly value my old friendships. Jeff and I go too far back to let him down. That's why I decided to meet up with him and Aliza at Paul's. She and I have history. Jeff wasn't aware of it until that night. Not until he picked up on how comfortable she was embracing me. I jumped in between them that night because I didn't trust her. It wasn't ego. I knew she traded in secrets and poisons as much as fine wines. I know Jeff likes French wines. He tended to get drunk whenever we were in Paris. Recognizing the folks at Tio's who had an interest in Jeff gave me a gut punch..."

"We know Tio is shady. But he is predictable. Paul is just a hustling musician. So, who else was at Tio's? Who else was at Paul's?" Jim asked. His eyes narrowed.

"Minor players, mostly. Steffan is not minor. He admitted to me when I saw him months later that he was there to make a deal with a Nigerian. He noticed Aliza arguing in Farsi with one of Tio's kitchen staff. He waited to see what her next move would be. The timing of the argument was key. He saw Aliza slip the man American dollars. Then he acquiesced and became quiet." Tyler nodded in Jim's direction. "I realized later through Steffan that the wine or the food was the way someone poisoned Jeff. Aliza was the source or the trigger. Before I knew the whole story, I took Aliza home so Jeff wouldn't. I wanted to find out what she was up to with him. Aliza was unwittingly for several months a dead man walking from the same poison. Over the years that I and Jeff had spent in Paris, we had each dated Aliza. I had in fact known her for several years prior to him, but he didn't know that."

"Maybe she left with you as a cover. Maybe you were covering for each other. Both of you can be bought." Jacquelyn sounded angry. "Why should we believe your story? Why?"

Tyler Patterson gave Jacquelyn an *I don't play, so don't waste my time* look. "There is a line that goes through this thing all the way to NASA. I have been connecting dots since the last time I spoke with Jeff. He called me twice. He thanked me for looking out for him with Aliza. He never trusted her either. He admitted that he had been sick ever since eating and drinking at Tio's. By the second call, Jeff knew he was in bad shape. He told me that he had been working on a 'Sun Ra code' dealing with satellites. It was no coincidence that he and I were at Paul's for that particular Sun Ra repertoire. We were connecting all of the dots—except for Aliza. Aliza was not in that loop. That's why she's dead now too. She never kept her alliances. I respected Jeff. Always promised him that I had his back."

Jim leaned forward in his chair. He slowly began. "The Nigerians have been putting more communications and military satellites into space for the past two years. The US government has been saying that the Chinese scientists are behind the technology, but Nigerians have been studying at premier universities all over the world for decades to position themselves to have top engineers and creatives for such enterprises. Quite a few have been Jeff's students. Nigerians understand Ra. The 'Uhuru Communications' is real."

"You think NASA killed my twin brother? And that Aliza poisoned Jeff but wasn't high enough up the chain to know why? Was she working with Tio or not? Can you trust Steffan Gunner? And we're supposed to believe that Jeff talked to you about 'Sun Ra codes'? Really?" Jacquelyn asked in rapid succession. "Tyler, I hope you are connecting the right dots."

Jim knew that Tyler was right. He also knew that alliances shift but remembered that Tyler worked closely with Jeff in Dakkaran and on other classified projects. Jeff respected Tyler and the skills he brought to the table.

"I trust that President Patori will help us find out who killed our brother. What can we do to garner strategic resources from him?" Jim looked pensively at Tyler as he spoke. President Patori owed both Jeff and Tyler a debt for life. That was a card Jim wanted to put into play on Jeff's behalf. Patori was now chair of the United Nation's Security Council as well as an "alt Five Eyes."

Jeff had formerly worked as a contractor for the top five countries combined super intelligence agency "Five Eyes." He was a satellite master coder. Jeff also developed the chips for IRC Global's Ivan Dogs. NASA had been blocking African countries in space exploration. Jeff had developed space-exploration codes for African countries. Jim and Jacquelyn always believed that Jeff was murdered by someone in their own government. NASA had him poisoned, as inferred by Tyler Patterson. They all would have to tread lightly in order to find answers. Jeff Ben Ivan had found himself as a casualty in the center of a global, and even space-jurisdiction, power storm.

Tyler looked Jacquelyn straight in the eye. "I'll handle this. I will handle whoever is responsible. No excuses taken."

Fort Washington, Maryland, June 5th

"Colt!" Colt's ears stood up. He was ready for any noise or movement. He stopped completely at his master's hand signal. "Yiza Colt." He responded to the command in Xhosa to come to his master's side. "Good boy, Colt! Good boy. Very good boy." Jim's voice was soothing but firm.

"Cosmos and Colt are improving almost by the hour. Good genes. Their mama, Crystal Black, was the best dog I've ever seen. Hell, who almost anyone has ever seen. Cosmos is almost ready to meet his host," Jim said proudly, smiling as he approached the dogs.

"Any better luck with the collar on Colt?" Jacquelyn asked.

"No. He hates it. He definitely needs a backup plan. Maybe an extra chip. Any suggestions?" Jim considered a new calibration.

"Where he can't chew it out? Like Jupiter? That depends on his true disposition." Jacquelyn replied.

Jim shook his head. "The one time that happened, Senator Bernard's assistant found the chip. The senator called to thank me. He thought that Jupiter found a chip that someone had planted in his den. I told him that some of the Ivan Dogs are trained to find computer chips as a part of their security training. The funny thing is, he gave me the chip and paid me to decipher it!"

"So, what did you tell him was on the chip?" Jacquelyn asked.

"I told him lucky for him that particular chip was flawed. Corroded, but that it was a government issue, top grade. I wanted him to keep his level of paranoia focused on his opponents. I told him that the chip made Jupiter sick. Then I could replace him until he recovered. I ended up with two dogs, Britt and Kenya, monitoring him and getting paid a bonus to do it! I think he wants to run for president. Harold Bernard. Watch that name." Jim seemed to warn Jacquelyn.

"I remember Jeff talking about him. He didn't like him at all" Jacquelyn said.

"Or trust him. Something inside that office is going to give us more clues to his agenda. He is the chairman of the Senate committee for Funding and Appropriations for NASA. Take another look at Senator Bernard's tapes for me. You're the next best thing to still having Jeff's eyes on things." Jim's voice trailed off.

"I miss him," Jacquelyn said, turning away from Jim so he wouldn't see her tear up.

"Come here, Jacquelyn." Jim pulled her to his side. He continued to speak softly. "I miss him too. But you know he is still here with us. In you. In all of his art, his software designs… I know you still watch his videos and that damn quirky hologram he never finished."

"Yes. I still remember how he would get excited about how the dogs learned how to be in the midst of a room full of people and discern their roles. Like hierarchy in dogs. Who was who in the room. Who was the alpha' and 'the pecking order." Jacquelyn smiled.

"Yeah. Some dogs gravitate to leaders." Jim nodded and pointed to Cosmos and Colt.

"I've got to work on finishing some codes. I have been stuck. Jeff's utter brilliance left us in the dust! His codes always blew my mind!" Jacquelyn begins to sing a hook from "Street Life" by Joe Sample.

Jim joined the song for a line, stopped, and taped Jacquelyn's arm. "'Street Life'…. 'That Sportin' Life.' Songs about being bound for New York. All written into his codes. Joe Sample was a master coder. Sammy Davis, Jr., too. No one could crack Jeff's 'James Brown codes' but you! The key was the horns, though. Jeff saved the best codes for IRC. I am proud to say I helped him on the codes of Coltrane. The "Sun Ra" codes were able to control satellite communications, Jeff was a threat to NASA and key players. There are a lot of moving parts." Jim shared his thoughts out loud.

"You introduced him to Coltrane. I actually helped him write the codes. Man!" Jacquelyn playfully punched Jim.

"All of the Ivan Dogs love 'Naima," Jim replied.

"Speaking of moving parts, let's get back to the office." Jacquelyn said. Jacquelyn, Jim, and the dogs crossed the field back to the building behind the tree line.

A wall of monitors filled Jim's office. He watched a particular screen to zero in on a special project he was monitoring. Ivan Dogs were on task. Their photographic and audio chips allowed them free access to places that would require the highest security clearances.

Jacquelyn's son Jamari was assigned to the east coast monitors. "Subject is entering his New York office. He is about to start a meeting of the alt Five Eyes. Looks like Harold Bernard and Patori are already there." Jamari pointed to a screen.

Jim told Jamari, "Be sure to make eight copies of the tapes. Put them in the safe and distribute them to the backup sites. Also, review the memo I left on your desk. Set up a meeting with Senator Kym Ramos-Kirby for your mom. She and your mom were roommates at Yale. We have got to stay on top of the NASA projects. No one is leaving us behind." Jim closed his eyes in deep thought. Sun Ra's music played in the background.

September 12th

"DC News 7. Breaking News! Senator Harold Bernard has died of an apparent heart attack. The senator collapsed today just thirty minutes after a campaign rally outside of Colin Powell High, on the Gulf coast of Florida. The Texas senator had recently announced his bid for the presidency of the United States. He was the chairman of the Senate committee for Funding and Appropriations for NASA. At this time, the only details are that Senator Bernard collapsed in his car, which was being driven by his wife Jasmine Franklin-Bernard, a former actress, known for her many television roles." Anneva Joilette was a seasoned newscaster, but she appeared shaken delivering this news.

Photos of Senator Harold Bernard and his wife flashed across the television screen. Video from the rally showed the senator freely mingling in the crowd, shaking hands and posing for pictures. Senator Bernard was known to dismiss precautions by his Secret Service detail to limit his crowd interactions.

Anneva Joilette continued. "A source for the campaign has verified that despite having a Secret Service detail assigned, the Bernards preferred to drive their own cars. The fact that Mrs. Franklin-Bernard was driving when the senator collapsed indicates that he may have been feeling too ill to drive. He suffered what has been described as a mild heart attack about five years ago. We will provide more details as they become available."

"This just in." Anneva Joilette forced a smile. "Congressman Blair Jones, former Vice-Presidential running mate of Senator Bernard, has announced that he is running for president. If successful, the New York Congressman will be the second African American elected since President Barack Obama. There is no word yet on who will be his running mate. Senator Kym Ramos-Kirby is stepping in as the new chairman of the Senate committee for Funding and Appropriations for NASA, replacing Senator Bernard as next in line." A recent clip of Senator Kirby-Ramos walking her dog Cosmos near the Washington Monument was on the screen.

Across news stations globally, photos and video of Congressman Blair Jones flashed. Tyler Patterson, the Congressperson's personal bodyguard, was at his side.

Train, Pain, & Naturals

Gavin Matthew

Thunder shook the Missouri terrain while lightning danced
across its vast scenery. Rain showered the night as if the sky was
in mourning. The Golden Rush, a luxury train by all accounts,
pierced through the falling water steadfast on its voyage. Ron
"Slim" Carter had already been onboard for the better part of
two days. In all that time, he had found absolutely no answers to
his problems. He had begun to curse the day the list arrived in
his mailbox. A simple piece of paper that had bred so much
trouble. Lives were ruined and destroyed behind it. It was not
just parchment. It was a curse. A dark omen that had haunted
him on to a train. Planes were too risky. Slim had spotted more
than a couple of black suits hanging out at the airport. His office
and apartment in Harlem had been ransacked. Gutted to the bone
and left bare. It was not paranoia when there was evidence that
someone was out to get you. It was survival. Survival that had
led him to the Golden Rush. A train ride that no man on the run
would think to take. After all, it was 1972. Who took the train
for anything other than relaxation and leisure? There would be
no reason for anyone to suspect he was onboard.

Slim quietly sat in the dining car, his hands clutched a little
too firmly around the edges of a newspaper. He was still wearing the burgundy bellbottoms and matching wide-collar shirt
from when he had first boarded. A nice purple vest and a clean
pair of Florsheim zipper boots completed his wardrobe. His full
crown of natural hair had fared the two days better than his
clothes, thanks to his Black Power fist comb. Normally, Slim
was very particular about his appearance. Coming up in Harlem
with barely anything to wear sometimes caused a tidy mentality.
Yet today, on the Golden Rush, his cleanliness was the least of
his concerns. His eyes scanned the newspaper from behind a

pair of large circular glasses, desperately looking for a distraction. Amongst the articles was Angela Davis's not guilty verdict and a recent scandal in Watergate. Both brought a grin to Slim's lips.

"Shit, you think you got some heavy stuff," he mumbled to himself as he flipped the page. A storm battered the world outside his window but he ignored it. Reading was always an effective distraction. No matter where or when, a good read was always the perfect medicine. Slim could feel his body ease into the seat as he skimmed through the articles. Minutes flew by and his thoughts were almost jovial.

"What? I missed the premiere of *Shaft's Big Score!?*" Slim said aloud with a smile. Films had become a hobby of his, thanks to the new wave of super Black movies. He figured the new Shaft flick could be a good treat for himself for when he hit Kansas City.

Down the way, the dining car door slid open. The sudden shutter made the man jump. His eyes trailed over the paper, subtly gazing just above the brim. A porter rushed through the car with a tray in hand. Slim was jumping at shadows a lot lately. He scratched his head as he thought about the list again. People had been dropping like flies for this information. Black people. Brothers and sisters in the struggle. What was he doing with it? He had never officially joined any group. As a writer, he more just hung out and rapped with the militants. Talked a bit too much, some might even say. So, why would anybody who had worked so hard to find this list send it to him? Slim had no qualifications for holding such a treasure other than he was notoriously stubborn and self-righteous. Features that his peers laughed about and said were the main reason he could never be an informant. Nobody could ever imagine Ron "Slim" Carter ever taking orders from a single human being. There were times when this was a feather in his hat. Then other times when it was a great folly. He was still on the fence on which it could be with this new chapter in his life.

"What's happenin', string bean?" Slim had barely noticed the woman approach his booth, having been lost in his daydreaming. Her sudden appearance startled the author in his seat.

"Sorry about that, honey," she said with a smile. "I didn't mean to scare you." Before Slim could object, the woman slid into the seat across from him. She was a full-figured woman blessed with a beautiful shade of onyx-toned skin and an afro. A form-fitting pair of jeans and a green dashiki did little to hide her voluptuous body. The sistah was a healthy blend of plus size and muscle. As much as there was something alluring about her, there was also a faint sense of something dangerous.

"Hi. My name is Patricia," the ebony beauty continued. "I couldn't help but notice you over here. You look real nervous. I've seen my share of nervous cats before, and you definitely fit the bill, baby. Why so uptight?"

Her smile was captivating. Slim's eyes focused in on her full lips and pretty round cheeks. Unimaginably beautiful. Black women were queens. The only thing that could distract the writer more than a good read was a good sistah. Patricia reached across the table and playfully pushed the man's glasses up his nose.

"Can't find your words, huh?" she joked, a coy grin hovering with her words. Slim's heart was starting to thump in his chest like an African drum in celebration.

"I'm not nervous," Slim finally said, his voice slightly cracking. "Just got stuff on my mind, is all. Folks dying in the streets for their beliefs, a country ripe with violence, and we still fighting pig politicians just to live in a decent home."

"Uh-oh, you one of those militant types. That right?" Again, more coy. It was almost as if she knew something he didn't. Slim wanted to be more cautious. He wanted to stay paranoid. Ride the train solo and be invisible. He wanted to be the protagonist in a new Ralph Ellison novel, skating under the radar but knowing too much. Still, this beautiful ebony goddess was just too damn intoxicating.

"I don't know. You're the one wearing the dashiki. That's got to mean something, right?"

"What was it that Chairman Fred said? I believe it was political power does not flow from the sleeve of a dashiki. Right? Right."

"So, you just like the look then?"

"No, but it does look good on me, though."

"Sistah, I'm sure anything and everything would look good on you," Slim replied, making the woman smile. "Or nothing at all, for that matter."

A moment of silence passed between them before Patricia exploded with laughter. Her hand softly caressed her chin as she cocked her head. Whether he noticed or not, he had made her blush. Slim been more than what she was already told to expect.

"Wow, now, there are those fun words that Ron Carter is known for," Patricia said as she sat up straight. "I wish we had more time to see how we would get down."

Slim's face slacked as he heard the woman's words. "I never gave you my name. You said yours. Patricia, right? But I never said mine."

Patricia sighed and shook her head. "That's because we don't have time to play games. I'm not the only tail you might have onboard this train. Matter of fact, it's because I noticed them that I'm even approaching you. My comrades in the underground sent you something because they thought they could trust you. A list of current ongoing FBI operations. Some of these programs are doing great harm to our people and their neighborhoods all across the country. Those details are extremely important. So, I just need you to hand me the list."

"I don't know what you're talking about. Besides, if I did, I don't know you! Everything you just said could be a lie."

"Really, fool?"

"Yes!" Slim said, hitting the table. "Dig this, I ain't got shit."

"I'm not playing with you, Slim. There are some serious cats on this train. They want what you have. They might have waited until Kansas City to get to you, but since I've made my move, they might just make theirs. Playtime is over. You dig?"

"Nope. Still no clue what you're talking about," he lied as he crossed his arms. The list was too risky to start openly claiming its existence. People had died for it. That he already knew too well. His secretary Beatrice and Gus, the man who cleaned the office building, just to name a few. Slim knew there were killers on the government payroll. Hell, anybody who was marching in the streets knew that by now. Some of those bastards shared his skin color. Was it paranoia or survival? That was how they got Malcolm. That was how they got Fred. Even Harriet had to safeguard herself from informants while saving lives. Who could Slim trust?

"Come on, man. I just told you I know who mailed you the fu—" Suddenly, a porter had approached the table. He was a clean-cut Black man with an immaculate mustache who stood a solid six feet. Slim was a bit taller but nowhere near as stocky.

"Is there a problem?" asked the porter.

"Actually, there is. This fine ass sistah here is disturbing me."

"Slim, that ain't a good idea," Patricia warned. Slim readied his mouth to reply but before he could say anything, the porter brought up his hand. The revolver shined under the train's fancy light as its long barrel threatened the writer's face.

"Oh, I am terribly sorry about your experience," mocked the porter. "Maybe if you hand me the list, we can see about ending your trip on a more positive note."

Patricia glared at Slim. Her face was a mixture of *I told you so* and *dumbass* but with no ounce of fear. She was the same cool and calm that she had been throughout their whole interaction. Slim did not have time to think about the woman's demeanor. The barrel of the gun hovering uncomfortably close to his forehead had stolen most of his attention.

"Hey, man. Could you not point that at me on a moving train? What if there is a bump on the tracks or something? One wrong jerk and that accident is my ass!"

"Then I guess you had better hand me the paper before you have an accid—"

Suddenly, a loud gunshot rang out as a hole blew through the porter's face, sending his hat tumbling through the air. Patricia quickly stood up from the booth with a smoking 9 mm in her hand.

"Slim," Patricia stated as she retrieved the revolver. "That chump came onboard with two other cats. Now, you got two choices. Either come with me and see if we can get out of this, or deal with the other killers who are here to cash in on your narrow ass."

Slim hummed to himself as his fingers fiddled at the heart of his afro. The ringing of the gunshot was still in his ears. Eventually, his trance broke as the whining disappeared. He took in a deep breath and sighed before his eyes met Patricia's steely stare.

"Do I really have a choice?" he said standing up, adjusting his glasses.

"Nope. Not really."

* * *

The train rattled below their feet as Patricia and Slim moved through the cars. Slim followed behind his beautiful protector. She moved as if she had a plan and a direction. Purpose was pumping through her veins like blood. Comrades in her personal cadre had died for this day. Shot, stabbed, and blown up. Patricia would be damned if their lives were snuffed out for nothing.

"Where are we going?" Slim asked.

"To the cargo car. I figure I can keep you alive longer in there. Closed quarters. One way in. If anybody comes looking for us, I got the advantage."

"Right on, sistah."

"Although it would be easier if you would take the revolver."

"Nothing doing. Trust me. Both guns are safer in your hands."

Slim had very little experience with firearms. The little he had mustered mostly involved the police jacking him up. The tone in his voice was all Patricia needed in order to drop the subject. She would hate to go through this whole thing only to end up shot by accident. For now, the two guns were snugly tucked at her waist under her dashiki. As they cleared the sleeping cars, Slim fiddled with his afro again.

"You know, you pick at your natural a lot," Patricia said as they moved.

"Nervous habit."

Patricia slid open the door to the cargo car. Several boxes and traveling bags littered the room. The car was barely presentable. Two dull lights struggled to illuminate the entire space. Luggage was cluttered everywhere, but a narrow path had been made to travel from one end of the car to the other. A few small cavities decorated different parts of the path. Patricia and Slim slowly meandered through the mess.

"Patricia," Slim said, picking once again at his hair.

"Pat. Call me Pat."

"Okay. Pat. I've been thinking. How about I give you the list? I mean, I'll still help you as much as I can, but at least you'll have it if anything happens to me."

"Really?" Pat chuckled. "Trying to get me out of your hair, huh?"

Patricia gave Slim a warm smile as she walked, but just as she cleared a cavity, a large figure flashed out from the shadows. A massive fist crashed into Patricia's gut, expelling all the air from her body. Large hands gripped at her throat and lifted the woman from her feet. The man was a mountain in a strained porter's uniform. His towering muscular form stood unmoved as Patricia struggled in his clutches. She felt as if her head would pop off at any moment. Her vision started to blur as her head throbbed in her own ears. Slim leapt into the air and delivered a hard punch to the giant's eye. The assailant grunted and tossed Patricia. Her body slammed against a set of crates before flopping to the car floor. A flash of lightning from outside played to the ferocity of the big man's next move. Like a freight train, his fist flew fast and hard. The blow exploded against Slim's jaw, lifting him off his feet. His glasses flew off his face and ricocheted against the wall. He never felt his head hit the floor or his mouth lose a tooth. All that his mind could recognize was the volcano of pain erupting from his face.

"How about I give you a chance?" grunted the giant, rubbing his eye. "You hand over the list right now, and things don't have to get really unpleasant. Hell, I'll even leave you and the lady alone."

The man had a Georgia drawl. Footsteps, heavy and solid, moved in next to where Slim was laying. Slim mumbled something as he spat blood to the side. The big man chuckled as he grabbed him up by the collar.

"What was that? I didn't quite catch it through the gurgling and shit."

"I said," struggled Slim, "you really should be watching the lady."

A gunshot echoed through the car as a bullet ripped into the giant's wrist. Slim dropped like a sack of rocks, landing supine against the floor. The man turned just in time to see the maverick crouched and aiming. Patricia unloaded a symphony of bullets from her guns. He took a volley of hits to the torso, head, and arms. She did not stop firing until her adversary had finally toppled over, his hulking form decimating a crate on the way down.

"You still alive, Slim?" Pat asked with a rasp in her voice. Slim raised his hand and gave a weary Black Power salute before dropping his fist back down.

"Good," Pat continued as she sat against a plaid luggage bag. "That's one less asshole to worry about, and we're almost in Kansas City. I think we could just wait it out back here. Get a little rest, you know."

Patricia tossed the empty six-shooter to the side. A difficult sigh released from her enflamed throat. It hurt to breathe but it beat the alternative. Slim slowly picked himself up. A pool of blood drained from his mouth as he made it to his feet. To him, there were three of Patricia sitting on the floor. Two more phantasmal than the first.

"I think I might have bit my tongue a little," Slim said as he spat more crimson ichor.

"Well, at least your hands are still good," Patricia said while rubbing her throat. "You being a writer and all, I would assume that was important."

Both Patricia and Slim strained to laugh but managed a pathetic chuckle. Deep breaths helped to exhale the fire from their bodies. As Slim extended a hand to help Patricia to her feet, a loud racking grabbed their attention. At the car's entrance stood a man in an olive-green suit with dark circular shades. He was a clean-shaven, caramel-colored man with a shotgun leveled at the ready.

"How about you toss that other gun before I blow a hole in someone?"

The man grinned like a viper, his words dripping with venom. Patricia thought about taking the shot, but the shadows obscured her target. It was too risky. She tossed the gun to the side, its small shape disappearing into the clutter.

"Groovy, baby. Groovy," said the man. Then his finger pulled the trigger. The large barreled beast barked with a deafening howl. Buckshot tore into Slim's gut and kicked him into the air. A mist of blood hawked forward as the stench of iron filled the car. Fire raged over Slim's abdomen. He let out an agonized yell as he lay writhing in his own fluids. The gunman simply giggled, feeding on the violence he spawned like a fiend scoring a hit.

* * *

The gunman forced Patricia and Slim to walk back to the dining car. He cared little about the passengers who recognized the weapon in his hand or the condition of his quarry. He simply told the gawking audience to keep moving and mind their own business. Patricia helped Slim struggle through each step. His skin was already getting clammy and sweat was coating his face. After arriving in the dining car, the hired gun motioned for them to sit across from another man. He was an older white man dressed in a grey suit, balding with no facial hair. He casually sipped coffee from a ceramic cup as Patricia slid Slim into the booth.

"I see you used your usual brand of subtlety, Mr. Gator," said the man in grey.

"I guess." Gator shrugged. "Anyway. They killed the cowpuncher. Darryl, too. I figured those ridiculous porter outfits were bad luck. Dumb, too."

"Yes, yes. You have made your views about their plan quite clear. I do not really care either way. Now, what I do care about, Mr. Gator, what I do care about is that list. You will have failed your hired duties if I do not acquire that list," the man said, emphasizing his words with each repetition. "Mr. Gator, how can I get that list if the one person who knows where it is bleeds to death?"

"Well, Stein, Mr. Stein if you prefer. You still got time to get your answers. He ain't dead yet, and in my experience, a lady is a good bargaining chip."

Stein sipped his coffee again. This time, he took a long drag of the hot liquid. Placing the empty cup on the table, he looked between the two people sitting before him. The writer was half-dead with his eyes roaming the car lights, while his revolutionary protector sat like a statue. From all accounts, retrieving the list should have been a milk run.

"Very well. Let's finish this," Stein said, twirling his finger in the air. Gator leveled his shotgun again and racked a round. He let out another giggle as he aimed at the center of Patricia's neat natural. The thought of the woman's head exploding brought a sadistic joy to his heart. He was itching to see such a thing. As if sensing the murderous vibes, she looked back and gave him a cold stare, shaking her head as she returned her attention to Stein.

"I don't know how well you think this is going to play out. Your green-suited lawn jockey over there pretty much killed Slim. The shock will be setting in soon, and then after that, he won't hear a thing you have to say," Patricia said.

"Then I guess we had better speak quickly," Stein replied. "Slim, is it? Mr. Slim, if you tell us the list's location and who else knows about it, then I can guarantee this young woman's safety. I will have Mr. Gator put away his weapon, and she will leave this train unharmed. What do you say that?"

"Douatinkitbe azgod?" mumbled Slim, his body slumping to the side.

"What was that? We didn't quite hear you. Could you repeat that for us, Mr. Slim?"

Slim shook his head to clear his consciousness. His eyelids felt so heavy and his upper lip felt so wet. It was too wet for his liking. He wiped his wrist across his face, drenching the sleeve of his shirt. That was odd, he thought. He dug the rain but hated getting wet. Why was he thinking about getting wet? Was he thinking about getting wet? What was he thinking?

"Mr. Slim," Stein interrupted, snapping his fingers. "What did you just say? You were telling us something. Just now. What was it?"

"Just now? Oh, right!" Slim turned to face Patricia and gave her a weak smile. "Do you think it will be good?"

Stein looked at Patricia, puzzled but waiting. She caught his insistent stare and looked back to Slim.

"What, Slim? What are you asking about?"

"The Shaft sequel. Do you think it will be good?" Slim repeated as his hand rubbed against the table. "Because I was thinking about asking you out. You like a man of action?"

Stein leaned back in his seat, annoyed. "Okay, enough of this."

"Sure," Patricia replied, giving Slim a heartfelt smile. "Who doesn't like a man of action?"

"Right on, baby. Right on."

In one smooth, quick motion, Slim swatted Stein's empty cup. The ceramic hurtled through the air and shattered against Gator's face. His finger pulled the trigger, but the cup had already thrown off the killer's aim. Stein's head exploded as a volley of buckshot obliterated his skull. Patricia wasted no time. Her fit form launched into the green-suited man, knocking the shotgun from his hands. Gator's head glinted off the edge of another table as they crashed down to the dining-car floor. Eventually, the gunman recovered to his knees. He was too dazed to see the last blow coming. Patricia picked up the shotgun and swung it as if she was batting for the Kansas City Monarchs. Gator instantly went limp as the hit struck a homerun.

"Pat," Slim whispered. "I got something for you, sistah."

Patricia watched as one of Slim's hands fidgeted with his afro. It almost looked like his arm was moving independently. Like the death throes of a dying beast. She sighed and sat next to him, grabbing his free hand.

"It's alright, Slim. At the very least, their plans are shook up. We did the best we could."

"Better than you think." Slim chuckled. His hand fought and tussled with the hair at the scalp of his afro. He yanked free a small two-inch cylinder and placed it in Patricia's hand. She gripped it tightly, a smile of hope beaming from her face. Wheels screeched and buildings slid into view past the window as the Golden Rush began to slow.

"I think this is your stop," Slim said, struggling to keep his eyes open. "I'll catch you on the Black-hand side."

Patricia stood up and gave him one more smile before pocketing the cylinder.

"Raincheck on the flick?"

"Sure thing, sistah. Sure thing."

Patricia leaned in and gave Slim a generous kiss, her full, comforting lips bringing a beat of jubilation. Then just as fast as she had entered his life, she was gone. The last thing Slim heard of Patricia was the dining car door opening and closing.

The author spent a few minutes in complete silence. Slim could not tell if Gator was simply unconscious or if he was dead. Either way, it did not matter. Resolved, the man rested his head against the train window and gazed out at Kansas City. Flashing red and white lights parked into the peripheral of his vision. Slim chuckled and briefly thought about what would happen if he survived. The questions. The looks. The downhill battle of litigation. So many ideas too pointless to ponder. He resigned himself to doing something much more important.

Slim craned his head back and forth to gauge that he was truly alone in the car. There was not a single person but him with two open eyes. Barely open, but open nonetheless. With his finger rattling on the table, Slim began to sing.

"*...Who is the man that would risk his neck for his brother, man? (Shaft!) Can ya dig it?*"

Slim freely sang to the tune in his head, his voice getting lower as his eyelids got heavier and heavier. Soon, it was just his fingers drumming to keep the funky beat. Then, finally, there was nothing at all.

Can you dig it?

Ace of Spades

Balogun Ojetade

Mahbas, Western Sahara

The man's normally fawn-brown skin had permanently turned the color of burnt sienna after spending over a decade handling operations in Northern Africa and the Sahel.

He looked to be in his thirties, athletically built, and a couple of inches over six feet tall. He might have been a Sahraw—there were certainly plenty of them in Western Sahara, the disputed zone between the Kingdom of Morocco and the Polisario Front controlled by the Sahrawi peoples. An AR-10 rifle lay by the man's side. To help blend in with the sand, he wore khaki tactical pants with a matching shirt and light brown suede waterproof tactical boots.

The tall man shifted his weight against the sandbags piled on the floor of the third-floor apartment, taking his eyes from the scope of the Barrett M82 for a moment.

"Need a break, Messiah?" a voice asked from behind him.

He looked down at his watch, then back at the big man reclining easily on the dingy apartment's bed. "Thirty minutes on the scope, Baron. Thirty minutes off. You know the drill. We switch in five."

Below them, street noise drifted up through the open window along with the smell of coriander, garlic and cinnamon.

* * *

Damage Control Headquarters
Atlanta, Georgia

"Give me some good news, y'all." Damage Control director Dr. Jared Franklin sauntered into the operations center, his dark eyes sweeping across the workstations until his gaze fell upon a Black woman with a short, curly pixie cut. She wore a navy blue twill slim pant suit that hugged her well-toned frame. "What's the latest from Alpha Team, Alonso?"

Lili Alonso plugged the USB cable into the back of her workstation and glanced up at her boss.

"Jones checked in at sixteen hundred hours, local time. Everything's still a go."

Dr. Franklin moved to the bank of plasma screens filling one wall of the op-center. Screens filled with satellite photos, their timestamps indicating their sequence over the course of the two months of Operation DEEP SLEEP. "How long before the LK-7 closes within range?"

"An hour away," Lili replied, referring to Damage Control's spy satellite. "The Lock will be in orbit over the target area for exactly ninety minutes—we'll have full-spectrum coverage, thermal imaging if necessary. That's our window."

A rare smile crossed the director's face. "It'll be good to have this over, bring the team back home."

"Folks are talking, sir—did the whole team have to be men? After Jones, Unachukwu is our best hitter," Alonso said.

"Are you one of those folks, Alonso?"

Lili smiled but didn't answer.

"Remember, we don't exist," Dr. Franklin said. "The whole idea is to make this look like a local job. The world can never know there's a group of Black men and women doing the kind of work we do to fight against global white supremacy and oppression."

Lili nodded. "All this money spent, all this work, and no one, not even our people, will ever know."

"Not in our lifetime," Dr. Franklin said.

* * *

Mahbas
Western Sahara
Kessler Jelks, aka Pär Öberg. Codename: VALHALLA—the founder and leader of the Order of Nine Angles operations in

Europe. Truth be told, Damage Control didn't know when or why the American-born Jelks had renounced his U.S. citizenship and expatriated to Sweden, just that he had formed the Order of Nine Angles and had used his considerable wealth and political connections to provide Morocco with weapons and resources in an attempt to tip the scales in their favor in the war for Western Sahara.

Pär Öberg was in his mid-forties, a genius, and made Arnold Schwarzenegger in his prime look like an anorexic schoolgirl. Thick bearded, six feet nine inches tall and easily three hundred fifty pounds of muscle, it was no wonder many thought he was a god—probably even Pär Öberg himself. For five years, Damage Control had worked to bring him down, with nothing to show for it.

If Pär Öberg's only daughter hadn't started sleeping with a young *Black professor* from England—if Pär Öberg hadn't then decided to *kill* his daughter...well, none of them would be there. He was now hiding out in Morocco, which made him much easier to get to.

Messiah Jones laid his binoculars aside, running a hand over his beard. Everything was in place.

A knock came at the apartment door and his hand inched toward the SIG Sauer P220 Legion .45 caliber pistol holstered at his side.

"Answer it, Baron," he whispered, gesturing to his partner. "I've got your six."

Baron Bailey was already on his feet, moving from the bedroom into the living room of the apartment. His suppressed Glock was clutched in two hands at a chest-ready position.

Baron moved with a grace born of training—he'd been a SEAL once, in a different life.

Messiah watched him in the cracked mirror as Baron advanced on the door, holding the gun at the ready as he opened the door a crack.

"Oh, it's you" were the next words out of Baron's mouth as the third member of the team entered the room. Messiah slipped the SIG's safety back on and exited the bedroom.

"As-salaamu alaikum, Seydou," he said with a smile, extending his hand.

The man at the door, Seydou Diatta, smiled at Baron, his beautiful white teeth seeming to glow in contrast to his blue-black skin. He clasped Messiah's hand in both of his. "Wa-alaikum salaam, my brother."

They'd worked together for so many years, dating back to the beginnings of Damage Control.

"Miss me?" Seydou asked.

"Hell nuh," Baron replied. "Laayoune TV is di bomb."

Seydou grinned. "Better than anything you can buy out there on the street."

That sobered everyone up. They were in the heart of Mahbas and pornographic videos were for sale everywhere—many of them from Morocco and "featuring" children. It might have seemed a strange place to be hunting the key player of a white supremacist terror network, but it was where he'd have his guard down.

Messiah cleared his throat. "You find anything actionable?"

"I met with BUNDINI BROWN," the Iraqi replied, referring to Damage Control's informant. "We talked things over in one of the downtown bars. He says the meet is going down shortly after nineteen hundred local—says Pär Öberg is already in the building, staying under wraps until after the meeting."

"Do you believe him?"

A pause, then Seydou nodded, an expression of distaste crossing his countenance. "He'd had too much alcohol to be lying." A practicing Muslim himself, Seydou didn't drink. It was the primary reason Messiah had chosen him to make the rendezvous.

Messiah gestured to the sniper rifle. "We've not been able to pick up much, just an occasional visual on the wife through the window. Thermal's useless; can't penetrate the thick walls. Long and short, we can't independently confirm. Pär= Öberg could be inside. So could a couple dozen Moroccans."

Seydou walked over to the window. "We have muscle near the door. Two guys, the big one has a pump—twelve gauge, but the small one's the leader. You can tell by the way they interact. Little guy's carrying a Beretta BU9 Nano."

Messiah snickered. Amateurs. You could tell a lot about hired muscle by their hardware. If they chose their weapons based on their "cool" factor, well, then, they'd been watching too many Western action movies.

Time to make the call. Over a decade as a Damage Control paramilitary operations officer and making these decisions never got any easier. They'd waited two months for this night, for this opportunity. But without independent verification…they were flying blind.

"Let's do this," he announced finally, looking around at his team. "Baron, get Atlanta on the horn. It's time we got the final go."

There was no comment, but he could see it in their faces, his own thoughts reflected in their eyes. They had a bad feeling about this…

* * *

Damage Control Headquarters
Atlanta, Georgia
"What's the deal?" As soon as Lili turned and saw the look on the face of the director, she knew the question had been ill advised.

I didn't even really belong here, the analyst thought. The Intelligence Division cut her checks, but with her skill set, she was being increasingly borrowed by the Suge Knights—the operations side of the house.

"Jones," Dr. Franklin responded, a heavy sigh escaping his lips. "They've been unable to confirm that VALHALLA is actually in the building."

"That shouldn't be a problem." She didn't see that it was. They'd planned for this. Multiple redundancy. "BUNDINI BROWN's wearing a wire. He confirms VALHALLA's presence, the team goes in. About as simple as it gets."

An unpleasant smile crossed Dr. Franklin's face. "That's what the Party thinks too, Lili. This isn't a game. Once you've got operators in the field, there's nothing simple about it. Anything could go wrong. Any one of a thousand things."

* * *

Mahbas, Western Sahara

"Roger that, boss. Yeah, I understand. Have Alonso monitor the satellite feed—let me know if any problems crop up. We'll give this a whirl."

Messiah hit the End button on his TACSAT phone and slipped it back in his pocket.

"What's going on?" Seydou asked, glancing over at his team leader.

Messiah laughed. "Atlanta's solved all our problems for us. Or they think they have. We don't *have* to trust him. Once BUNDINI BROWN is in place, they're going to run voiceprint analysis on the conversation to determine whether VALHALLA is really in the room."

They both knew what that meant. "Five minutes?" Seydou asked.

Messiah shook his head. "More like ten."

There went the *quick* part of it. Sometimes, plans didn't even survive contact with your allies. Forget the enemy. They walked back into the bedroom, where Baron lay manning the Barrett. "The target window opens in twenty minutes with the arrival of BUNDINI BROWN," Messiah said. "We need to be ready to strike the minute we have target confirmation, hard and fast. From shots fired, we've got thirty minutes to clear the area." He smiled. "The local *pigs* may be too corrupt to put in an appearance, but the same thing can't be said of the Nine Angles' muscle. They'll be all over us."

"Tell me again why we couldn't get a camera on the inside?" Baron asked.

"Too risky." Messiah reached down and picked up a pair of high-powered binoculars, aiming them down the street, watching the pedestrians, the shoppers moving in and out of the myriad of storefronts. Dusk was falling, the dirty, faded buildings casting long shadows in the setting sun. "They're bound to have swept the room before the arrival of Pär Öberg. They find a cam—game over."

"Al'awghad," Seydou whispered behind him, uttering an Arabic curse under his breath. "Bastards. These people really think Pär Öberg is Allah."

Messiah didn't take his eyes off the street. He smiled. "Better than Allah." He loved riling Seydou up.

"Better than…" Seydou walked over to the window, gently pulling back the shade. "Allahu akbar!" he hissed. "Allah is the greatest!"

Messiah turned his head away and chuckled.

* * *

Damage Control Headquarters
Atlanta, Georgia

It was a beautiful way to fight a war. Lili leaned back in her desk chair, peeling the rest of the wrapper off a Kit Kat bar.

Movement on-screen caught her eye, and she keyed her communications headset. "We have the package, ACE OF SPADES. BUNDINI BROWN's entering the target area—look for a gray Mercedes…E-Class."

"License number?" Messiah's voice said from over four thousand miles away.

The analyst's eyes narrowed as she tapped a command into the keyboard, watching as the satellite image zoomed in on the moving vehicle. "Here we go… Uniform-Zulu-Whiskey…niner-five-one. He's about four klicks out."

Five million dollars US. Cash. Non-sequential Ben Franklins. Lili interlaced her fingers behind her head. It was Damage Control money, "liberated" from banks and corporations around the world through a little "Robin Hood action," as Dr. Franklin called them. Five million dollars in the back of that gray Mercedes.

The man codenamed BUNDINI BROWN was a longtime player in Western Sahara. A businessman—a middleman, really, willing to deal in most anything. If you wanted enough guns to start a small war, enough heroin to corner the market in New

York, or enough young Thai girls and ladyboys to start an un-
derage escort service, he was your man. A facilitator. It had
been five years since the FBI had caught him leaving LAX under an assumed name. Four years since Damage Control had
broken him out of federal prison and flipped him, sending him
to Western Sahara with a new identity, plenty of money, and a
job working exclusively for them. Yeah, they'd put a perverted
wheeler and dealer back on the street.

That was the nasty side of the spy business. Lili made a face,
throwing the rest of the Kit Kat bar into the trash. She had lost
her appetite. "ACE OF SPADES, you should have eyes on
BUNDINI BROWN any minute now."

* * *

Mahbas, Western Sahara
"Boss, we've got a gray Mercedes inbound from the north."
It was Seydou, standing well within the shadow of the apartment's window. Messiah moved to his side, taking the binoculars from him.

The crowds had dispersed from the street with the setting of
the sun—leaving behind the detritus of the bustling district, the
neon lights of a distant bar flashing in the gathering darkness.
Messiah's binoculars picked out the shivering form of a half-na-
ked young prostitute standing beneath the harsh glow of a street-
light. She was doing her best to look seductive, but it came
across as desperation. She couldn't have been more than thirteen.

He looked away, refocusing on his target. Sooner or later,
you had to realize you couldn't save the world.

He switched on the night vision and zoomed in on the Mercedes as it pulled into a parking space in front of the target
building.

The passenger door opened, and a short, balding white man
exited, holding a briefcase. His light jacket did nothing to con-
ceal his growing paunch.

"I have visual identification on BUNDINI BROWN," Messiah announced, more for Atlanta's benefit than their own.

The Nine Angles muscle moved from the shadows, advancing on BUNDINI BROWN. *Not bad*, Messiah thought, watching them as the big man flattened BUNDINI BROWN against the hood of his car, frisking him head to toe and back again. His partner turned his attention to the briefcase, ostensibly checking it for explosives.

Messiah aimed the binoculars at BUNDINI BROWN as they hauled him to his feet, adjusting the focus until he could see the sweat on the businessman's cheeks. *Stay calm*, Messiah thought. *Stay calm.*

* * *

Stay calm, the man called BUNDINI BROWN told himself. It was what he'd been telling himself ever since this hellish ordeal got started.

He took a look around as they pulled him to his feet. The street was deserted except for a few drunks and the hooker. She looked familiar—then again, all prostitutes looked alike to him.

Anyone but the neo-Nazis, skinheads, and other racist nutjobs. That's what he'd told them when they'd broke him out from the feds. He'd do business with anybody but these psychos. That was what he'd kept telling them—until the leader of the Damage Control team had laid his choices on the table.

Convey the money to Pär Öberg, or back to the feds he'd go…or worse.

So, here he was, working as a courier again. The money was supposed to be from some two-bit Saudi prince known to secretly loathe Black Africans, especially the wannabe Arab ones.

What was his name? Crap.

The little guard pushed open the door of the apartment building and waved the Beretta, motioning him inside. He glanced back to see the big guard still standing by the Mercedes. Good choice. There were four more identical briefcases in the trunk of the Mercedes. A million each.

Enough money to have set him free. Leave, go somewhere in Europe, Eastern Europe preferably, out of reach of blasted

Damage Control. Eastern Europe, a cash economy with women almost as cheap and desperate as Southeast Asia. To start anew.

Freedom. He licked his lips nervously. It wouldn't work. Damage Control was tracking the money. How, they wouldn't tell him.

He heard metal on metal behind him, a pistol slide being racked. His heart almost stopped at the sound.

"You don't have to do this," he whispered, instinctively raising his hands. "Please, God, don't."

* * *

There was no warning. No time to react. The explosion hammered their eardrums, the sound of a pistol being discharged only inches from the microphone. Baron ripped off his headset with a curse, throwing it against the wall. "What's going on?"

A second pistol shot followed the first. They could hear BUNDINI BROWN struggling to breathe, hear him cough, a rough, hacking sound. The sound of a man dying.

Messiah's face hardened, watching the second sentry, by the Mercedes. He hadn't moved, despite the gunshots. He had been *expecting* them.

And in that moment, Messiah knew—a disconcerting flash of certainty. A sixth sense, warning of danger. "Scratch this," he announced, "we've been played."

He saw the look of shock on Baron's face. "Leave the long gun where it is; it's sterile—nothing to connect it with us. Alonso, are you getting this?"

"What's the situation, ACE OF SPADES?" Lili said.

"BUNDINI BROWN's dead and I'm calling an abort on DEEP SLEEP. My authority. They have to know we're here."

"Wait one, ACE OF SPADES."

There was no time. Messiah moved to the apartment's dresser, wedging his fingers around the bowed wood, jerking the drawer outward. A small leather attaché case lay inside, and he pulled it out, dumping the contents onto the bed. Three envelopes. "Clean passports, Nigerian. The entry/exit stamps will be verified by our people if you're questioned. Standard E&E protocols apply."

Escape and evade. Last resort.

Baron placed a hand on Messiah's arm as they moved toward the door. "If anything goes wrong…"

He didn't say anything more. He didn't have to. The SEAL was the only married man on the team. Married, with two girls.

"We got you," Messiah replied, meeting his friend's eyes. "Luisa and the girls—they'll be good."

Police sirens sounded in the distance, confirming his worst fears. They'd been set up.

"Don't stay together, whatever you do," he admonished, tucking his SIG inside his jacket. "And remember—as much as I know you want to, the pigs are off-limits…for now. Let's roll…"

* * *

Damage Control Headquarters
Atlanta, Georgia

Two months. Two months and three days, to be exact. She'd been detached to Clandestine Service for the duration of DEEP SLEEP. In reality, the fun was only starting—the fun of figuring out what had gone wrong. It seemed disturbingly anticlimactic, Lili thought, leaning back in her office chair.

"Nothing like the movies, is it?" She looked up to find Dr. Franklin standing behind her, staring at the LCD display of her workstation.

She shook her head. "Has the Party been told yet?"

"That's happening now—has the money been moved?"

"That's a negative," Lili replied, bringing up an active window. "There you go. All the trackers are online and stationary."

"Any chance that Pär Öberg will be able to detect or disable them?"

The analyst shrugged. "Not according to the fam in Sci and Tech," she said. "The trackers cost almost as much as the cash they're supposed to keep tabs on."

That got a laugh from Dr. Franklin. "They were meant for the short term—Pär Öberg's going to get them banked and electronic before too much water goes under the bridge. Kiss the bills good-bye."

"Another five mill in the Order of Nine Angles' war chest," Lili said.

There was silence between the two for several seconds, then Dr. Franklin cleared his throat. "I know it's tempting, Lili, but never allow yourself to second-guess the operator in the field. Leaving three bodies on Western Saharan soil wouldn't have accomplished squat."

At that moment, Dr. Franklin's phone rang, and he stepped away, leaving Lili lost in thought.

Movement on the screen caught Lili's eye, and she focused her attention on the trackers. They were moving. She pulled up the streaming feed from the LK-7 on her second monitor, focusing in on the doorway of the apartment.

It was the two Order of Nine Angles heavies from before, plus three more. Each of them carrying one of the briefcases. Weapons drawn as they moved out into the street.

Then, behind them, it looked like a woman, a silk scarf draped over her head and shoulders. Lili tapped a command into her keyboard, and the resolution cleared up. The woman looked more European than Arab. Two little boys clung to her hands as they followed the armed men toward one of the parked vehicles.

There was no question about it—it was Pär Öberg's wife Maja, well known to Damage Control, and their sons.

The sight was strangely unnerving—to see the family of the man they'd been tasked with killing.

And they were on the move.

Dr. Franklin swept back into Lili's cubicle, grabbing up a communications headset off the desk.

"What's going on?" Lili asked.

"We've been overruled," the director replied, his face tense and drawn. "DEEP SLEEP is to proceed at 'all costs.'"

Lili shook her head. "Huh?"

"The Council's orders." Dr. Franklin sighed. "Get me a line to Jones."

* * *

Western Sahara

Messiah glanced carefully in the rearview mirror of his Renault Clio, checking for a tail. Nothing.

He shook his head in disbelief, knowing he was going to have to come up with an answer. Sooner rather than later. He took a deep breath and keyed his headset mike.

"Seems like I remember a day when there was an agreement with the Council about *not* micromanaging field ops."

"Different time, Jones." Dr. Franklin sounded tired, even from four thousand miles away. World-weary. "We've located a Sweden-flagged King Air 350 on the tarmac at Dakhla. Got a flight plan filed for Cabo Verde. I'd bet the money in your wallet that VALHALLA's family is headed to meet him there before going off-grid."

"What do you want me to do?" Jones asked. It was perfectly obvious, but protocol demanded that he hear the order. No misunderstandings.

"Collect your team. We'll do everything we can from here to keep that King Air 350 on the ground until you can mobilize." There was no indecision in Dr. Franklin's voice. Just a cold, calculating certainty. "Once you're in position, eliminate VALHALLA."

VALHALLA. It didn't sound like a man's name, and it wasn't supposed to. *Dehumanize your target*. That was always the first rule. Made it easier to carry out the mission.

"It'll need to be close in; there won't be time to set up a long-range shot—if they were tipped off, they'll be expecting a team, not a single man." Messiah paused, as if weighing his decision. "I'll do this myself; Bailey and Diatta will have enough to do getting out of the country. Have Alonso send everything to my phone. I'll need satellite imagery of the King Air 350 and the surrounding area, security arrangements. The works."

There was a long moment before Dr. Franklin responded. "We'll do this your way. Just remember—don't get caught."

That went without saying. It was always the way: if he succeeded, no one would ever know. If he failed, no one was

126

coming for him. No glory in this. He closed the phone without saying good-bye.

* * *

Dakhla Airport

It had been Lili's advice. *Go straight in, through the front gate*. It saved time, if not money.

Fifteen hundred dollars had gotten Messiah through the security fence, around the metal detector and the scanners. Bribery was a way of life in Western Sahara. From the look in his eyes, it hadn't been the first bribe that guard had accepted.

"What's my situation?" he asked, turning on his headset.

"ETA on VALHALLA's family is five minutes," Lili replied. "Everything is ready for your departure. Once VALHALLA has been eliminated, give me the code *Firefly*. I'll release the virus."

Messiah often wondered if Lili had been a hacker in a previous life. Either way, Damage Control was in place to release a computer virus into Western Sahara's power grid, focusing on a substation three miles to the south of Dakhla Airport. Within ninety seconds of the go code, the sector would be plunged into darkness.

"Be advised, the satellite window closes in fifteen," Lili went on. "We'll no longer be able to provide real-time updates when that happens."

"Fine." He'd worked without them before. He could do so again. Three storage containers were lined up near the security fence, a forklift parked beside them.

Messiah knelt beside the rear wheel of the forklift, pulling his backup weapon from its holster, which was strapped to his ankle. A Glock 43—a subcompact semiautomatic chambered in 9mm Luger. Six shots, plus one in the chamber. Every shot had to count. Every shot would.

He tucked the pistol into the left thigh pocket of his tactical pants. It was going to be awkward, a weak-hand draw from his pocket, no less, but he was counting on surprise. It would be his only ally.

From his crouching position he could see the King Air 350 parked in front of the hangar. The stairs were pulled up into the fuselage—he could hear the whine of the turbofans. This was going to be close—was VALHALLA going to wait for his family? Was he even onboard?

The uncertainty of field ops. He stayed where he was, staring out toward where the King Air 350 sat beneath the glare of the airport's lights.

Two minutes. Nothing. Messiah glanced up to see a pair of cars moving down the access road toward the hangar, with the familiar gray Mercedes in the lead. A calm, slow approach— they weren't looking to draw attention to themselves.

"You should have eyes on the package, ACE OF SPADES," the voice in his ear intoned.

"Roger," Messiah replied, staying crouched.

Forty meters of open ground to cross. No cover.

"All you need to do is take out VALHALLA; do not, I say again, do *not* try to recover the money."

He hadn't intended to. What he didn't expect were the next words out of Lili's mouth. "The Western Saharan police have been alerted to the presence of VALHALLA and the money—he needs to be dead when they arrive."

Messiah slammed the palm of his hand against the forklift's tire. "How much time do I have?"

"Probably ten minutes out. Fifteen, tops."

"And you were planning to tell me this when?" he demanded, taking another cautious look around the tire. A bearded giant was descending the steps of the King Air 350, a smile on his face as he approached his family. Pär Öberg.

"No choice, ACE OF SPADES. There's no way you could retrieve the cash, no way we were going to leave it in the hands of terrorists."

"Roger. Out."

A sound struck his ears—the delighted shriek of a child hoisted in the air by their father. He rose from his crouch, watching as Pär Öberg hugged first his sons, then his wife, the flowered cloth of her headscarf fluttering in the turbulence of the jet engines.

To kill a man in front of his family…he'd never done it before. Not like this.

Focus. Dehumanize. *He's not a man, he's a target.* Just a target. That lie never got old, no matter how many times you told it to yourself.

He felt the weight of the SIG in its holster on his right hip, the ice-cold bulge of the Glock 43 in his pants pocket. To kill a man…no, *not* a man. Not a father. A target.

Bile rose in his throat, and he choked it back, forcing himself to remember.

Standing in a morgue in Rabat a year before, staring down at the stripped, mutilated body of a young half-Arab, half-white woman, according to DNA. She was no older than seventeen—a girl, really. They'd found her body covered with stab wounds, already decomposing.

Also according to DNA results, she'd been raped—by at least five men. Including her father.

Pär Öberg.

Time to move. *Focus. Think.* He was going to need a diversion if he was to have a prayer of escaping. The blackout wasn't going to be enough, not by itself. He rose from his crouch, spying an oily rag laying on the driver's seat of the forklift. A T-shirt.

Acting on experience and instinct, he ripped the T-shirt lengthwise, twisting the soiled fabric into a single long strip. He took another look around the forklift and screwed open the cap of the forklift's gas tank, feeding one end of the rag into the opening.

His target was still in place, in front of the King Air 350, one of his little boys in his arms, but it was clear. Time was running short.

Kneeling there in the darkness, he pulled his lighter from his pocket and depressed the button. He'd never smoked, but you never knew when you might need a good fire.

A spark and then flame sprang from the tip of the lighter, igniting the cloth. Lighting the fuse.

No more time for hesitation. The moment of truth.

Messiah rose to his feet, covering the ground in easy, unhurried strides as he moved toward the King Air 350.

Thirty-five meters.

His hands were only inches away from his weapons.

Twenty-five meters, moving from the shadows now. Two Order of Nine Angles muscle within the threat matrix, two more near the back of the plane. The fifth had disappeared up the stairs. None of them were *visibly* armed. The Western Saharans might look the other way for many things, but an open display of weaponry? That was pushing the envelope.

Fifteen meters.

He saw VALHALLA glance his way, concern registering on his face as they made eye contact. The terrorist spoke into the ear of his son. He lowered the little boy to the ground.

It was now or never. "Hej, Pär Öberg," Messiah called out in Swedish, still moving forward, his arms outstretched in greeting. He was painfully vulnerable now.

Ogun—the God of War—favors the bold.

He could see the bewilderment, the indecision in the eyes of VALHALLA and the two Order of Nine Angles lackeys. Fatal indecision.

The little boy peeped out from behind his father's legs, regarding Messiah with a childish curiosity. An innocence.

"How do you know my name?" Pär Öberg shouted.

Messiah shrugged, watching the lackeys out of the corner of his eye. One big one from the safehouse had a hand inside his jacket. His short companion was on a shortwave radio, talking to the rest of the team, undoubtedly. Zero hour.

"I come from Stockholm," Messiah replied in perfect Swedish. *Nine Angles.* "My name is Nils Andersson. I am the liaison to bring your initiatives to Africa."

An expression of pleased surprise broke across VALHALLA's face. "Hej, my Negro friend."

Disregarding his bodyguards and his common Swedish use of the word *Negro* to describe Black people, he took a step forward, his arms outstretched. Messiah glimpsed the little boy standing a couple of feet behind his father, his thumb stuck firmly between his lips.

Messiah's left hand slipped down to his pocket as he and Pär Öberg shook hands. The man wore no body armor; he could tell that from the freedom of his massive arms when they shook hands—there was just flesh beneath the terrorist's shirt.

The Glock-43 slid smoothly from Messiah's pocket, and he drew Pär Öberg in close, jamming the gun into his ribs. He could feel the man's body tense against his and he squeezed the trigger once, twice. Point-blank range. Hollow-point slugs ripping through muscle and tissue.

Blood and bits of bone sprayed into the air as VALHALLA staggered toward his daughter, clutching at the wound. Messiah shot him twice more with the Glock 43, high in the chest this time. He fell backward, splayed out on the tarmac.

A woman's scream rent the air, shock and sorrow mingling. Time itself seemed to slow down. He glimpsed the bodyguards reacting, the big man coming out of the back of the Mercedes five meters away, the pump-action shotgun in his hands. *Primary target.*

The SIG materialized in Messiah's right hand.

His first shot went wild, the suppressed .357 sounding like a hammer blow—drowned out in the roar of the King Air 350's turbofans.

Steady, he breathed, hearing the cold, metallic sound of the shotgun being racked.

Adrenaline flooding through his body, he threw the nearly empty Glock 43 away, bringing up his left hand to steady his grip on the .357. He squeezed the trigger, a slow, steady motion.

The heavy slug smashed into the lackey's throat, sending the man staggering against the side of the car, clutching at the gaping hole in his neck.

A bullet flashed past his ear. The smaller bodyguard stood there, his Beretta blazing fire. Messiah threw himself behind the Mercedes, taking cover. He rolled over onto his stomach, staring across the tarmac at Pär Öberg's wife.

Tears streamed down her face as she knelt there on the asphalt, cradling VALHALLA's head in her lap. Her fingers caressed his cheek, coming away stained with blood.

Their youngest son lay across her father's chest, weeping as he tugged at his father's shirt with all of his five-year-old might. The eldest son, just a couple of years older, sat crisscross applesauce at his father's feet, rocking to a rhythm that only he heard. The picture of grief. Lives destroyed in the mere seconds since he'd fired those first shots.

It was at that moment that the flame reached the forklift's fuel tank. The explosion assaulted Messiah's ears, a fireball boiling into the Western Saharan night.

"Firefly. *Firefly!*" He rose up from behind the Mercedes, catching the lackey distracted and silhouetted against the flames. "Execute!"

The lackey started to turn, started to react, but not soon enough.

Messiah fired. Two shots resounded as one. The small man reeled, crumpling to the tarmac, his legs kicking spasmodically.

Messiah looked back, watching as a pair of guards came around the wheel of the King Air 350, responding to the threat. More than a little late. He squeezed the SIG's trigger. *The lights.* Why were the lights still working?

In return, automatic-weapons fire filled the air around his head. The pair were armed with AK-47s. Messiah dropped to one knee behind the Mercedes' engine block, hitting the magazine release on his pistol and slamming a fresh magazine into the butt of the SIG.

He was seriously outgunned, and he knew it. Time to leave. *The lights.* He needed the distraction to get away.

Sirens split the night. A pair of police cars sped down the access road toward the hangar. The *cops* were off-limits to him. But not to the Order of Nine Angles.

He heard the AK-47s on full automatic, saw the windshield of the lead police car explode into a thousand shards of glass.

The car slid off the road and into the embankment. Apparently, the Moroccans had come prepared for an arrest, not a firefight.

Fools. It was going to get them massacred.

The price of still having a conscience. In that moment, he made his decision, raising himself up over the hood of the Mercedes.

Only one of the Order of Nine Angles lackeys was still in sight, and he was reloading, having already emptied his rifle's banana-shaped magazine. Less than five meters away. Close enough to see his face, the look of panic in his eyes.

The SIG came up in both hands. Training taking over.

The lights went out suddenly, darkness falling over them like a physical weight. He could have let it go, could have walked away.

He squeezed the trigger a single time, the scream in the night confirming his hit.

The pistol still held at the ready in his hands, Messiah walked forward to where the lackey lay dying, bleeding out on the asphalt.

He couldn't have been more than twenty-one, twenty-two. A kid. Too young for this.

Messiah's face hardened into a pitiless mask. It was the price of war. Nothing more, nothing less.

It would take time for the *police* to recover from their casualties—time for them to regroup and establish their perimeter.

By that time, he would be long gone. Messiah tucked the SIG back into its holster. He set off across the airport runway, walking slowly away from the scene of the crime. Ten meters, and the darkness had swallowed him up…

* * *

Damage Control Headquarters
Atlanta, Georgia
One day later

"You might want to take a look at this, boss," Lili said to Dr. Franklin.

The director took in the peculiarly satisfied smile on his analyst's face and rounded the edge of the cubicle.

CNN was streaming live on Lili's terminal, with *Breaking News* scrolling along the bottom of the screen and an announcer providing voice-over. "…this morning, we are reporting on the death of alleged Order of Nine Angles leader Kessler Jelks, aka Pär Öberg. According to Moroccan authorities, Pär Öberg was killed at Dakhla Airport in Western Sahara last night following a brief firefight with the local police who had attempted to arrest him. Here with us this morning to comment on the impact of the death of the Order of Nine Angles leader, I welcome Senator Emmanuel Werner…"

"Are they really fools enough to believe that?" Lili said.

"The Western Saharans? The Moroccans?" Dr. Franklin said, smiling. "Not for a moment—but it's a feather in their cap. And it suits our purposes to give them the credit. What's the status of our field team?"

"They made it out of the country safely; that's all I have for you. From here on out, they'll be off the grid until they reenter the States."

* * *

A playground
Stone Mountain, Georgia
Eight days following DEEP SLEEP

It was a beautiful day, the chill bite of fall just beginning to enter the air. Messiah turned off the Jeep Wagoneer's engine, glancing out the tinted windows of the SUV toward the playground. He knew she'd be there. His eyes scanned the crowd, the children running to and fro—the mothers keeping an anxious watch.

There. Black yoga pants and a blue windbreaker, sitting on a bench near the swings. A playful gust of wind toyed with her curly brown hair, revealing a familiar profile. It was her.

He grabbed his shades off the dashboard, pushing the door open with painful reluctance.

The laughing shrieks of kindergarteners filled the autumn air as he passed like a ghost through their midst, making his way toward the woman.

This—this was America. He felt like a foreigner in his own land.

The cool air bit at his naked cheek, an unwelcome reminder that he had shaved clean for the first time in two months.

"It's a beautiful day."

The woman looked up at the source of the voice, the shadow of dread passing across her features.

"Baron." Her voice caught. "Is he…"

"He's just fine, Luisa," Messiah replied, knowing she couldn't finish the question. He took his seat beside Baron's wife, leaning back against the bench.

"When will he be home?" she asked, her voice still brittle. Life in the Teams had been hard, but the SEALs had nothing on Damage Control.

Messiah looked over into her eyes. "A couple days, three at the most. He wanted me to check in on you and the girls. Give you his love."

She laughed, wiping away a tear from the corner of her eye. "They're fine—as you can see. They miss their daddy, but I'm sure a visit from Uncle Messiah will perk them right up."

He followed her glance, just in time to watch six-year-old Kadence emerge feetfirst from a slide. "I forgot to bring them anything," he said, a sheepish smile passing across his face.

The six-year-old straightened, in that split-second staring directly across the playground at the two of them. Eyes filled with that innocence that only a child can know.

A child. Swung high in the arms of his father under airport lights. A child. Standing there on the tarmac, his thumb in his mouth.

A child. Bent over his father's corpse, his little hands bathed in blood, hot tears washing away that innocence forever. Paradise lost.

Messiah's throat felt suddenly dry, as though he was trying to swallow and couldn't. He turned to see Luisa looking at him strangely.

"Are you okay?" she asked, putting a hand on his arm. "You look like you've seen a ghost."

The adrenaline that had sustained him in Western Sahara was gone now, remorse taking its place. He hopped to his feet, uttering a lie. "Yeah, I'm fine."

He made it back to the Wagoneer in a daze, leaning back into the seat as he fought the urge to vomit.

And he knew. He would see those faces again, in his dreams. The faces of those little boys.

He took a deep breath, fastening his seatbelt as he put the SUV in drive. Toward Atlanta. Back to work. It *was* war for the liberation of the African diaspora. And there was only one thing certain about this war. It was far from over…

Three of Clubs: Centimeter

Guy A. Sims

He braced himself against the wall. After an hour and a half of near-unconsciousness, the return of his senses also brought physical pain and an unusual level of anxiety. The musty smell of the abandoned warehouse escaped him, as the focus was solely on lowering his heart rate. He fell back on his training, re-laxing his mind, a type of self-hypnosis. Slowly, the BPMs decreased until his mind cleared and his breathing eased. He could now begin. He inspected himself. Considering the estimated fif-teen-foot fall through the ceiling skylight, no bones broken. He moved his legs, leaned forward, rotated his head. He was still mobile. His clothes had taken a beating but were none worse the wear. Off to the left was his supply box, contents scattered on the moist floor. He tried to use his arms to push himself up from his seated position, but a painful, burning sensation in his left arm forced him to remain. He peeled away the shredded piece of bloody jacket sleeve to reveal a long, jagged laceration, deep, dirty, and bloody. He mentally rearranged his priorities. With a struggle, he leaned to gather the contents from his supply box, grimacing as he put more pressure on his wound. Moments later, with all items secured around his leg, he began his first task. He sorted out the dented can of water, a double-A battery, and the partially opened first aid kit. He held the kit up to the light and saw that the standing water of the warehouse had gotten inside, wetting the contents.

He popped the top of the water, drinking it fast and hard, only leaving enough to rinse the wound. With the can empty, he flat-tened it, bending up the edges to form a bowl. He reached deeper into the kit and fished out a couple of dry cotton balls and gauze pads, a tube of benzyl alcohol balanced on his knee as he picked up a needle from the ground. Placing the cotton and one of the larger gauze pads on the can, he retrieved a lighter from his jacket pocket, igniting the contents in his makeshift cradle. As the fire quickly caught, he passed the needle through the flame until the tip turned a bright red. With this task done, he returned to the first aid kit and pulled out a wrapped ball of cat-gut suture. He took a breath. He was ready. He squeezed the contents of the tube into the wound. Suddenly, his arm felt like it was on fire. Sweat appeared from out of nowhere on his fore-head, stinging his eyes until the pain subsided. He threaded the needle, and before piercing his skin, he placed the battery be-tween his teeth and clamped down. As he drew the needle from one side of the laceration to the other, he drew his thoughts away from his task to avoid the pain.

Bang... Bang... Bang...
The final three shots rang out, followed by laughter.

"You laugh, but you need to work on your long-range hand-gun technique."

The target floated on the wire and returned to the two agents. The taller man removed the target from the clasp and inspected it. He pointed. "See that, Tre'? Off by two centimeters. That means a miss, if not a wound. You need to focus your efforts on being a better shot." Tre' smiled as he removed his safety goggles.

"I focus on *not* getting shot." The taller man did not blink. "C'mon, Ocho, I'm kidding. I'm on it." Ocho removed his goggles as well.

"When your application first came into Club Division, I had high hopes for you. I told Deca that you had the potential to be a solid agent. Back then, he didn't believe me." Tre' offered a puzzled look as he secured his sidearm. "You had high scores…but not the highest. The agency normally takes those who are tops in their class, former Rangers, SEALS, Be-rets…you know…that ilk. But I lobbied for you. Want to know why?"

"Why?" Tre' only asked because Ocho grinned as he slipped on his jacket.

"Because you always struggled. You came from disadvantage and competed against those with privilege and resources…and you held your own. Your military record is strong, shows initiative…but also unnecessary risk-taking and limited ascension in the ranks. You also have just enough insubordination issues to make you unpredictable…and that unpredictability can prove to be useful in the field."

"I don't know if what you're saying is a compliment." Ocho smiled as he guided Tre' out of the range and into the corridor.

"That's why I volunteered to serve as your mentor. Everyone in Club Division could use one." The two reached a fork in the corridor. "Gotta go, Tre'. But before you return to your room and relax with mindless television, I procured a little assignment for you. Simple and clean. Comes straight from the Jack himself." Ocho removed an envelope from his jacket pocket. He handed it to Tre'. *Simple and clean.* The two men shook hands and departed. As he walked slowly to his quarters, Tre' opened the envelope and removed the contents, both familiar. The first, a few sentences on the standard letterhead:

D.E.C.K.
CLUB DIVISION

After that, the text was so boilerplate, he disregarded it. His eyes went straight to the closing signature, *Jack of Clubs*. Tre' knew that was big. His attention was drawn to the other item, a nondescript playing card. The back of the card had a traditional paisley design. Flipping it over to the front he saw his identifier. The black number 3 in the upper left and lower right corners. The center was a large club symbol. Using his fingernail, he peeled back the club to reveal the face of a man and an imprint for scanning. Tre' placed both items back in the envelope and moved quickly to his quarters.

Tre' looked at the handiwork on his arm; crude but got the job done. He took the additional gauze and wrapped his arm. Looking up at the broken skylight, Tre' laughed to himself, remembering the desperate move not to be spotted by the on-coming helicopter. Rather than risk running to find a more suitable entry, he blindly flailed himself through the skylight. *Well, it worked.* He looked at his watch. It was time. He pushed himself to stand and soon was up, standing by the window. He could see across the street. Below, two cars pulled up to the adjacent abandoned warehouse. Two figures exited one vehicle and three from the other. There was a brief conversation, and soon all five entered the building. Moments later, they entered a room across from Tre', directly in his line of sight. Tre' reached into his jacket and cradled his custom CZ P-09 and silencer. He kept his eyes on the men as he checked the chamber. He was ready. One last time, Tre' removed the card from his pocket and looked at the face on the card. He turned away from the card, and that same face was now in his view. His eyes narrowed as he squeezed the trigger…knowing he had half a centimeter to spare.

Rundown in Jamdown

Russell A Smith

It's always a treat to get a rum punch on Negril Beach for a few days before the inevitable and far colder West Berlin assignment. But nothing ruins that rare summer break as much as getting a message to say one of the most infamous mercenaries on the planet has shown up while you're trying to enjoy yourself.

Well, I got a message to let me know as much. I had been slightly concerned that it hadn't come from Control's usual channels, but it was always foolish not to take those things seriously. My handler, Dennett, contacted me not long after that to confirm that Oliver Parks, better known as "Dust," speculatively because that was all he ever left behind him, was on a home visit. "Keep an eye on him, Rivers," he said to me. "We've had intel that he's about to pick up a big hit from a contact in Coronation Market. Get your magnificent eyes and ears over to Kingston and see what you can find out, will you?"

"Couldn't he just have been over visiting his mother?" I asked, more in hope than prior knowledge. "He was born in Trench Town, after all."

"Correct. In 1945," came the gruff voice over the payphone I'd secured with a device I really wished was smaller. Could hardly stuff it down the back of my bikini, so I felt a bit odd carrying a tool bag across to the booth. Maybe I should have put some overalls on first.

"And no, he isn't. She died in '78. He hardly ever comes back here; believe me, we've been monitoring. Which is why this is such an auspicious occasion. Would hardly have wanted one of the rookies on this assignment, eh?"

"His 40th birthday this year then. That's practically a miracle in his profession." I sighed. "Fine, I'll get my coat." It was easily thirty-three degrees Celsius out there. I may have been lying about the coat.

* * *

It took the Land Rover a few hours to get down to Kingston, but I didn't mind; we were both determined to enjoy what little I had of this poor excuse for annual leave. I'd changed out of my beachwear and not gone with the overalls in the end; for all my efforts to not look like a tourist, the locals just *know,* so I stopped making any. My flattop afro was very much in the Grace Jones style, and I wore a loose-fit pink shirt and trousers, just as comfortable. Luckily for us government agents, we could abuse the power of Q Branch for pockets anywhere I needed them too.

I got into the flow of the market crowd, like water in a stream, and enjoyed letting the smells of fresh fish and curried goat wash over me. A little too much, actually. I caved and picked up a lamb patty while on the moving stakeout. I blew hard on it after my first bite and savoured the taste as I scanned the area for a broad, shiny-headed fella, hopefully still wearing the dirty brown hide cape he always seemed to have on in pictures. Nobody dressed like that around there, but then, he liked to stand out. Heck, the man commuted in an eighteen-wheel tanker, and seeing one parked casually around the other cars hinted that Dust might just be nearby.

The grainy monochrome images did him no justice. His arms were as thick as some of the palm tree trunks around there. He wasn't a tall man, probably just above my 5'8" in flat shoes, but he had a look which reminded me of a shark on the hunt. I kept my distance, but so were most of the others in the market. Something about him just didn't lend to going near him. Maybe others sensed him smelling blood too.

He was clutching something in his left hand, and I could see a glimpse of wires on the inside of his arms. I knew from the file Dust knew his way around explosive ordnance, but without knowing where any bomb was, I had to keep an eye on this. I took my patty and weaved my way through the bustling crowd. He stopped. Was he *smiling*?

"SIMONE RIVERS!" he yelled, loud enough to silence the entire market. He still hadn't looked over my way, yet he seemed to know I was there. "YOU'RE DEAD!" He sloughed off the hide and revealed a shotgun. The crowd scattered, screaming, and I threw myself over a table just before the shotgun blast ripped through the air. I got out of the way just in time, though I got less lucky with the landing, failing to clear the wooden table, which shattered under me with my weight suddenly adding to that of the food it already held. Unluckier still, as I went to break my fall, my hands slipped on rolling coconuts and I hit the ground face-first, knocking me cold.

* * *

I can't have been out for long, as the sound of sirens remained distant. As I first untangled myself from the fruity, splintered mess, I straightened up and drew my pistol, looking for Dust or any associates. I refused to believe he had eyes in the back of his head; therefore, he must have had company. The market had been mostly vacated save for one man who I might have mistaken for a local, though his own afro and clean-shaven look had a distinctly military look, even with the fade. Not the physique of a super soldier, though. Actually, it was the dull grey shirt that gave it away. Brother from Langley, perhaps? He nested in a position of decent cover of his own making with a couple of carefully tilted tables, looking in the distance to what was my left. And the Agency didn't use Kalashnikovs unless they absolutely had to. The yelling of insults in Russian also threw my initial guess out a lot.

I took aim and, even a touch shaken, felt confident I could have taken him before he spotted me. But he wasn't aiming at me, and I needed to know why. "Who the hell are you?" I asked. He spun around and I fired at the top of one of the tables, close to his hands. "Don't!" I ordered, and he took one hand off the AK-47 and slowly raised it.

"Simone Rivers?" he replied. Definitely sounded Russian.

"No, that's me." I sighed. "Does everyone around here know my bloody name?" Then I remembered, thanks to Dust, yes—they probably did. "Who are *you?*"

He raised his head slightly. "Valery Okandi. Got a message to say you needed help."

"Why would Soviets be helping *me?*" I asked, as much voicing aloud as anything else.

"Message was not from Soviet intelligence."

I shook my head. "Then who?"

"Do not know. I was hoping you'd be able to tell me. Whoever it was saved my life, too."

I couldn't tell him anything at the moment. Too many variables for me to know as well. I asked the obvious ones. "How did you know I was here?" And more importantly, once I thought about it, how did Dust know I was coming? He must have known. And the only ones who knew I was there, at least until not long before, were Dennett and perhaps his superiors.

"They told me to protect you from Oliver Parks. And where he would be. That was all."

I lowered my aim and looked away from Okandi as a sickening thought entered my head, the one all operatives hate with a passion.

He's about to pick up a big hit from a contact in Coronation Market…

"Shit. *I* was the hit, wasn't I?" I said aloud, barely realising I'd done so. "But why the hell does my government want me dead? I'm one of their best agents, and well I know it."

"Hmm. One of their most modest, too," Okandi said. I had to admire humour in a life-or-death situation. Can't have been his first mission.

"Modesty gets people like you and me killed," I replied, then made an effort to stand up. The sirens were getting a touch louder, and I didn't want to leave things there, but nor did I want to risk detention when I'd just been burned. "I need to leave."

"And I need your help."

I thought for the second or two I could spare. Passengers were a bad idea in this situation, but the man did just save my bacon, so I owed him that much.

"We'll walk and talk," I said to him. "There's a safe house not too far from here, and someone I trust there, but I can't take the Landy if they're looking for me."

"I have a motorcycle," Okandi said. "But I don't know where I'm going. Can you ride?"

"Been a while, but yes. Shall we?"

*   *   *

"So, you know something I don't?" I asked him at the safe house, in truth no more than a large garage with a rough mattress and a reasonably stocked working fridge. I threw him a bottle of fizzy grape juice just as I popped a second open for myself.

"Many things," he said, as he caught the bottle and looked quizzically at it for a moment before popping the top with his teeth. I rolled my eyes. "But to better answer what you are really asking, I believe yes, Dennett sent you here to die. Just as my former superior did me."

It wasn't healthy to have that kind of additional paranoia in a world already this dangerous, even if it did keep you alive. The other thing that kept you alive? Information, and this man had it, I thought. He was younger than me, I could tell, likely in his twenties to my early thirties, yet I could also see in those eyes of his that he'd seen a lot, even in this early a career. I imagined he could have gone some places they couldn't have sent any old Soviet intelligence officer. A counterpart to me in many respects, I thought. "How did you root out your rat?" I asked.

He looked away, down, sighed. "Was my immediate superior. I caught him out when he gave me the order to come here. Yes, Walter Dennett was the name he gave me, along with an assassination order. Said I could get closer to him than other operatives. I am no assassin, so this made no sense to me. Then he told me Dennett planned to meet with Parks and organise a threat to Moscow which we could neutralise here if someone reached on time. Although orders are orders, I could not see how he knew so much about what was happening here unless he already had someone who could get close to Dennett's operations.

I did some digging. I do not believe British Intelligence, even at their worst, would hire an outside contractor as messy as Parks to do their dirty work."

I took several large gulps from the glass bottle even as Okandi took a sip after all his talking. "The whole thing was a setup. But why not just do it the old-fashioned way and car-bomb me? Or at least have just played me off against you before we realised what was going on?"

He shook his head. "Probably the plan. Except it failed before they signed the paper. I believe they underestimated us both."

"And what happened to your commanding officer ~~captain~~?" I asked.

The Russian cleared his throat. "*I* happened to him. I went above his head and found no such order had been given from there. So, I took the matter into my own hands."

I gave a nod. Couldn't say whether it was of acknowledgement or approval, but I at least knew why he was there. "Oh. You can't go home, can you? Not unless you clear your name. Were you planning to defect? Only, I'm going to have some bother, clearing the paperwork for that myself at the moment."

"As you say, it is not that simple. You at least have the luxury of being assumed dead whilst we figure out what your former boss and mine were up to. And besides, the protection of the great 'Blue Angel' is nothing to be turned down."

I let out a big sigh. "Well, I could be doing my job better. Everyone knows I was here now. I'm supposed to be a spy."

"You're a very good one. It just happens I'm a very good intelligence officer. Speaking of which, I happen to know there's a good chance your man Dennett *is* on the island. For business like this…"

"…Dust likes to do business in person. Yes, good point. Also, I'll take the compliment." I huffed, finished the juice with a careful burp, and pointed to a map on the table. "Now, if we're going to catch ourselves a rat, we're going to have to move fast."

* * *

We couldn't move much faster than by what I hoped was in the other lock-up nearby. My memory served me correctly, and we soon found ourselves facing a slightly different shape in the forestry in my line of sight. I waved Okandi down to a crouch as I saw some movement close to the mound. A thin, bearded man with no shirt, faded and worn short jeans, and grey dreadlocks sat on a stool, to the casual eye slicing a hole into a huge green coconut. My more-trained eye could see that he sat on a quiet sentry duty and had clocked us at least a few steps back, though he didn't want us to know that. Okandi started to reach into his pocket, but I gently waved to stand him down. I smiled, mostly to myself, as I considered I had no chance of identifying the passcode. I thought I might try something, though, given this was at least my third operational visit to Jamaica. "Bet you don't see many angels round here," I said. Hopefully, he was as familiar with my callsign as Okandi had been, perhaps more so, given who I expected he was.

The dreadlocked man continued to chop away with his small knife until he had an excellent point on the top of the coconut, along with what I assumed to be a wide hole. Without looking up, he then reached for a far larger machete, the blade of which briefly glistened in the sun. He twiddled the handle back and forth with quite deliberate movements for those he had truly intended to be watching. I knew now we had more pairs of eyes on us, with a rough idea where they might be positioned, but if they were as well camouflaged as the base, they'd find me long before I found them. "Do *not* draw your weapon," I whispered to Okandi. "In fact, don't move at all."

"Da," came the whisper back. The dreadlocked sentry finally looked up, just barely. "Me never see many duppy round here, neither."

"*Duppy?*" whispered Okandi.

I chuckled quietly. "Me look dead to you?" I called out, sounding every bit like a Londoner with Jamaican parents rather than local. Again, I stood out anyway and had given up hiding it.

Our sentry laughed. Whether at my reply or with me, I did not know. "Nuh yet," he said.

"I'll take that," I told him.

He held the machete at an angle for the blade to catch in the sun once again, but this time he left it in that position for a second before placing the weapon gently back on the ground. Sometimes, you're better off not messing around with old codes and just saying who you are without saying who you are. "Him with you?" the sentry asked and pointed directly behind me at Okandi.

"Yeah, I guess so," I replied. "He's the reason I'm not haunting you at the moment, Lion."

He snorted, then took a gulp of the coconut water. "The Lion, the Angel and the Wolf," he said, and as he did, Okandi's eyes widened.

"Wait. Did you give me the message to save Agent Rivers?" Okandi asked.

The sentry shrugged with a smirk. "What message?" I looked at Okandi, who looked back at me. We didn't find much between that exchange. "Well, if you're not dead, you must have come here for something?"

"Yes, I need to 'debrief' with my old boss. Seems he's the one who *wanted* me dead in the first place."

"God help him when you catch him. Come." He waved us over. We complied. Once we had reached him, Okandi turned to the guard and asked, "How did you know who I was if you didn't send the message?"

"You want to ask me questions or Mr. Dennett?" he replied. "You know, if you hurry, you might catch him. Takes an agent not meant to be here a lot of time to get on a boat with the wrong papers. Even a boat that's not meant to be there." He moved to a thick-roped pulley on a nearby tree branch and started to operate it. The flat, leafy front of the mound lifted up like a garage door. "You know, I wonder why the damn fool didn't just take a plane like any sensible murderer in a hurry. Ah. Maybe because someone told him they were looking for him at the airport, too."

"They?" I asked.

He just winked. "I heard some friends wanted to buy you some time to find him." Once the ropes were up and the doors open, he reached for a hanging hook inside and then pitched a set of keys at me. I pressed a button on one of the two silver plastic fobs, and a set of yellow lights flashed at me. I took the other off the ring and pocketed it. "This isn't the Aston Martin," I said, raising an eyebrow.

"Me know," said Lion. "Everyone asks that. But this is rarer."

I took a quick look at the vehicle. He was right. "Porsche 935," I said. "Not many of those to be had on the roads at all. Anywhere." It was a silver, grey, and white triple mix that looked magnificent. "But I'd take a milk float if I thought it had half a chance of catching that bastard."

"Close enough," said Lion. "And my mother shop in that market every other day. If her foot weren't sore from a fall the other day, she would have been there. I don't even want to think about it. Bruk him neck fe me."

*   *   *

The winding roads of Mount Rosser quickly reminded me to respect the near eight hundred horses pushing this Porsche along. I almost warped the paintwork on some of the corners as I tested my limits. We'd hopefully reach Montego Bay quicker than a tanker, and tuning myself to the car and the roads was almost perfect meditation. I was getting so into it that for a moment, I forgot I had a passenger with me, not least one I might have had to consider keeping a gun trained on.

"Did you see the motorcycle cut down the hill behind us?" Valery asked.

"I really have to look where I'm going," I answered. But now that he mentioned it, I did remember one bike it seemed like was trying to keep up with us for a while. I didn't let up, though, and left the rider behind a truck I passed. Or so I had thought. Just as I was mulling this over, I noted the next truck I was coming up on was veering across each side of the road as if the driver were drunk. Yet given the tight roads and corners, had that been so, then the truck would have hit a wall or building by now. The driver was trying to slow me down, and it was working. I had no room to pass like this.

It decreased speed, and I had no choice but to follow. I matched for distance, looked for a gap or a fork in the road. "Get a weapon ready," I said, without taking my eyes off the truck. I watched the tarpaulin on the back ruffle in a way which had nothing to do with the wind and everything to do with the cargo being prime ambush. "And pray this is armoured."

"What?" Valery said, still looking behind.

"DOWN!" I said, crouching out of sight as the veil burst open and automatic fire chattered our way. Bullets hammered at the front, and I slung the gearstick into reverse, throwing the wheel with my other hand. We spun halfway, only to see another truck edge around the previous corner, with no interest in stopping. I cancelled my previous plan and decided to take my chances up ahead. Still, bullets showered us, hammering into my side of the thankfully reinforced vehicle.

"Get me a clean shot at the gunner," Valery ordered. While I had been working on evasive action, he had readied a sidearm and reached one finger to the dash in front of him. Looked like he had taken it as a targeting reference. I slammed my foot down and wheeled into a drift to try and grant his request. The wheel-spin created a smokescreen as he lowered the window and let three rounds rapidly loose at the rear guns, breaking to reload. They did not fire again. I straightened the wheel and went straight for the front cab and the tight gap left in front of it. I stopped feeling any kind of precious about the paintwork as I squeezed the racer through a space marginally smaller than it was.

"So much for the element of surprise," I grumbled. "Guess I'm back to the land of the living."

Okandi pulled himself back upright in his seat after the impact. "Good. Keep it this way for both of us."

"Not for them." I pressed one of the switches I had taken a moment to study before leaving the garage, and the large fin at the rear tilted forward as I heard a *pfff pfff pfff* behind. I accelerated hard to put some distance between us and where we'd been.

Three far, loud explosions rendered the ambush truck a fiery roadblock. It had the desired effect of a few minutes of uninterrupted navigation of roads quite treacherous enough without the aid of people actively trying to kill us.

* * *

We'd neared Ocho Rios, so I knew to head west. On this road, I could really put my foot down. Hard enough to pin Valery right in his seat. And for all else I happened to be feeling, I couldn't hide the grin this put on my face. It had the desired effect of leaving the other pursuers coming after us in large and heavy vehicles in our dust, without having to resort to any of the "usual refinements" buttons. They may have harmed as many civilians, and I didn't want that on my conscience.

We spotted Dust's tanker just within line of sight, pulling into Runaway Bay. I couldn't think of anywhere more appropriately named for an extraction point.

As we slowed and came off the A1, the hide-clad figure casually pulled a green tube from his cab and lifted it in our direction. Screaming bystanders scattered as I realised what was happening. "RPG launcher!" I said, cursing as I slammed the brakes on hard and threw the wheel into a hard lock.

"BRACE!" I yelled, hoping I'd done enough to evade, but as the car spun left, I heard a loud bang as we flipped into the air. We came down hard, upside-down, front-first, and helpless.

I didn't know how long it took to recover, but the first thing I caught was a whiff of smoke and oil and the awareness of blood rushing to my head and then dripping from it, upwards. I removed the five-point harness with some gratitude for it being there and put my left arm out with a gnarled wince as I let gravity take its course. I reached for my pistol, then took the butt of it and bashed out what remained of the reinforced but unhinged glass. I didn't have time to be thankful for that already being loosened from the impact, or to do anything other than crawl out. If this thing was going to blow, I'd have to check on Okandi once I got upright, *if* I had time.

As I escaped the prospect of a fiery metal tomb, I heard a series of hammering thumps and realised Dust had been taking potshots at the car with his assault rifle on single yet rapid rounds. He couldn't have seen me; otherwise, he'd have targeted me instead. The screen of smoke and oil the vehicle was belching out seemed to be a final act of protection for me from this one-off work of art. It would have been awfully ungrateful to not have passed up the opportunity it afforded me. I staggered clear, hoping to get a clean shot at him, but I couldn't see a damn thing either. If he got the jump on me, I was dead. Even at full health, Dust would have given me the kind of run for my money I couldn't call in a fight, but as I was, he'd have snapped me in two without breaking a sweat.

I saw his cloaked shape emerge through the smoke just in time to double-tap. But my vision and my aim were both off. I had to settle for glancing his shoulder. It was hard to tell if that did anything at all, because he barely flinched. Thankfully, it did enough to take his rifle away from hitting me too, and I swung a thrust kick at his weapon arm to make sure it stayed that way, too. The strike did enough to knock it out of his grip and onto the floor, but he closed in way quicker than someone his size had any right to before giving me the kind of backhand that sent me spinning back to the ground. When I looked up, I saw two of him; unfortunate, because I couldn't take *one* more blow like that. Still, prone as I was, he swung a foot back, ready to punt me in the head. For all the good it would do, I covered my head with my hands and waited for the inevitable.

I heard a clang, alright, but I didn't feel anything, and the lights hadn't gone out on me. With the little time I'd been granted, I looked up…and saw Okandi holding a bent exhaust pipe and Dust holding the back of his head. Okandi hadn't reacted to him still standing, though admittedly that caught me on the hop, too. "Hit him again!" I croaked, and Okandi eventually attempted just that. With the attack telegraphed, though, Dust caught the mangled muffler in his hands and just flicked. The Russian hurtled backward. I took the opportunity to scramble for my dropped pistol, roll, and empty what remained of the clip into Dust's chest. He staggered back with each round but still remained on his feet. I could see why he had the rep that he did. I dragged myself back up to my feet and, before he could recover, ran at him and launched myself into a one-footed dropkick. That did it. Like a felled oak, he crashed back onto the tipped car front. I didn't trust him to *stay* down, though.

"Valery! Over here, now!" I barked, and the Russian complied immediately. As soon as he was close enough, I grabbed him and swung us both backwards and to the floor as I reached into my pocket for the other key fob. I pressed both the lock and unlock buttons simultaneously twice in quick succession. Finally, the car *did* explode, though of my own choosing.

"Don't suppose you can drive an eighteen-wheeler, can you?" I asked Okandi. Dust was Dennett's last line of defence, there to buy him some time. I started to believe I could catch him.

Okandi coughed, and shook his head. "Nyet. But get me a chopper and we'll talk."

"Chance would be a fine thing," I said, and rolled around, amused. Right up until I noticed that for all the fire and debris, I couldn't see any sign of Dust. I prayed to myself that I'd at least taken him out of the fight. Trouble was, so were we unless I could figure out another way to track our traitor. "I guess it wouldn't do us any harm to at least check the truck…"

* * *

I was really glad I said that. It turned out he had made plans to fly out of Montego Bay after all. But all these explosions had made it a simple job to get on a payphone and call in what sounded like a pretty credible bomb threat. "Thing is," I said to Okandi as we arrived at Freeport Police Station not much over an hour later, "Six sometimes send me here as one of their better agents to 'blend in.' Thought I'd call up a few contacts while I was at it."

Okandi's mouth upturned into a small smile. "Hmph. This is still my best ever vacation. I may be forced to extend if Dennett does not confess."

I thought of rum punch cocktail glasses and Negril Beach, then smiled back. "I'll get it out of my new commander, but it might take a little time."

"That's good. Maybe I hitch a ride to Lagos and visit the university my parents met at. Maybe even visit my grandmother. Maybe I even find the person who warned me my old boss wanted me dead."

At least for a short while, the Cold War was frozen for the two of us.

The Standing Death

R. Turner

Nakisisa loathed the smell of boiled cabbage. There was no place in Freeport where he could escape the odor. The residents cooked it in the market, in their homes, and in the taverns. Nakisisa even fancied that the women used the foul scent as a perfume, a thought that made his scowl deepen. Six days he had been waiting on his contact. Six days he would have rather spent in a brothel, had the brothel not also stunk of boiled cabbage. Instead, he bided his time in a waterlogged dockside tavern called the Drunken Dolphin that also reeked of the vegetable.

The door opened, letting in a gust of chill wind and rain. Nakisisa heard the hot winds of the savannah and the lush hanging gardens of Queen Nnenne's palace call to him with the lustful whisper of a lover. He missed drinking tej with his brother until they could not see straight. He chased the thoughts away with a deep pull of the local bitter ale. Homesickness was routed by his belly churning in protest of his choice of libation. Nakisisa chided himself for his moment of weakness. Tears of longing would not slit High General Bannon's throat.

The queen knew that the high general's death would not prevent the war as the council suggested, but the selection of a new high general would delay the Houses of Gouvene long enough that the victory of Qefat would be assured. "A single life in exchange for thousands," the empress had written, and Nakisisa knew that Her Highness was not speaking of Bannon's life but his own. This mission, his most important murder, was meant to be his last.

Another draft rousted Nakisisa from his memories. This blast carried another scent to his nostrils: tobacco, a Qefati variety. The smell belonged to a tall man, his clothing a haphazard mishmash of Gouvenian wool, Imperial silks, and brightly colored Qefati cotton. His pale fingers were adorned with large

155

sapphires and rubies, some as large as a cow's eye. He reminded Nakisisa of a bird looking for a mate.

"A round for everyone and a roast duck for myself!" The newcomer tossed a purse onto the bar. "Keep the ale flowing until the money is gone!" The crowd cheered and raised their tankards in salute, except Nakisisa.

"I would have preferred a more discreet meeting, Hanif," Nakisisa grumbled as the merchant eased himself into the seat across from him.

"A happy drunkard is less likely to take notice a wealthy merchant having dinner with a lone, brooding Qefati." Hanif chuckled and lit his pipe. "Smoke?"

Nakisisa shook his head.

"I heard that a Gouvenian caravan was attacked near the border."

Nakisisa hid his smile in the mouth of his tankard. "Shame to hear."

"They say the Devil of Serpent's Fang Pass was responsible," Hanif whispered.

"Devils do hound the feet of the unrighteous."

Hanif slapped his hand on the table and laughed, pleased that the cloaked figure remembered the code phrase after all these years. Nakisisa was relieved that none of the patrons had taken notice. "It is good to see you, old friend." Hanif clasped Nakisisa's wrist. "A pity it is not under better circumstances...or better weather."

Nakisisa leaned forward, "What of the high general?"

"There is a small fortified villa just to the north of the city used as a residence for visiting officials taking advantage of House Hames's neutrality and hospitality. My first mate reports that Bannon's ship docked before dawn. A dozen or so men in his retinue. Experienced swordsmen supported by spear levies, from what I understand." Hanif took a drink and Nakisisa began to rise. "There is more." Hanif coughed and began to dab at a patch of ale that had dribbled onto his tunic.

Nakisisa sat down. "I'm listening."

Both men paused their discussion to allow the serving boy to place the roast duck and a pair of fresh tankards on the table.

The smell made Nakisisa's mouth water, and he realized that it had been at least three days since he had last eaten. He reached out and ripped a leg off the fowl. The serving boy's eyes went wide as he noticed Nakisisa's umber-colored hand.

"What's the matter? Never seen a Qefati before, kid?" Nakisisa growled in the sailor's tongue. The boy ran back to the bar.

"Well," Hanif chuckled, "if you ever retire, you could have a fabulous career as a nursemaid."

Nakisisa almost choked at the mental image of himself tending to squealing children. The thought made him feel that his current line of work was much safer. "I'm waiting."

"Yes." Hanif wiped his mouth. "I cannot vouch for the accuracy, but I am told that the high general is carrying the seal of House Duchard. If the queen could obtain that…"

"This war would be over before the first arrow is fired."

* * *

The rain had become heavier in the time Nakisisa watched the outer wall of the villa and he wondered if it was ever sunny in the Barony of Orsic. Flashes of lightning illuminated the spear tips of the patrolling guards, making them glow as if they were composed of white-hot flame. The spy had scouted the location days before he met with Hanif, its being the most obvious place to house a visiting official. Bannon possessing the seal changed the game. Nakisisa watched as both guards turned on their heels and marched toward opposite corners of the wall, the opening in the pattern Nakisisa required to get into the compound. He raced across the open space between the wall and his hiding place. As soon as his hands touched the stone, he began to scale the wall. He paused at the top, crouching to make his silhouette as small as possible.

Nakisisa took in the view of the inside of the compound as quickly as he could. Everything on the ground level was covered in mud. Guards stood at their posts, slouching under the soaked wool of their cloaks, spears hanging limply in their hands. These men were exhausted. The why of the situation, while an interesting topic of speculation to Nakisisa, was unimportant. Across from where he crouched Nakisisa could see a large stone building. Warm, oily light seeped from the windows, steady compared to the sputtering torches that cast a miniscule radiance around the guard posts. The situation was almost perfect.

Lightning illuminated the sky overhead; the storm was about to worsen. Hanif assured him that his fastest ship would be available for an immediate escape, but Nakisisa did not believe that they would be able to depart in this storm. Escape did not factor into his original plan, but he was comfortable with improvising.

Nakisisa dropped off the wall, a roll of thunder masking the sound of his landing. He quickly slipped behind a rain barrel, watching the guards for any sign of reaction. The man closest to him simply stared straight ahead, eyes glazed. Nakisisa crept forward, staying just outside the guard's frozen gaze in case it was a ruse. The guard seemed paralyzed; the only sign of life was a faint wisp of shallow breath in the chill night air. A simple wooden cup lay at the soldier's feet. Nakisisa retrieved it and sniffed it. No smell. He ran his finger along the inside and licked it. A faint but familiar taste numbed his tongue: spiderroot. Someone else had been in the compound, someone familiar with Qefati flora. The guard breathed a final labored breath and fell face first into the mud.

* * *

Nakisisa made his way through the compound, searching for the best entry point into the villa. Along the way, he encountered a number of Gouvenian soldiers. All of them dead from the spiderroot poison. The Standing Death, Nakisisa's teacher had called the tactic. Whoever the mystery assassin was, they were well trained and efficient. For a moment, Nakisisa felt as if he was following his younger self through the compound. He expected to stumble into the high general's chamber to find himself standing over Bannon's corpse. He scowled at this folly. He had been exiled from his homeland for a long time. Perhaps the queen was unsure that he lived and had sent another agent. Dark thoughts entered Nakisisa's mind. If there was another assassin, they would have to meet their end for Nakisisa to return to the land of his birth.

A timely clap of thunder covered the sound of Nakisisa shattering the window that led to a study, walls lined with thick leather-bound tomes and piles of scrolls. A simple wooden desk sat in the middle of the gloom. A forgotten oil lamp burned the last dregs of its fuel, illuminating a parchment map spread out over the top of the desk. Nakisisa squinted in the dim light. The map was of the border between Gouvene and Qefat. Dark ink outlined the potential routes the army could take and how long each would take to reach the capital. One was highlighted. A treacherous mountain pass that led to the headwaters of Mother Darya, the river that ran through the heart of Qefat. The climb would be too difficult carrying rafts, and there were no trees suitable for making them once the army had made the ascent. What would the Gouvenians gain from such an arduous route? He was pondering the unusual strategy when he heard a bowstring drawn taut.

Nakisisa whirled into the shadow next to the desk, crouching and spreading out his cloak to obscure his silhouette. The arrow struck the bookshelf behind him. The dying lamp did nothing to help identify his attacker.

"You needn't worry about the high general or the signet ring. Neither were ever here," a voice answered Nakisisa's unspoken question. "But you took the bait."

Nakisisa seethed. "A ruse. Why?" He hoped he could keep the traitor talking long enough to devise a way out.

"You deserve to know, since it is your plan, after all. A body count worthy of the reputation of the great Nakisisa." The speaker stepped forward into the dimming glow of the lamp. He was a Qefati man, near to Nakisisa's age, but his features and the pattern of his robes showed that he was a man of the upper class. "The Gouvenians plan to poison the river. Mother Darya will be corrupted by my own special version of the Standing Death poison. Many of our people will die slow, like the men outside. My friends, the Gouvenians, will offer aid, including access to the antidote, under the condition that the Immortal

Queen abdicate. In her supreme compassion, she will bend knee to Lord Duchard rather than watch her people continue to suffer. Alas, we were too late to stop the man responsible, the traitor, Nakisisa, before he enacted his plan."

"You'll never get that much poison into the river," Nakisisa growled through his teeth.

"You are a fool, assassin. We've been poisoning the river for months."

A cluster of Gouvenian soldiers burst through the door, two of them with crossbows levelled where Nakisisa, now illuminated by torchlight spilling in from the hall, crouched. Nakisisa rose, hands raised as if he were defeated.

"A well-considered plan, but there is something you forgot to anticipate."

"What is that?" The traitor responded.

"Me!" Nakisisa snatched the lantern and flipped the table to deflect the crossbow bolts. What remained of the oil caught fire when the assassin smashed it against the dry wood of the floor. Flames raced along the planks and licked the walls far more quickly than Nakisisa had anticipated, but the chaos would afford him the opportunity to escape.

"End him!" the traitor screamed over the roaring fire, and pushed his way through the soldiers spreading out into the room, short swords drawn.

Nakisisa avoided a thrust, grabbed his opponent's arm, and smashed his elbow with a hard palm strike. He caught the falling sword and finished off the attacker with a deep slash to the neck.

The assassin waded into the remaining soldiers, parrying and thrusting with the accuracy of a viper. Blood soaked through his clothes and filled his nostrils with the coppery stink of battle and death. He burst into the hall with a roar. Nakisisa saw the traitor urging a pair of soldiers forward to face him. He scooped up a second sword and raced toward the two men. He threw one sword. It buried itself to the hilt in one of the guards' chest. The second guard attempted a wild slash that the Qefati easily sidestepped. Nakisisa lopped the man's sword hand off at the wrist before slicing his neck and continuing his pursuit.

The Gouvenian soldiers did their best to protect their ally, but none could stand against the wrath and skill of Nakisisa. They fell, two or three at a time, many dead before they hit the mud. A few fled in terror, cowardice being the only balm they could muster against the Devil of Serpent's Fang Pass. There were more than Hanif reported. Nakisisa hoped he would be able to get through them in time to prevent the traitor from making an escape.

Bloodlust burned white-hot in Nakisisa's chest, enabling him to ignore the sting of superficial wounds from Gouvenian steel. The storm had grown as intense as the assassin's fury, drowning the din of the fray beneath the roar of thunder and the crashing of waves against the rocks. Nakisisa mounted the stairs to the ramparts facing the ocean. The traitor was trapped.

A lone spearman's weapon bit deep into Nakisisa's shoulder. The spearman drew back to deliver a second blow, and Nakisisa slammed the pommel of his sword into his jaw, smiling at the satisfying crack of bone. The soldier fell and Nakisisa extinguished his life with a hard stomp to the chest.

The assassin turned and strode toward the traitor. Lightning flashed, revealing his narrowed eyes, hardened from rage and battle. He tossed the captured blade over the wall. Though this man quaking in fear before him was a traitor, he was still Qefati and deserved to die with honor.

"Give me the formula for the antidote," Nakisisa demanded.

"It will die with me." The traitor stood defiantly, but his voice wavered.

"Why would you slaughter your brothers and sisters? How could you support them?" Nakisisa motioned to the fallen Gouvenian soldiers. "They would overrun our birth-land like vultures on a battlefield. They would strip all Qefat's wealth and bind us in chains."

"I would have had wealth, power, land, and the queen herself as a pet. They promised me all these things. Go ahead! Take my life, but know that Qefat dies with me!" A smile crossed the traitor's lips as the sound of alarm bells rose from the town. "They are coming for you, great Nakisisa."

"You are a traitor and a fool! The houses would never install you, even as a puppet. Your lust for riches and status has dulled your sense." Nakisisa looked out over the raging sea. In the darkness, a single pinprick of light bobbed: Hanif's ship. It was Nakisisa's turn to smile. The assassin charged, tackling the traitor and sending them both over the wall and into the surf.

*   *   *

Nakisisa sighed as he basked in the sun on the deck of Hanif's ship. His body ached from the battle, but his wounds were healing quickly, thanks to the merchant's skill with herbs. The cries of shore birds echoed as they navigated circular courses in the azure sky. Turquoise waves crashed against the rocky shore. "Qefat," Nakisisa whispered, "I've missed you."

Hanif plopped down on the deck next to his friend and passed him a bottle of tej. They sat, drinking in silence for a while before the merchant spoke. "The traitor will be delivered to court to face justice."

"And the antidote?"

"My men can be very persuasive, my old friend. The formula should already be in the hands of the Royal Brewers, if my pigeons are worth the gold I paid for them."

Nakisisa laughed. "And my fate?"

"As far as the court is concerned, you were lost to the Deep." Hanif rose and pulled Nakisisa to his feet. "Unofficially, welcome home, son of Qefat."

The Bonds That Bind: A Pogue Institute Case

Dennis R. Upkins

The boys said nothing. Lips busted, jaws swollen, the two alternated between nursing their wounds with ice packs and scowling at each other. Sophomores Cameron David and Robbie Rodriguez sat fuming in the guidance counselor's office. Their mouths clenched, silence seemed to be the one thing the two Black teens both agreed on.

"We can stay here as long as you like," Ms. Summer said, "But no one is leaving until we resolve this."

The two students glanced at the new petite guidance counselor. She was the preferable alternative to the other figure in the room. Leaning against the wall with his arms crossed, Mr. Zephram easily mimicked a Sicario. More than once Cameron watched Coach Adkins, a former marine, abruptly exit a room whenever the new science teacher entered. This was also why neither he nor Robbie mounted any resistance when he broke up the fight and separated them. Cam glanced at the digital clock on Ms. Summer's desk. *Odd*, he thought. While the time was correct, 11:45, he noticed the year was set to 2042. That wasn't the only thing that was weird to Cam. He noticed both Zephram and Summer wore identical necklaces that had an arrowhead as its pendant.

"Now, you both know we have a zero tolerance for violence, and Mr. McCall wanted to suspend the two of you, but I convinced him that I would get to the bottom of this," Summer said. "Now, this isn't like either of you. You're both honor-roll students, and between the two of you, you're involved in almost every extracurricular activity offered. So, what's going on here?"

Robbie and Cam pursed their lips and gazed at the opposing walls.

"You hear her talking to you?" Zephram snapped. "Answer her!"

"Ask Robbie," Cam said. "All he's done is rag on me the whole year. He keeps giving me crap because I'm adopted."

"Is this true, Robert?" Summer asked.

"No," Robbie replied. "He's lying. I don't care about him being a charity case."

"Careful," Zephram warned.

"It's true," Cam continued. "He hassles me every day. I've tried ignoring him and steering clear of him, but nothing works. He's even managed to turn most of the school against me. I also think he hates me because I'm gay."

"Dude, my cousin is gay," Robbie snapped. "I don't care who you're into. You're a loser. It's not my fault no one else likes you."

"Right, just like it wasn't your fault when you jumped me today?" Cam said.

"I told you, something shoved me into you," Robbie replied.

"We heard," Zephram said. "Some invisible force picked you up off your feet and chucked you into Mr. David."

"It's the truth!" Robbie cried, before sheepishly adding, "Except for the invisible-force part. Maybe someone shoved me. I don't know! It wasn't my fault."

"You see," Cam said. "He's always lying. I was at my locker, and as usual, Robbie shows up and starts ragging me. I didn't say anything. I just ignored him and grabbed my books. The second my back was turned, he tackles me to the ground. I had no choice but to defend myself."

"I really want to resolve this so no one gets suspended and no one's parents are called," Summer said.

Robbie scoffed, "Like they'd care."

Tucking a tendril of red hair behind her ear, Summer cast Zephram a glance, who in turn arched an eyebrow.

"Oh," the guidance counselor said, peering at her file. "Today is your birthday, Robert. Now, I know you don't want something like this to ruin your day. I'm sure your parents have something special planned for you."

"What the hell do you know?" Robbie exploded. "You don't know anything! Go ahead, tell my parents! I'll call them for you! You know what they have planned for me? Not a damn thing! Same as last year! They didn't even remember!" Tears streamed down his light brown cheeks. "You know why? Dad's too busy being a cliché, banging his secretary, thinking we don't know, and Mom's too worried about making partner at her stupid firm. They can't be bothered with little things like their son. Call them! Be ready to sit on hold for an hour."

He kicked his chair into the wall and stormed out of the office. Silence fell upon the stunned room.

Zephram turned to Cam, "Go get him."

"You think that's a good idea?" Cam asked.

"You think questioning me is a better one?" Zephram replied.

The sophomore darted out of the office.

Zephram yelled, "And don't come back without him!"

Cam's trek ended underneath the stadium bleachers. Sensing he was no longer alone, Robbie quickly wiped the tears from his brown face. "What do you want?"

"They wanted me to find you," Cam said.

"Well, you found me. Now get lost."

Cam turned to leave but paused. Rather than feeling triumphant, he studied his foe with empathy and confusion. Cam prepared to depart again, but the opportunity for answers proved too compelling.

"I wanna know why," Cam said. "Why me? The truth. I don't think it's about me being adopted or being gay. Not anymore. Why do you really hate me? Just tell me. Man to man. I mean, I don't get it. You're popular, you're loaded, you've got everything. What did I ever do to you?"

Robbie scowled at him. Cam tensed. For a moment, he thought round two was about to commence. Instead, Robbie gazed at his sneakers.

"Truth is, it was never about you," Robbie said. "I guess it took until now for me to realize that. Beginning of the year, a few days after you transferred here. Your foster dad dropped you off at school. You two were laughing. He hugged you and wished you luck. You aren't even flesh and blood, and they love you more than my folks love me. I'd kill to have my dad treat me like that. I don't get it. I make good grades, I'm captain of the hockey team, and it's like they couldn't care less. What's wrong with me? Am I really that bad?"

Cam took a seat next to Robbie. "I know what it's like to have your birthday forgotten. My biological mom overdosed on heroin, and before she died, she frequently missed birthdays and Christmases and everything else."

Robbie gazed at his classmate in disbelief. "I didn't know. Sorry."

"For the longest time, I used to blame me too," Cam continued. "I used to think I was being punished and I deserved my mom being sick because something was wrong with me. Because mothers don't treat their sons like that, so clearly, I was the problem.

"Living with the Wilsons, I've come to realize it wasn't about me. I think my mom loved me as much as she could, but I wasn't the problem. She was sick. I'm sure it's the same for you. Your parents' issues aren't yours. Yeah, it sucks being on the receiving end, but that doesn't mean there's something wrong with you, or either of us."

"Why are you being so nice to me? Especially considering all of the crap I've given you? Not to mention we were kicking each other's asses not two hours ago."

Cam laughed. "I don't know. Maybe all those sermons on compassion and forgiveness from my youth minister, Mr. Parker. Maybe I can relate to how parents can really mess you up. Or maybe it's because I used to think that my life would've been so much better if it was more like yours. Nice home, two parents. Truth is, maybe, we're not that different."

"God. I knew today was gonna suck."

"Oh, yeah, happy birthday."

Robbie scoffed. "Best one yet."

"Maybe. Maybe we can salvage it."

"Huh?"

"Mr. Zephram said not to come back until I found you. He didn't say I couldn't check the mall and the movie theater."

"Cameron David, the Boy Scout, is gonna play hooky?"

"Do you really feel like going back to class after everything that's happened today?"

"No, I really don't."

"You in?"

"I only celebrate birthdays with friends."

Cam sat stunned while his classmate strode off. Robbie paused and turned around, "You coming or what?"

Cam shook his head and laughed. "Dude, you're a real piece of work."

"Yeah, I know. I'm sorry for being such a douche."

"It's cool, man."

Robbie rubbed his jaw. "By the way, you got a vicious right hook."

"Sorry."

"You ever thought about trying out for hockey?"

Summer beamed from atop the bleachers as she and Zephram watched the two departing teens.

"Looks like the timeline has been restored and the Pogue Institute just crushed another case," Zephram said.

"I have to say, Zephram, telekinetically slamming Robert into Cameron was pretty ingenious," Summer said.

"Thanks, sis. There's nothing like a healthy dose of violence to get little boys to open up and share their feelings."

"Don't I know it."

"Ha-ha. Mentioning the birthday and the parents was a nice play as well."

"I figured he needed one more push...so to speak. Looks like they did the rest themselves."

"The doctor and the senator," Zephram said. "Who would've ever guessed it would be those two down there. Two of this century's most important figures. They have no idea what's ahead of them. Neither of them are going to have easy lives."

"No, they won't," Summer said. "But the bond they forged here today is going to help them weather all the storms and all the battles they're going to face in becoming the leaders they're destined to be. What those two are going to accomplish will be nothing short of greatness."

"And I take it Agent Parker will be keeping an eye on things?"

His sister nodded. "Brendan will maintain his cover as a youth minister and report back if any problems arise."

"Excellent. Another case closed for the Pogue Institute. Now that we've played Dr. Phil-good, can we please get back to the assignments we should actually be doing: kicking demonic ass and saving the world? This after-school special is giving me hives."

"Oh, admit it, Zef. Helping people battle their inner demons may not be as exciting as fighting the physical kind, but it's just as gratifying."

"Only if there's an exorcism involved. Otherwise, I admit to nothing."

Summer shook her head. "All right. Let's go."

Zephram waited until his sister had descended the bleachers. Once the coast was clear, he glanced back at the teens one final time and grinned.

A Bullet from a God's Gun

Napoleon Wells

I am Emaje Bul. I am Bilawa. I was letting those two truths
flow out and over me every few seconds. I was born in the Bilawa Lands and could travel almost anywhere. No one could
come to the Bilawa dimension, not even the Matrons. I was in a
trance here in Shadow, dream-like, watching. To the east of me
were visions of craft landing, and voices raised, and the forming
of words and the gift of life and fire. I could see it all, warming
and filling my consciousness. I had to retrieve my truths. I was
firing my known truths off every ten steps of my time in
Shadow, and every ten seconds that I was on top of my current
perch. Being in Shadow for long periods could eat away at the
knowing and sanity of the most skilled Usuiku, and those who
knew of the gift considered me a fair Usuiku, Shadow Walker.
Still, my mind faced all of the same vulnerabilities as every
other human Shadow Walker, and so, I reminded myself of my
name and my people, yet again. I drew out both facts. Tasted
each in word and thought, and sent them running away. I was
whole.

I had entered this Shadow space from a broad corner of the
Shiftcraft that I had been a passenger on, flying at about 900
drops per thirty standard. I had activated my Shout and made the
leap as soon as security forces from Bahir had begun making
their rounds in earnest. I had seen the fracas coming. I had felt
it, and the Shadow began calling my attention. A group of five
soldiers from Bahir, monitoring the craft, had been performing a
sweep. One of the five had been a Mage, and he had discovered
a passenger wearing a veil. The Mage spoke a word of Power
and ripped the veil away. The passenger was an undocumented
Shifter. This one was a woman, and a Mongoose. I couldn't see
any plans she had to get to Bahir other than desperation and
hope. She began her Shift, tearing at the armor of the front two
soldiers, baring tooth and claw, just before the one Duhuman
soldier with the security force extended their hand, it

transforming into something like a minigun, and fired off a single burst of pulsing rounds which tore through the Shifter. She was torn nearly in half. There were a few screams from other passengers. There was an army of averted gazes. There was the whirring of gears as the Repurposer opened its maw in the middle of the Shiftcraft and appeared to swallow the broken body whole. There were still another twenty drops to Bahir. Far too long.

I had taken a series of steps back toward the Shadow while all of this was happening. It had taken mere seconds. A commotion. A roar. Life ending. The nanites flowing frantically through my body and over my suit had surged upward, obscuring any recording or scrying of my movements. I didn't have much time. The distraction stoked by that quick breath of violence would soon pass. I needed to be off this shuttle when it did. I waited for the chorus of sounds to return to something like their normal levels and uttered my Shout. It drew the Shadow to me, the dark opening to me like a tunnel around a bend. One of the benefits of taking a Shift into regions like Bahir is the anxiety of all those traveling, and how it generally led to beings shutting themselves off to anything save what was going to get them to their destinations alive, and something resembling safe in the process. There were passengers who had seen me step into Shadow, no doubt. They would admit this if braced by an Inquisitor, or faced with death or profit. But in these confines, and with security patrols now stalking the craft? Silence, for nearly all aboard this craft, was the only sure covering in the cold.

When I had first been given this assignment by Layna, my handler, she would say, I had explored every image and synth that I could find in the Amhara Region. Since the Waking, it was a region generally left to its own devices. Very few of its residents had ascended to the Citadels, floating cities, above Earth. I had never been curious enough to explore why that may have been. Perhaps the region had offended the Black Gods. All of what had formerly been Kenya, Eritrea, and Ethiopia were reformed into what was now Bahir State. Even here from my place in the Shadow, approaching its borders in hushed tones, I could see why so many had been drawn to the nation-state.

The city of Bahir was massive and brilliantly lit. It was nestled in the hands of what appeared to be a sleeping colossus. That had been Loaja. She was an emissary of the Great Goddess of the tides. She had torn Bahir from the Earth itself, lifted it in her massive hands skyward, and held it there. She had been kneeling when she had done this, and was there still. Her skin remained a black so profound and complete, one was left to wonder if the night itself had been birthed by her. There was movement all over her skin, what appeared to be stars being born and dying. Strange, eldritch creatures peering back out at the world away from her body. Her hair was a wild riot as black as her skin, wreathed by an ocean of colors flowing in every conceivable direction. She had done her time in battle following the Waking, and she had tallied many scalps. She had journeyed across Afriq and stopped at Bahir. Lifted it in her hands. Kneeled. She had not moved since. Many Gods and Powers had left or fled Earth altogether. We had learned after the Waking that anything, any being, could die on this plain of existence. Gods and man bore that in common.

There were fingers of flame and light surrounding Bahir and off in the distance. These were usually the small, wandering tribes of beings from all over Afriq, and other forsaken parts of Earth, petitioning for entry and Bahir citizenship. Others were offering themselves as labor, or slaves for Bahir royalty. Others were roving bands of predators, feeding off of the smaller, weaker tribes and vulnerable cities as they frantically tried to be effectively absorbed by one nation-state or another. The Waking had changed the fortunes of many.

The fortunes of my people, the Bilawa, were directly tied to those of the Matrons, and all those chosen as direct agents of the Black Gods. Those few were the voice of the Black Gods and Powers on Earth, and above, and in the Steppes and Ways. We Bilawa were scorned and feared by most who knew of us. We had magics, and power and tech, and mission. The Earth, for all intents and purposes, was the child of the Matrons to govern in the absence of the Black Gods. As a Usuiku, I had been detailed to surveillance, tracking, and clandestine operations. Rarely did I simply surveil or track. If Layna activated my comm and agreed to my regs and bonuses, there would be a reckoning of one kind or another for some being, Power or sovereign, so-called. I had been able to get into, and out of, most places that I needed to, and my completion rate was absurdly high. I was certain that I was the best of the Intelligence Functionals available to the Matrons, and I didn't particularly care. I was skilled and wealthy. Those two, I did care about, deeply. I understood my role in forwarding the objective of the Matrons and tightening their grip on terra Earth. I had slipped into keeps to help and topple sovereign nations. I had assassinated identified threats. I had stolen and claimed secrets and private lies told between Powers. I had prevented and started wars. I was clear on my turn in the way of the Wheel.

Part of my success had to do with the fact that there was almost no way for any being to glance at me twice and believe me to be a Functional of any stripe. An initial glance right at me revealed a being with medium black skin, a short, neat, graying beard, large black spectacles, and a frame built for reading at the large desk I kept in my study. I affected more the professor and less the Functional. It would do. Most of the bright, growing buildings of Bahir looked rather like the one I occupied in New Dar Es. The buildings here were occupied by millions of beings. I could see a Mage school in the distance from my perch. I could see a great temple, the capitol, and crowds upon crowds of beings crowding the streets. All nation-states had been terraformed with living architecture by the Black Gods. It was the only act of benevolence on behalf of those stranded on terra Earth by their new rulers. These cities could accommodate as many residents as they held. There were also instances where, like in Kinshasa, an angry god would destroy the entire city, snuffing out all life, only to rebuild it seconds later.

I was wearing a heavy wool black suit. Black shirt, tie, and boots. It felt weightless here in Shadow. My nanites had armored it, reinforcing it. Very few Earth-made weapons would penetrate it. I needed to take all precautions, considering how heavily armed and patrolled Bahir was. Layna had indicated that she had sent in another Functional and had not heard from her in four days. I was to find out the what, and why. The Royals in

Bahir were hosting some event, one which had brought dignitaries from several other nation-states, and the Matrons wanted to know why. The limited intelligence that Layna had provided for me suggested that each nation-state was required to bring tribute, and each had gladly agreed. Odd. It was scheduled for four days from her last transmission. Today. Now. From my perch heavenward I could see no fewer than twelve Mohane Giants roaming the perimeter of the Royal Keep. There were thousands of Duhumans, gleaming human/droid mixes, patrolling the streets. My Sight in the Shadow allowed me to see the wards and fetches arranged by the Mages. Why so many? Odder still was how bright the Lifesparks were in the Keep's bottommost levels. I could barely keep my eyes focused on it. It was blinding. I imagined for a moment a god striding about down there, but that wasn't possible. Interesting.

I had found a deep well of Shadow just beyond the foyer on level three. About three stages above the event. I had opened a way through Shadow for my nanites to scour the area before me for anything that my Sight may have missed. They counted several Loxodonta, elephant Shifters, standing guard in rows in front of all of the levels leading down to the event. I ran through my weapons preparation with my nanites. I had several repeaters, bullpups, and stargazers ready to be called. I had two Akan blades and a ganga ram for close-quarters work. I hoped that it wouldn't come to that, but one never does know, does one? I extended the Shadow several klicks to the darkened border that I could make out around the Keep. Shadow was always just next door to the world as we know it. It pulled me along as if I were flying, and I was at the Keep in moments. I opened my comm and sent a silent pulse to Bahati. She was my Mwalima, essentially my on-site intelligence and spotter. Anything I needed to know in the moment, she was to gather for me. Her mind opened up to me, and I could see that she was examining herself in a mirror. Her dark eyes glanced over her brilliant gold dress, made entirely of mail, and the Bantu knots arrayed around her scalp. Her dark skin appeared cool and dry, and I could see the tether to her Locker, a small pocket dimension where she kept weapons and supplies, tucked firmly in her palm. She thought to me severely, *Are you here yet? They have already started things down there. This buffoon I am with is stumbling about and nearly staggering out of my control.* We had "secured" a wayward son of a regional lord and mind-tapped him. Bahati was his companion. I could sense her broad mouth frowning and broad shoulders tightening. She was near killing him; that much was certain. *I'm coming in now, get me some dark on the bottom level. There are a troop of Loxodonta patrolling. I've no desire to dance with those bastards this evening. Hell, any evening.* She paused at my reply, clearly thinking, before saying. *Hold tight.*

We had learned a lot in four days. Mostly through whispers from sources and rival nation-states. A small, isolated outpost like Bahir was now flush with power, influence, and troops. But how? And how so quickly?

There was interference in our comm link, due in large part to the work of the Mages and unending tech, and whatever was being projected out from the bowels of the Keep. I repeated my name again to myself while I waited. I reminded myself of my kin, the Bilawa. I pictured the abbott alive, her blindfold and tonfa appearing before our enemies as a terrorist threat. I picture Baba and the Blink, charging into battle. I pictured the Fall, that day. The day we swore fealty to the Matrons, I remembered, the rage and pain visiting me yet again. My focus was torn back to my place on the perch as the comm flared open, angry and frantic. I heard a crash, sensing that Bahati had knocked something over. I could sense broken glass and spilled food through her thoughts. It was bright on this level. I could see the ornate doors of the Keep's bottom hall. I could see glass windows all around, and brilliant blue sea on all sides. I knew that they had worshipped several sea Powers, so this should not have surprised me. Bahati briefly opened her Locker and let a small clear box hit the floor, just outside of a foyer. A single thought from her would activate it. It was a Corner. An item of my creation. I had managed to draw several of my nanites around bits of Shadow once I realized they could survive it. They could store it until I needed it released. That one tiny clear box had approximately eighty million nanites prepared to release their hold and give me the sliver of Shadow that I would need to make my way in. This had to be timed just right.

As she straightened up and let the various servants tend to the mess she had made, I heard the doors to the hall behind Bahati open. All of the guests I could see from her view had turned their attention to the doors and the two women who had emerged from them. I recognized Siyana immediately. She was the eldest daughter of House Bahir, and while she was an understated beauty in most images I had seen of her, something was off tonight. She appeared to be radiating and reflecting light, her eyes feverish. Bahati thought out at me, *Are you seeing this?* I was, while also sending my nanites out through their kin holding the box to collect information on all who had attended. They were able to get to nearly every corner of the Keep, but not through those wide-open hall doors. The being behind Siyana was massive, appearing female, nearly as tall as the Loxodonta that she was presently striding through. Her armor was fully black, save her arms which were a café au lait tone. She was wearing a helmet, and the eyes which peered out were as feverish and urgent as Siyana's.

Siyana let out a great laugh, all of the blue-skinned Loxodonta and guests regarding her. She said, "Great comrades, friends and neighbors. Welcome. Like you, we have kept our worship of the many Gods and Powers devout. Like you, we have called out to them, begged, and asked why. Like you, we have never received an answer. None which would satisfy our searching minds, anyway." There were uncomfortable shuffles all over. One did not question the Black Gods. "They are all we have, after all. We are their children. When they woke, they chased and slaughtered all other gods. There is but one Pantheon!" She raised her hands and shouted this last, looking up at the ceiling, which was a flowing tapestry of images of ocean goddesses and Powers. They began to writhe angrily at this last from Siyana. "Come. Let us consider that." She turned and began to stride into the hall, which began lighting up as she entered it, all of the guests following her. Bahati was one of the last through the entrance, and I could feel the doors shut behind her. She was disturbed by what she was seeing, and thought this all the way through to me. I was unsettled, no doubt. There were floating globes arrayed around the hall. There were beings in each globe, floating in what I knew to be celestial amber, the cursed substance which had been used to trap the Black Gods ages before. It had all been destroyed in the Waking, hadn't it? Where had this come from?

Bahati and I both noticed Layna's former Functional all at once. She was frozen in one of the globes. Nowhere near as powerful as her many neighbors. Her face was a frozen mask of pain. I captured the scene with my nanites and memory.

I opened a line to Layna, being sure that these images were being relayed to the Matrons. I never knew what they did with the information, as they so rarely acted on things directly, but surely this was another matter. I could make out a man made completely of stone, a Botswanan Gargoyle. None had been seen on this plane in decades. I could see beings of Air and Fire. This was why I could not see into this level. My nanites began flaring, a rush of information hitting my consciousness. There were children of Lightning trapped in these globes. I could see a Death Power and several Billi spirits. Bahati was stunned. I found myself curious, filling with questions, when Siyana spoke again, her voice rapturous and booming: "I wonder what we children know of the Pantheon we serve. They speak of our dedication to them, but they give us a life full of distraction, and families full of tumult." As she spat out her last, a group of twelve humans were dragged out into the center of the hall by one of the Loxodonta. They were a riot of shades of black and brown, all nude, bleeding from various cuts and abrasions. They appeared to all be starved and emaciated. There were a rush of sensors and private security calling on weapons at this. Siyana raised her hands to settle those assembled. Her smile broad and manic. "Friends. Your Bahir Royals have lost their way. They have, by their own will and deed, abdicated their seats in the House. Living here, trapped by the very Gods we worshipped, was yet another Godkind."

Before she had finished. I followed Bahati's gaze as a Shadow started to grow out and back behind the high table. From behind it strode a small woman. She appeared to be of middle standard human years, but her gaze felt far more ancient. Several of the beings trapped in amber began to rock and shrink away from her. Her eyes were the same feverish black/grey as Siyana's. Siyana immediately took a knee. The newcomer reached up, and a flask appeared. Small clusters of light emanating from the flask were linked to each of the globes. The tall figure which had first appeared with Siyana went to stand just behind this new addition. This new being glanced about the room, haughty. She grabbed the flask, put it to her mouth, and began to drink. The beings trapped within the globes began to shake. Some were literally disappearing as we watched. Others let out screams, some frozen in place in agony. Some were clearly dying. What were we seeing? I sent the images back to Layna at greater speeds.

She withdrew her mouth from the flask, and I could see an army of color dance across her dark lips. She was wearing a heavy three-piece suit, the vest low-slung, her small breasts barely disturbing the cut of the suit. It was an earthen crimson. "I am Imbegele. The Left Hand. What you are seeing here, these many captives, leeches, and traitors, are being drained. They are my Menagerie. My gifts, given to me by my new children. Each is feeding me their life. I need it, you see, if you are ever to be free. All of you. While you looked skyward at all of those moons during the Waking, you saw Gods. At that very same time, Ways had been opened. They needed to be closed before the Forgotten had come. They still want to come now. They are just at the seams of your world. You can hear them if you listen. Your Gods have left to try and find the Source. The first of us has risen, you see. Somewhere near your Sudan, she woke and ran, Somewhen. She woke everything. Both the Gods and the Forgotten. After I had slain so many and closed so many Ways. They trapped me in this same amber, with the aid of many of the traitors you see here. I was made weak, and hidden. This child"—she motioned to Siyana—"found me and released me, that I may save this world." Her voice kept changing. It sounded as if she were speaking with a chorus of minds, all at once. "We are not here to celebrate this evening. No. We are here to consecrate and plan. Better then that even my children have come to attend and witness this moment." She looked directly in Bahati's direction, and I felt a chuckle in my thoughts. Could she see me?

"This, you see, allows me to drink of Gods, to become a more ready and powerful God." She raised her left hand, showing us a mouth in her palm full of pulsing silver teeth. Power leaked outward, searching for more life. It was frightening.

A corner of her mouth had curled up, and I saw a bit of what appeared to be fang, and what appeared to be lava flowing about it. She slowly walked about the front of the Hall, aiming her hand out ahead, at one of the globes to her left. A creature was trying to stir inside of it, horrified. It was shifting slowly between a number of animal forms. It was a Chimera, one of the known Shifter Powers. Even from my perch I could feel Imbegele calling power as the being cowered. I could see larger and more defined versions of what looked like my own nanites forming around Imbegele's palm. Faster than I could track, she had crafted a gun, a pistol as red as her suit, and fired a single shot. It pierced the globe, striking the Chimera. She left her hand extended, drawing what appeared to be the very soul out of the Chimera into that mouth. She was chanting. I hadn't noticed it earlier. This being had found some way to drain Lifespark. I found my body shaking and my nanites reacting to her presence and power. Her chanting slowed. The amber flowed out of the makeshift cage. I knew that we had all just witnessed a bullet end the life of a Power. We had been told it could do the same to all the Gods. She tucked her hand, making as if to stow her fabricated weapon.

There was stunned silence everywhere. She continued: "I don't need your wealth or slaves or lands. No. What I need is your prayers. I need altars and temples built to the Left Hand, the Maiden of Iron and Ways. I need you to direct me to any of these weak, pretend Powers in your borders"—she waved her hand at the globes—"or bring them to me. I have all I need to do the rest." She walked slowly past the twelve Bahirs, light draining from them and into her, her bare feet making no sound as she drew their Lifespark. Each died as she walked past them. Each was an empty husk. She looked around the room, smiling that same mad, benevolent smile. "I wonder what all of you would sacrifice to see to it that your world is free. What would you sacrifice to bring those Matrons low? Hmmmm? How many throats would you cut to feed me and see their time at an end? I can tear open those fishbowls they live in. I can make them kneel before you. What would that be worth to you?" She looked around the room, drawing the silence around her as power. "I can find the First of Us. I can remake this world."

Several thousand of my nanites had been activated by the power swirling around the room. Something about being in her presence had fired them. Several had latched on to her; they had drawn several images, which stunned me. I saw what she spoke of. The pain, the betrayal, and what she intended to do. I shouted "No!" and forced open the Shadow. I dived through it. I saw where she was headed next and what she meant to do with every God and Power she came near, including this First that she referenced. I could feel my nanites dying, chased and destroyed by her power. She was aware of them. Several made it back to me with all of the intelligence that I needed. I swept up into the light with two of my bullpups drawn. The Loxodonta charged me. Bahati kicked her companion away, drawing the two Vektor pistols that she kept near. There were too many enemies. I could feel my own Shout being strengthened simply being in proximity of Imbegele. She looked at me, watching the chaos bubble up and around. Two hundred elephant Shifters headed for us, some maintaining their near-giant human forms, otherwise shifting fully into animal forms, others shifting to a middle warrior form.

I couldn't focus enough to shift all of the information back to Layna. I had to let her, let everyone everywhere, Matrons and Gods included, know everything that I had seen and heard. I drew everything I had into my Shout, crying out "Unimayale!" activating all the life in my Shadow. As the Shifters drew near us, it felt as time slowed. The world around us appeared to be overtaken by dark and Shadow. I had never erected a Shadow this size. I could feel the Shadow pulsing. It was alive and frantic. It wanted to wash over these intruders. I let it. I called for my weapons, and versions of my bullpups appeared all over the Shadow, sighting on the Loxodonta. I squeezed my finger as if pressing a trigger, and the sound of all of the makeshift weapons was riotous. The Loxodonta fell everywhere. Bahati moved to stand behind me. The Shadow appeared to absorb the falling bodies, feeling sated. I could feel something pushing at the edges of my Shadow boundary. It was still touching Bahir. I began to withdraw it, fighting the powerful will of what I knew to be Imbegele's powers.

I let out a Shout again, one that pushed all the way to Layna's tower. She would need this report in person. As we ran through Shadow, I could feel tethers from the Citadels linking with our destination. I could see an afterimage of a young woman in a Ways journey suit fleeing. Power and fear were radiating off of her in equal measure. I could feel other Shadow users the world over drawing their attention to me. I had changed something. I could feel Powers stirring. I had done my job. I had gathered my intelligence and had forwarded it on to those who could act on it. I was not so certain that I had done a good deed, or that my mission was rightly accomplished. Bahati and I kept our comms open, shooting thoughts at one another as we ran. We each understood, without saying, the Gods were certainly returning. The Stirring, just over our head in the Ways, suggested that the Forgotten were coming too. I wasn't sure that Shadow would keep me safe. I wasn't sure that any place on this world, and this When, were safe. I was an agent, no doubt, but soon, I realized, I would need to be a warrior. I had to hope that that would be enough.

Ghost

Milton J. Davis

-1-

A cold drizzle settled on Seaboard Industrial Boulevard, ushering in another miserable January night in Atlanta. The lights still burned at Gentech, a small genetics laboratory tucked behind a cluster of naked maples, an odd sight for a Friday night. Bryce St. George sat at his desk inside, wrestling with a genetic sequence that played hard to get. The brilliant Jamaican loved the challenge; it was something that was rare in his life in the outside world.

Bryce was a blessed man. At twenty-eight he stood six foot four, carrying two hundred and twenty pounds of natural hard muscle on his bones. He was a gifted athlete who had excelled in sports throughout his life, earning a football and academic scholarship to college. After graduating, he turned down the physical challenges of pro football, soccer, and basketball for the mental challenges of genetic engineering. With dark chocolate skin, dreadlocks that lifted over his head then fell to his broad shoulders like a lion's mane and deep green eyes, Bryce was a woman's dream. If his looks didn't capture her at first glance, his deep, melodic patois usually sealed the deal.

The glare of car lights interrupted his scientific scrutiny. He looked up from the stereoscope and recognized the red Honda Accord pulling into the parking lot. A knowing smile creased his face. Briana had returned to "surprise" him. He went back to his desk and pretended to be busy, ignoring her clumsy attempt to quietly open the front door. He kept his back turned as her heels clicked across the vinyl floor. Warm honey-brown hands slipped over his eyes.

"Guess who?" she purred.

"The cleaning lady?" he answered.

"Bastard!" she exclaimed as he smacked him on the head.

Bryce spun his seat around to view his boss's latest assistant and his soon-to-be latest conquest. Briana posed in a black trench coat pulled tight against her body.

"You ready to play?" she asked. She opened the coat slowly, revealing a sheer chemise, then eased onto his lap. Their kiss was wet and full.

"Not here," Bryce whispered. He picked her up suddenly and she yelped. He carried her into Lenny's office and her eyes widened.

"We can't do it here!"

Bryce smiled. "Yes, we can."

He was placing her down on the sofa when he noticed Lenny's monitor. Instead of the usual screensaver of his boss's family, there was an unfamiliar emblem flashing.

"What's this?" Bryce went to the screen. "Vanguard?" This was something new.

"Bryce?" Briana sat up on the sofa with a frown. Bryce flashed a smile, then sat at Lenny's computer.

"Give me a minute, Bree. I need to check this out." Bryce's fingers flashed across the keyboard as unfamiliar data streamed past his eyes.

"Lenny, you naughty boy," Bryce whispered. He jumped out of the chair, ran to his desk, and returned with a flash drive. He plugged it into the computer and began downloading files.

"What are you doing?" Briana asked.

Bryce turned to her and began to remove his shirt. "The question is, who am I doing?"

They nestled into the sofa; the room illuminated by the flashing monitor lights.

Leonard Steinberg arrived at Gentech Monday morning just as the snow flurries began to fall from the blanket of grey clouds overhead. This was too early for this kind of weather, he thought. Snow usually came to Atlanta in February, sometimes as late as March. It was the reason he moved down from upstate New York years before despite the wailing of his family. Gentech was the type of business you could run from anywhere in the country, and at fifty-five, Leonard had his fill of shoveling snow and grueling drives to vacations in south Florida. Georgia was an excellent compromise as far as he was concerned. Besides, there was Bryce. He refused to relocate any farther north than Atlanta. Gentech was nothing without Bryce.

The building was empty; Bryce and the other technicians usually didn't arrive until after nine. He hummed as he shuffled to his office, briefcase in one hand and the *Journal-Constitution* stuffed under his arm. He opened his office door and was assaulted by the aroma of Glade Morning Mist.

"For God's sake, Bryce!" he barked. He looked at his sofa, his pale face crinkled as he imagined what had taken place the night before in his office. He knew Bryce used his office as his office tryst station; he knew that Bryce knew he knew. But Bryce also knew his own value to the company.

"I'll have to call the upholstery cleaners," he mumbled. As he sat his briefcase down, he noticed his monitor still on. His pale face became paler.

"No, no, no," he stammered. He sat in his seat and hit Enter. Vanguard options jumped on the screen and he dropped his head. He didn't log off yesterday. Bryce and Briana had been in his office. Maybe they were too hot with each other to notice. As he logged off the system, his phone rang.

"Gentech," he answered.

"We have a breach," the voice said.

Leonard took the receiver away from his face and cursed silently.

"There was no breach," he replied. "I forgot to log out, that's all."

"This was not log error. This was a breach. Files were entered and downloaded. Important files. Sensitive files."

Leonard's head began to sweat. He waited for the next words.

"I need names and information."

"He's too valuable," Leonard replied. "Everything you have from me, he created."

"No one is too valuable. Everyone is expendable, including you. Besides, the project is nearly complete. I need names and information."

Leonard pulled up Bryce's file on the screen. He gazed at it for a moment, regretting the terrible act he was about to commit.

"I'm sorry," he whispered. He opened the secure e-mail and attached Bryce's file.

"Anyone else?"

Leonard closed his eyes. "Yes, a woman, but she's fairly new. I'm sure she wasn't involved."

"That's not your decision to make."

Leonard attached Briana's file to the e-mail and clicked Send. The was a moment of silence before the caller spoke again.

"You have a week to shut down operations. Your new facility will be in Sao Paulo. No more mistakes."

Leonard rubbed his head. "Yes, I understand."

"Goodbye, Leonard."

The caller hung up. Leonard placed the receiver down, dropped his face into his hands, and cried.

-2-

Malik Cooper sat in the stall of the NSA building, staring at a picture of Tisha and the twins. He was doing it for them, giving up a storied career as a deep-cover agent for his soon-to-be family. He rubbed his head, brushing his close-cropped hair back and forth, and sighed.

"It's the right thing to do. The best thing to do."

He exited the bathroom and marched to Sheryl Jennings' office.

Sheryl saw Malik enter and ended her phone conversation immediately.

"Sit down, Malik," she said, gesturing to the chair before her mahogany desk.

"Thanks for seeing me, Sheryl," Malik said.

"So, there's no changing your mind?"

Malik shook his head. "No, Sheryl. I need to do this."

Sheryl leaned back in her chair. "Need to?"

"Don't try any psycho-talk on me today," Malik warned. "I'm quitting effective today."

"She must be something."

Malik took the picture from his jacket and placed it on Sheryl's desk. "They are."

Sheryl picked up the picture and smiled. "You'll make a fine family."

They stood together as if on cue and shook hands.

"When does your flight leave?"

"This afternoon."

"You'll be missed, Malik. You're the best."

Malik shook Sheryl's hand. "Thanks for everything, Sheryl. I won't forget it."

Malik left the NSA building for the last time. He was heading to Atlanta to start a new life, a real life. The deception and killing were done. He had no regrets. He was in a cab heading for Ronald Reagan when his Android buzzed. He looked at the message and grinned.

How long does it take to quit a job? Longer than it takes to get fired from one, LOL!

His phone chimed and he answered.

"What's up, Bryce?"

"Nutten, bruh. When you coming?"

He must be at home, Malik thought. Bryce always fell into patois when he was relaxed.

"My flight leaves at 1:10."

"Good. I'll meet you there. We'll go to the Patty Hut and get some good food in you. There's a new sister working there that will give you a righteous welcome home if you talk to her right."

Same old Bryce. "Got to pass, St. George. My ladies are waiting on me."

"So?"

Malik laughed. Bryce never gave up.

"So I can't. I'm engaged, man!"

"All the more reason, my brother. Your days are numbered!"

"I tell you what; we'll hook up tomorrow, okay? But no women for me."

"Cool, bruh. Tomorrow at Two Urban Licks. Peace."

Bryce set down his iPhone and focused on his desktop screen. The files were almost done uploading. If they contained a fraction of what he glimpsed in Leonard's office, he'd hit the jackpot. His project needed some enhancing, and the new data could be the perfect addition.

The computer chimed. Bryce hit Enter and the contents of the file were revealed. His cool countenance dissipated as the data emerged before him.

"Either I hit the lottery or I'm in serious trouble," he whispered.

He picked up his phone and speed dialed Kandace.

"What?" she answered.

"Meet me at the lab, Kitty. I got something to show you."

"I can't. I'm at work, and I told you to stop calling me Kitty."

"Fake sick or something. You really want to see this."

"I'll stop by at lunch. It better be good."

Bryce smiled as the sequences danced on his screen. "It's lovely, Kitty. Really it is."

Leonard was cleaning out his desk when the black Infiniti FX45 eased into the Gentech parking lot. He looked up, watching the occupants exit from the vehicle as sweat formed on his forehead. He'd made the announcement earlier that morning to his employees, then stood silently as they reacted. Some cried, others cursed him out, while some just shrugged and asked for their severance. Bryce didn't show; Leonard shuddered when he thought of what had happened to him.

The four men entered the building. One man was tall and pale, his fading red hair flecked with gray. He looked about with piercing green eyes that finally settled on Leonard. The other three were dressed identically, long black wool coats with black hats and shades, their faces obscured by their turned-up collars, their hands covered by black leather gloves. They walked with a fluid grace that reminded Leonard of the dancers at the Atlanta Ballet. They studied everything in the office but seemed uninterested in Leonard.

They entered his office. The red-headed man took off his gloves and extended his hand, his expression cold despite his smile.

"Leonard? I'm Leif Thorvaldsen. I'm from Vanguard."

Leonard shook Leif's hand, the appendage as cold as his face.

"Hello, Mr. Thorvaldsen. You came sooner than I expected."

"Time is of the essence, Leonard. I suspect the dismissals went well?"

"As well as something like that could go."

"Any takers to relocate?"

Leonard scowled. "No."

"And Mr. St. George?"

"What about him?"

Thorvaldsen's expression shifted to serious. "Was he here?"

Leonard looked puzzled. "I thought you..."

"No. We didn't. The address you gave us led to an empty warehouse."

Leonard detected the implication in Thorvaldsen's voice.

"That's the address he gave on his application. It's the only one I have."

Thorvaldsen tilted his head, and the other men moved closer to Leonard.

"Bryce has worked for you how long, five years, and you never checked him out?"

Leonard became defiant to hide his fear. "The man did his job, damn well, I might add. I had no reason to doubt his credentials."

"I see. Where is his office?"

Leonard led them to Bryce's office. Thorvaldsen's companions scoured it, examining every part and piece. Leonard wasn't sure, but it looked like they smelled the personal items. The men finally finished, then returned to Leonard's office.

"It seems your man Bryce is into more than just genetics," Thorvaldsen said.

He reached into the coat and extracted plane tickets.

"All the arrangements have been made. We expect you to be out of the country by midnight."

Leonard took the tickets. "Thank you."

"And I'll need the employee files."

Leonard was stunned. "Why?"

"That's none of your concern." Thorvaldsen nodded and his companions quickly dismantled Leonard's computer.

"Enjoy Brazil, Leonard."

Thorvaldsen and his men left the office, climbed into the Infiniti, and sped away. Leonard dropped his head and closed his eyes.

"God forgive me," he whispered.

-3-

Bryce stepped out the cab in front of the Vortex Bar & Grill at Little Five Points, the usual lunch spot for him and Kandace. He trotted through the cold air into the gaping mouth of the skull entrance, finding himself among Atlanta's fringe culture and the best burgers in the city. Kandace waited for him at their table, ponytails sticking out from the sides of her head, with loud red lipstick announcing her full lips. Her mocha legs extended from beneath the table, her manicured feet wrapped in a pair of knee-high leather platform boots. Her black skirt was so short it seemed she wore nothing below her tight black jacket.

"Still rocking the punk look, I see," Bryce commented.

"You like it," she purred. She leaned towards him as he sat, and they kissed. They were friends with benefits, as some like to say.

Kandace's face became serious. "Now show me what you got. I don't have a lot of time."

Bryce took out his netbook, logged in, then slid it across the table. Kandace took one look at the screen and whistled.

"Damn, boy!" she exclaimed. "You are in so much trouble!"

Bryce leaned back, folding his hands behind his head. "No, I'm not. Leonard won't touch me. He fires me and Gentech folds. I'm the ace of spades at that place."

Kandace peeked up from the screen. "I bet you didn't go to work today, did you?"

Bryce smiled and shook his head.

"Damn fool." Kandace pushed the laptop back. "What are we going to do with all this?"

"I figure we can enhance Ghost with it. Tweak it a bit."

"Some of this stuff looks promising. You going out tonight?"

Bryce frowned. "Got to. Funds are getting low."

A waiter came by but Kandace waved him away. "I can't believe you. You make six figures and you still can't keep a dollar."

"I'm living life, baby. I didn't hear you complaining when we went to Shanghai last month."

Kandace smiled. "Yeah, that was fun."

She looked at her watch. "Shit! I gotta go. I'll see you tonight."

She stood and Bryce's eyes got big. "Damn! I see you now!"

"Kiss my ass!"

"With pleasure."

As Kandace walked out of the Vortex, a black Infiniti FX45 cruised by. Four men were distracted by her briefly, then refocused on their task.

"Are you sure he's here?" Leif asked.

His companions nodded in unison.

"Too many people. We'll pick him up tonight."

The FX45 sped away, merging into the lunchtime traffic.

-4-

Some habits are hard to break, especially the ones that have saved a life. Malik sensed the exact angle of the Delta 727 took as it made its final approach to Hartsfield-Jackson International. He knew where all the exits were located, the number of people on the flight sorted in his mind by sex, gender, age, nationality, and sexual orientation. He noted the location of the Homeland Security marshals and the other undercover agents on the flight. Most of all, he noted that he was coming home.

His mind shifted from deep-cover mode as landing gear met tarmac. Atlanta had always been a haven for him, a cover stop between assignments. Here, he was an international businessman with a comfortable home in the Sugarloaf subdivision, surrounded by other successful professionals. His neighbors never came calling and he never complained, using his time to rest, heal, and review his next mission. That all ended one fall Saturday morning when he decided to take a run and found himself stride for stride with a lovely, divorced lawyer that changed his life.

Malik jumped from his seat the moment the plane parked at the A gate. He grabbed his overnight bag from the overhead bin and pushed his way through the other passengers, ignoring their silent and vocal complaints. He was on the train in minutes, a smile growing wider on his face with every second. By the time he stepped off the escalator at the main terminal, he was practically giddy. His ladies were waiting, Kelly and Michelle holding a lime green sign with the words *Welcome Home, Daddy!* scribbled in red marker. Tisha stood behind them, her welcoming smile and sparking eyes letting him know that this was all real.

"Hey, queens!" he exclaimed. The girls dropped the sign and rushed him. He scooped them up into his arms, and they assaulted his cheeks with kisses.

"Hey, Daddy!" they shrieked.

Tisha picked up the sign and sauntered to them. He leaned to her and they kissed lightly for the sake of the girls.

"Hey, baby," she said. "You really did it."

Malik smiled. "I told you I would."

Tears welled in Tisha's eyes. "Come on, let's go home."

So, this was normal life. He had a beautiful wife, two gorgeous daughters, and a well-paying government job with liberal holiday time. There were no covert missions, no life-threatening dilemmas, and no close calls. So, when his cell phone buzzed and he saw it was Sheryl, he almost jumped for joy.

Tisha looked up from her book.

"Who is it, baby? Bryce?"

"No. It's Sheryl," Malik said with a false frown.

Tisha rolled her eyes.

Malik answered the phone.

"I thought I was retired," he said.

Sheryl laughed. "You are. How's peacetime treating you?"

"Can't complain. What's going on?"

"Bryce St. George. You know him?"

Malik lost his smile. "I do."

"Our agency received a report on him. Seems he's involved in a situation that may have national security implications."

"Bryce? I doubt that. He's not perfect but he's not a spy."

"I didn't say *spy*. When was the last time you two talked?"

"A few days ago."

Malik hesitated to ask the next question. He knew the answer could draw him back into his old life.

"What do you have, Sheryl?"

"I can't tell you, Malik. You don't work for us anymore."

"So, why did you call me?"

"No reason; just thought you'd like to know. You take care, Malik. Tell Tisha I said hello."

Sheryl hung up. Malik stared at the phone. Sheryl was trying to lure him back. This must be a deep one, one that required his expertise. He glanced upward, thinking about the ladies whose life he was a part of now. He put the phone in his pocket. He'd do a little digging and call Sheryl if he discovered something. He'd begin by calling Bryce.

-5-

Bryce ordered two Spanish Fly burger plates and a large Coke. He had to fill up if he was going out with Ghost. His funds were extremely low, which meant his night run would be longer than usual. The waitress smiled, working her hips as she left his table. She wasn't his type, but apparently, she thought she was. The punk look only worked for him when Kandace wore it; she was so fine, she would look good in a potato sack.

He stuffed down the meals then leaned back in his seat, un-buckling his belt. He called the office but got no answer. That was odd; Lenny was always at his desk and always took his calls. He shrugged it off and texted Malik. Malik didn't respond; he was probably with his "queens," practicing fatherhood and married life. The boy was truly in love. He got that dumb look whenever he talked about Tisha, and he took to the twins as if they were his own. Bryce was jealous; he'd had plenty of women but none that made him consider settling down. He was a good time to them, as they were to him. They desired him, but they didn't care about him. Well, Kandace did, but she was different.

He ordered an Alpine Steak House Burger to go. The waitress brought him his receipt and her number; the receipt he kept, the number he tossed as soon as he stepped outside. He caught the MARTA to Clairmont Road then transferred to the GRTA shuttle to Gwinnet County. He got off at Gwinnet Place Mall; he could walk to the hotel from there. Kandace had given him the key and the room's number a couple of weeks before. She rented the room for a month, as always. Inside was the usual set up. He went into the bathroom, closed and locked the door. The Skin floated in the nutrient filled tub, a thin, translucent wonder of genetic biotechnology. Bryce stripped naked, then slipped on the suit. He waited as the loose material tightened, pressing against him like a second skin. The tingling swept his body as the contacts pierced his flesh in a million places, connecting to his blood vessels and nerve endings. He walked to the bed as the tingling subsided, pulling back the sheets to find the tablet. Kandace had updated the blotter. There was a suspected drug house only a few blocks away.

"Perfect," Bryce said aloud. "This shouldn't take long."

He opened the desk drawer and took out the loot bag. The Skin activated, and he watched as his hand and the bag disappeared. By the time he reached the mirror, he was completely invisible.

"Showtime." Bryce looked out the window, then slipped outside. He was cold but not extremely so; the Skin adjusted to the temperature by increasing its flesh-to-fat ratio. He boarded the bus, standing between the unsuspecting passengers with a smile on his face. He wondered how they would react if the Skin failed and a naked man suddenly appeared between them. The bus reached his stop, the entrance to a neat middle-class neighborhood. The Mexican drug boys were hiding their stashes in rented homes close to the interstate these days. The police were on to the scheme, but it was still difficult to spot the weed among the flowers. Bryce strolled by the stakeout car, walked up to the nondescript two-story house, then went around to the back. He was climbing over the fence when a patch of grass lifted and two men emerged. This was even better; the house was a decoy. The real stash was underground.

Bryce slipped into the hidden chamber before the men closed it. It was well lit; he bypassed the stacks of bagged meth and weed and went straight for the money. He opened his loot bag, filling it with money. He wasn't greedy; it would take them a while to notice, and when they did, they would blame each other. He closed his bag and waited. The men returned an hour later, grabbed a few bags of money, and left. Bryce left with them. He followed them to the undercover stakeout car across the street from the house. The officers rolled down the window and took the money. So much for law enforcement.

Bryce hit two more drug houses before calling it a day. He went back to the hotel and stripped off the Skin. He transferred the money into a backpack and caught a taxi back to his condo. His phone rang while he cruised down I-85.

"Speak," he said.

"Bryce, it's Briana."

Bryce grinned. "What's up, baby girl?"

"Something's wrong. I went into work late today and everything was gone."

Bryce's smile faded. "What do you mean, 'gone'?"

"I mean gone, empty. No desks, no lab equipment, no computers, nothing."

"Somebody broke in?"

"No, Bryce. Everything was moved. I tried to contact Leonard, but his phone is disconnected. Bryce, I'm scared."

"Where are you?"

"I'm in the lobby at your place."

Bryce took the phone away from his mouth to curse. "Look, stay right there. I'll be there in a minute."

"Okay, Bryce. I'll wait for you."

Bryce tapped the window between him and the driver. The driver peered and him through the rearview mirror.

"What?"

"Change of plans," Bryce said. "I need you to take me to the airport."

The cabby frowned. "I thought you said..."

"Just do it, okay?" Bryce texted Kandace, leaving her a message worked out between them a long time ago. *GET GONE*, it read.

Bryce sunk into his seat. The good thing was over. It was time to go home.

Bryce had just closed his phone when the taxi jerked right.

"Where the hell did you learn to drive?" he shouted.

The taxi jerked again. Bryce looked to the left out the soiled window and saw a black Infiniti FX45 speeding alongside them, the windows sliding down.

"Speed up! Speed up!"

The driver didn't need any encouragement. The taxi lurched forward, throwing Bryce back into the seat. The driver wrenched the wheel and they cut across three lanes of traffic, jumping off the next exit. The taxi barreled down the exit, then stopped.

"Get out!" the driver yelled.

Bryce's eyes went wide. "What? No!"

The taxi driver turned his head, his grizzled face full of anger.

"Get the fuck out! I'm not getting killed over a fare!"

Bryce unzipped his backpack and took out a handful of money.

"It's yours, man, all of it. Just get me to..."

Bryce heard a crash and flew into the taxi shield, smashing his face against the Plexiglas. He fell back into his seat dazed, his ears ringing from the explosion of the airbag. The passenger door opposite him flew off the hinges, and a man in a black coat, black hat, and feral eyes reached in and grabbed him by the collar. Bryce's response was automatic; he reached into his back pocket, pulled out his straight razor, and slashed, cutting the man's wrists and neck in one fluid motion. The man howled as he fell back. Bryce reached back and opened the opposite door. He fell into the street; someone lifted him to his feet.

"You cut my friend," the man said. Bryce was suddenly airborne, landing on the curb.

"Stop," another man said. "We need him alive until we find out what he knows."

Bryce rolled onto his back. The man was coming for him. He was dressed like other man, possessing the same catlike eyes. The man reached for him then jerked, a fountain of blood spewing from his hat.

"You wrecked my cab!" the driver shouted. He held a Glock in his trembling hands. He was spinning to his left when he was engulfed in white light, his body shaking and smoldering. The light dissipated and the driver collapsed in a smoking heap. Bryce looked to his right. A tall, pale man with red hair stood a few feet away from the driver, his glowing fingers smoking. The man looked at Bryce with a frigid grin and started for him.

He was impeded by another cat-eyed man. The man spoke in a language Bryce didn't understand; the red-headed man frowned.

"Let's go," he said. He stared at Bryce for a moment, his fingertips glowing as he raised his hands. A siren wailed in the distance; the man lowered his hands and walked quickly to his dead companion. He lifted him like a broken doll, tossing him into the FX45. His companion appeared with the man Bryce had sliced and threw him inside as well. They jumped into the SUV and sped away.

Bryce didn't have time to process what happened. The police were coming. He staggered to the taxi for his backpack, stuffing it into his heist pouch. He stripped off his clothes and donned Ghost, disappearing as Atlanta's Finest exited off the highway.

-6-

Kandace took a long drag on her joint, bobbing her head to Janelle Monáe while DNA sequences mutated and twisted before her glazed eyes. Beyond the screen, a vat of nucleic acids simmered, prodded by minute changes in temperature. It was simple, but then again, it wasn't. Genetic engineering was almost like cooking with calculus. The thought and the joint made her burst out laughing. The laughter stopped when the new genetic codes emerged on the screen. Molecules twisted and turned in unfamiliar patterns, forming paths that almost blew her high. This was brilliance, engineering far beyond anything Bryce ever dreamed up. She realized her partner was an amateur compared to whoever developed the sequences spinning before her.

Her iPhone pulsed in her pocket, and she read the text.

GET GONE.

"Damn it, Bryce, what you done got into this time?" Kandace didn't budge. If Bryce was in trouble, he'd be coming to her. Their lab was in the safest place in the A, deep within an abandoned industrial complex and protected by the best thugs money could buy. They didn't realize that the money they took was probably theirs, but they didn't ask. If the guns didn't scare anybody off, the smell did. Genetic engineering was a funky process, literally.

It was almost time. Kandace struggled out of her chair and staggered to the edge of the pool. The skin was taking shape, its crinkled form rising from the muck. She had no idea what it would be capable of; Bryce fed her the formula this time, so she had to trust him. Thinking of Bryce reminded her he hadn't shown up yet. It had been at least an hour since he called. Bryce was never late. Suddenly, her high was gone. She paced, rubbing her hands together.

"He's in real trouble, which means I am too!"

She ran back to the control board. Thirty more minutes before the skin was ready. She slipped into the back room and changed into a pair of baggy jeans, big shirt, huge jacket, and a Braves hat. She was going butch for the next few days until she found out what was going on with Bryce. She reached into the back of the closet and took out a backpack heavy with bills. Farther in the back was her P90. She secured it under her jacket and trotted back to the pool. The skin was as ready as it was going to be. She took it out, her nose crinkling with the smell, then stuffed it in a small plastic bag. It took her fifteen minutes to dump the pool and shut the lab down. Her thugs appeared as she emerged from the steel door.

"Here." She handed them a backpack. "Nobody comes in here unless they're with me. There's another one for you when I get back."

They took the bag and stepped aside. Kandace rambled down the metal staircase and disappeared into

-7-

Leif Thorvaldsen looked out the canopy of the private chopper as it descended on the platform surrounded by stunted evergreens. He hated Albania but understood the logic in locating Vanguard headquarters in the decrepit country. As the poorest country in Europe, the government was easy to persuade and eager to ignore anything that seemed questionable.

He glanced to the rear of the chopper. Two body bags filled the small space. His surviving assassin watched over them, his face showing little emotion. This was a botched operation, two prototypes dead and nothing to show for it. There would have to be modifications.

The chopper landed and was met by a military-style truck with no markings. Two men in Vanguard security uniforms ran out to meet them.

"Sir," one said to Leif. "Mr. Constantinides wishes to see you immediately."

"I'm sure he does," Leif replied. "I brought the bodies back. Take them to the lab for autopsies and genetic analysis."

The man glanced at the remaining assassin. "What about him?"

Leif looked at the surviving assassin and frowned. "He's defective like the others. Dispose of him."

No sooner than he gave the order did the other man extract a handgun from his jacket and shoot the assassin in the head. Leif nodded and went to the truck. Another vehicle emerged from the woods, a black Hummer with chrome wheels. Leif entered and was taken immediately to Vanguard HQ. The squat grey building hid under clump of old oak trees surrounded by a triple barbed-wire fence. Observation towers rested at fifty-foot intervals. The facility resembled a prison, and in a way it was.

After an extensive security check, they entered the compound. The Hummer worked around the main building to another building in the rear, a two-story structure that resembled a traditional office. Lucy Lundy, Leif's assistant, met him at the door.

"How did it go?"

"Terrible. I need you to pull up the genetic sequencing on my computer. Ask Himmel and Stryker to link up as well."

"Modifications?"

Leif glared at Lucy, and she took a step back. She was brilliant, but sometimes she angered him with her naive questions.

"I'll see to it right away, sir," she said and hurried away.

Stephan Constantinides, a rotund, olive-skinned man with fading black hair, was waiting at his desk when Leif entered his office.

"What the hell, happened, Leif?" he snapped.

Leif sat before answering. "The prototypes failed."

"You failed," Stephen corrected.

Leif ignored the jab. "The prototypes performed well physically. The problem is mental capacity. We need to increase their decision abilities."

"That will make them more difficult to control."

"If we plan on using them as assassins, it's a risk we'll have to take."

Stephan leaned back in his chair. "Maybe we could implant a destruct module."

"We would have to."

"What about the man who escaped?"

Leif frowned. "He seems to be a man used to trouble. He had a plan, which caught us off guard. I contacted our inside people. Apparently, he has a friend that recently resigned from deep intel. We've informed the friend of Bryce's situation. We expect him to lead us to him."

"Don't screw up," Stephan warned.

"We won't. We'll be using normals on this operation."

"I want you there personally."

Leif nodded. "Of course."

Stephan waved him away. Leif held his composure until he was out of the office, then his hands began to smolder. Of course he would go on the operation. He had a score to settle with this Bryce character.

-8-

Bryce sauntered down the cargo-ship gangplank, his relaxed gait disguising his fear. His eyes darted back and forth as he searched for anything suspicious. He managed a laugh as his feet touched the concrete. He was home, but not the way he imagined it. He dreamed of stepping out of first class to the admiration of his relatives, a rude boy done good. Instead, he was slinking back incognito, hiding from whoever it was trying to kill him. It was just the way his grandma told him it would be.

The docks swarmed with people, but the three he expected stood out among the rest. They were dressed simply: blue jeans and T-shirts, each shirt representing a different American baseball team. They wore shades, their dreads spilling from under their baseball caps. The tallest of the three walked up to Bryce and shoved him.

"So, you come back now, huh, cousin?" he said.

Bryce shoved him back. "Yeah, me come back."

"What trouble you got?"

"Deep trouble."

His cousin grinned. "I guess you need to go deep, then?"

Bryce nodded. "As deep as I can."

"No problem." The men turned and walked away, Bryce trailing behind. They led him to a battered Toyota extended cab. Bryce climbed into the cab with his cousin. The other two jumped in the truck bed.

"Grandma said you'd come back like this."

"Shut up, Nathan," Bryce barked. "Where you taking me?"

"To the countryside, up into the mountains. I got some Maroon friends who will keep you company for a while."

"I need you to do something else for me." Bryce gave Nathan a piece of paper.

"He's a friend of mine. Tell him where I am. When he gets here, bring him to me."

Nathan looked at the paper. "I don't know, cousin. If he ain't blood, you can't trust him."

"Just call him. He's the only one that can get me out of this."

Nathan shook his head. "You must be in some deep shit."

Bryce rubbed his forehead. "Yeah, cousin, I am."

The black Lexus SC400 cut across eight lanes and streaked up the West Peachtree exit. Five cars spun as the car zipped down the one-way street the wrong way, then cut over to Spring. The wild drive ended at the parking lot of the W, the young valet dropping and shaking his head, his dreads swishing from side to side.

Kandace stepped out of the Lexus in an outfit that labeled her either an actress or a stripper. The valet's humor was shut down by his hormones.

"Damn, girl! How much?"

"Shut the fuck up and park my car," she spat.

The valet shook his head. "Why you got to be like that, K?"

"Because I can. Now park my damn ride."

Kandace strutted through the entrance, happy with the commotion she was causing. After three weeks waiting for Bryce to contact her, she figured he was in too deep. Whoever was looking for him was probably looking for her, too. But she wasn't about to spend the last days of her life hiding in the hood. If she was going out, she was going out right. She jumped on the elevator with a tall young brother sporting an indigo silk suit. She'd seen him a few times in the building, and now he was seeing her. Every inch of her. He looked her up and down a few times and frowned.

"A little over the top, don't you think?"

Kandace grinned. "You criticizing me and you don't even know my name."

"Kandace, I believe," the brother said. "My name is Jaleel."

"Well, Jaleel, I was about to ask you to come by tonight for a drink, but since you think I'm over the top, I'm sure you wouldn't want me on top."

Jaleel grinned. "I can always make exceptions."

"I bet you can."

Kandace stepped off the elevator. "Nine o'clock. Take your vitamins."

The first thing Kandace did when she entered the room was check her cell. She didn't know why; maybe from force of habit. There were no calls. Bryce was still MIA. The second thing she did was go into the hall bathroom to check on the skin. It hung over the bathtub, swaying with the air-conditioning flow.

"I might as well," she said. She stripped off her clothes and donned the skin. It hung loose for a moment, then slowly fitted itself tight against her skin. She felt like she had a bag over her head, then the feeling dissipated. But the real shock hit her when she looked into the mirror. She was invisible.

"Damn," she whispered. She reached out at the blank mirror and a bolt jumped from her fingers. The glass shattered.

"What the hell?" A wave of fatigue hit her; she was suddenly famished. She peeled the skin off and stumbled naked into the kitchen in a desperate search for food.

"This skin ain't right," she said as she dumped a box of corn flakes onto a plate and ate with her hands.

"This ain't right."

-9-

The cargo plane landed with a thud on the dirt runway, miles away from the tourist destination of Montego Bay. Malik jostled in his seat, but his expression didn't change. He was destroying his life for a friend. He could still see the look on Tisha's face when announced he was leaving and refused to tell her where he was going, why he was going, and how long he would be gone. The words that spewed from her mouth were meant to hurt, and they did. His response was clichéd.

"Trust me, baby," he said. Even he didn't believe the words when he said them.

The cargo plane taxied to a stop before a tin building. Malik gathered his things, then walked toward the cabin. The pilot, a scruffy-looking red-faced German, looked back at him with a sly smile.

"Should I wait?" he asked.

"No. I have another ride," Malik replied.

"All you have to do is make it worth my while," the man said with a wink.

Malik sneered. "If I see your plane here five minutes after I leave, I'll come back and kill you with my bare hands."

He reached into the duffle, took out a stack, then tossed it at the pilot.

He went to the rear of the plane and climbed out. The pilot was off the ground and gaining altitude before Malik reached the shed.

"I'll be taking that from you now," someone said.

Three men emerged from behind the shed, guns in their hands. They wore jeans and T-shirts, their heads crowned with dreads. The man in the middle, a short, wide man with bulging muscles, stepped toward them.

"Drop the bag and put your hands behind your back,' he ordered.

"This is a shitty way to treat a friend," Malik remarked as he did what he was told.

"You're Bryce's friend, not mine," the man replied.

One of the other men stepped behind him and tied his hands together. The other came with a blindfold.

"Come on," Malik said. "Really?"

"Shut your mouth," the short man said. The lanky man tied the black fabric over his eyes. They led him to a vehicle, then hoisted him into the back. He lay on a bed of straw.

Malik didn't know exactly where he was, but he knew which direction they traveled. He was trained to know such things, but his captors didn't know. They headed west, following a winding road that climbed into the highlands. They were either headed to Maroon country or somewhere near. Bryce was making a good try at not being found.

The truck halted after two hours. Malik heard the truck door clang.

"C'mon, boy," the short man said. "My cousin been waiting for you."

Malik slid to the edge of the truck and was helped to the ground. His hands were freed and his blindfold removed. He stood in the middle of a camp surrounded by marijuana fields. There were four buildings, one serving as some type of office while the others were warehouses for the illicit harvest.

"Man, I ain't never been happier to see you!"

Bryce ran to him from the office and they bear-hugged.

"I didn't think you was gonna come," he said.

"I may have lost my marriage over you," Malik said. "But we're boys, so I'm here."

"Come on in, man," Bryce said. "You must be tired."

The office was neat and orderly despite its remote location. Bryce was a stickler for organization. A man with secrets had to be organized to remember them all.

Bryce sat in a huge chair, then lit a blunt.

"I'm in some deep shit, bruh. Some real deep shit."

"So, what's new?" Malik replied.

Bryce extended the blunt to Malik, but Malik waved him away.

"I figured it must be serious. I've never seen you run from a jealous husband."

Bryce shook his head. "I wish that was all it was. I think it's got something to do with my job."

Malik sat up. "What did you do, Bryce?"

"I was working late and came across something that was interesting. I downloaded it."

Malik was puzzled. "You work for a mom-and-pop lab. The worst they can do is fire you."

Bryce laughed. "They couldn't even do that. I'm the brains of that place. Fire me and you might as well lock the doors. But we do work for some heavy hitters. I think I might have taken something from one of them and they ain't happy about it."

"What happened, Bryce?"

"I was on my way home and got jumped by some weird shit."

"What's that supposed to mean?"

Bryce took another toke. "It means just that. I don't know they were men or dogs or what. All I know they were strong as hell and trying to kill me."

Malik scratched his head. "This has something to do with genetics."

Bryce nodded.

"Look, Malik, I figured you could look 'em up, then threaten them to leave me alone."

Malik cursed the day he let Bryce know his profession.

"It doesn't work that way, Bryce. I can't just terrify folks just because you're in trouble."

Bryce seemed distracted.

"Shit, I need something to drink. Clarence!"

Bryce assumed that was his cousin's name.

"Clarence!"

"Look, Bryce, I …"

Bryce stood up then stormed by Malik. He was pissed, no doubt about it.

He pushed the door open then turned to face Malik.

"Why you come here? Huh, Malik? You come all this way to tell me you can't help me?"

Malik walked outside.

"Look, man. I'm…"

He saw Bryce's cousin lying behind him in a pool of blood.

"Bryce, get back in!"

"What are you talking about, fool?"

Bryce's head exploded into flesh and bones. Malik was running into the building when something hot streaked across his forehead and threw him inside. He hit the ground hard on his back, slamming his head into the floor. His world was heat and stars just before he passed out.

When he finally came back to the world, his head throbbed, light flashing in his head with each pulse. He couldn't move; his eyes were open, but he couldn't see. He didn't know how long he lay there until his sight returned. The building was black except for a faint beam of light entering through an open window. He moved his head and pain flashed, but he was determined to move. He slid his hands to his sides, then pushed himself upright, his eyes clenched to the pain. He touched his head; the wound had stopped bleeding, the blood caked over the crease.

Malik grabbed the door, then stood. Bryce lay before him, his head destroyed.

Malik opened the door, then stumbled to the nearby building. He needed a weapon, something to defend himself. He opened the door, revealing stacks of weed. He searched it from corner to corner but found nothing. From there he went to the next building, searching it as well as he could. He paused, sitting hard as his head spun, making him nauseous. He was about to continue his search when he heard voices.

"Make sure they're dead!" the voice said. "Every last one of them."

He had to escape. If he killed any of these men, whoever sent them would know the job was not complete. He eased to the ground, then crawled across the ground into the nearby foliage. Malik continued to crawl deeper, flinching every time he heard a shot. They were shooting everyone again to make sure the job was complete.

"Burn it," he heard someone say.

Malik continued to crawl away. The sound of crashing wood was replaced by the roar of a huge fire. As he reached the top of the wooded hill, he dared to look back. The entire compound was in flames. Malik took a hard look at every person involved. He wanted to remember every face so there would be no doubt in his mind when he hunted them down and killed them. One man stood out, tall with sickly white skin, gray eyes, and red hair. Malik couldn't be sure, but it looked as if his hands glowed.

Malik faded into the brush. He had to find out what the hell Bryce had done to bring a high-level hit down on him. This wasn't underworld; this had the precision of a military operation. The only way he could find out more would be to reopen old contacts. He'd be reneging on a promise, but he had no choice.

"Damn you, Bryce," he whispered. "Damn you to hell!"

-10-

Kandace checked her phone again as the RV pulled into Smit's Garage. It had been two weeks, but still no word from Bryce. He told her to run, but he didn't tell her what the hell she was running from.

"That's your baby," the man standing next to her said. "I told you it was sweet."

Tamarious's hand brushed her ass. She elbowed him hard in the ribs.

"Shit, girl!" he said through his clenched teeth.

"Watch your damn hands," Kandace said. "I paid you, and money is all you gonna get. Unless you make me shoot your ass."

"Aight, aight," Tamarious said as he rubbed his side. "She'll be ready in two weeks."

"Two weeks? Mothafucka, you told me one week!"

"I lied," he replied. "Really, though, we had some parts come in late. Ain't never done a mod like this one."

"Well, hurry up," Kandace said. "I got places to be."

"Where you trying to go?"

"None of your damn business. Just fix the bus."

"Aight, aight."

Kandace was striding back to her car when her phone played Bryce's song. She pressed the phone to her ear.

"It's about damn time! Where the hell you at?"

There was silence for a moment.

"Who is this?" the unfamiliar voice asked.

Kandace pulled away from the phone, her face crinkled.

"Who is this?" she asked.

"Are you Kandace?" the man asked.

"Look, I don't know what's going on, but if you stole my boy's phone..."

"Shut up and listen to me very carefully. Bryce is dead. The people who killed him are coming after you. If you want to stay alive, you'll meet me as soon as possible."

"Bullshit!" Kandace said. "I'm off the grid. I don't need no help."

"Yes, you do. If you don't come to me, I'll come to you."

"Try it," she said. She dropped the phone on the pavement, then stomped it to pieces.

Kandace marched back to Tamarious's office.

"Change of plans; I need that bus right now."

Tamarious took off his headphones. "Really? I'm still fleshing out the interior. Wait till you see the bed!"

Kandace tossed the backpack on his desk. "Here's the rest of the money. Give me the keys now."

Tamarious unzipped the back, then took out a handful of hundreds.

"I need to count this," he said.

Kandace whipped out her P90.

"Give me the goddamn keys!"

"Shit!"

Tamarious tossed Kandace the keys. She scrambled into the cab, started the RV, then barreled out of the parking lot, side-swiping two cars along the way. She didn't give a shit. She was sure Bryce was dead and whoever killed him was coming for her. She would head west; yes, that was what she would do. She had no family out there, so no one would know to look for her. As soon as she was settled, she'd change her hair, change her clothes, then leave the country. She had enough money to lie low for a few years and let things settle, whatever things were. Or so she hoped.

"Fuck you, Bryce," she yelled. "Fuck you!"

Malik watched the RV careen out of Smit's Garage, into the street, then onto Interstate 20. He stuck his phone into his pocket and pulled down his helmet visor. He knew the call would cause her to panic and run. He started his Harley, then eased into traffic. There was no reason to hurry; the RV was as conspicuous as cherry in a bowl of milk. As he exited onto the highway, he felt his phone vibrate against his thigh. A wave of guilt caused him to shudder. It was either Tisha or Sheryl, and he couldn't speak to either one. He'd called Sheryl as soon as he got out of Jamaica and asked her to trace Kandace's phone. When Sheryl asked why, he wouldn't give her any details. Sheryl did it anyway but made him promise to fill her in as soon as he confirmed the threat. Tisha was a deeper matter. Someone had tried to kill him, and when they discovered he was still alive, they would try to kill him again…or someone he loved. He had to find out who had killed Bryce and why before they discovered he was still alive.

He trailed the vehicle for ninety miles before it exited in Oxford, Alabama. Malik followed it to a hotel parking lot, then watched Kandace scurry into the hotel. He cruised up to the RV; it took him five seconds to unlock the door, then climb inside. He settled behind the driver's seat, then waited. Moments later, the door opened and Kandace climbed in.

"Shit!" she said. "That damn bathroom was nasty as shit!"

Malik reached around the chair then grabbed Kandace's throat.

"Motha…"

Her voice faded as she fell unconscious. Malik eased her out of the seat, tied her hands and legs, then propped her up in the passenger seat. He found the key in her bag, then hurried outside to his bike. He wiped it clean, then re-entered the van. Before he could get in, two feet smashed into his face. He fell out of the van and his head struck the pavement hard. He lay stunned for a moment, then sat up, shaking his head.

"Help! Help!" Kandace screamed. "This motherfucka is trying to kidnap me! Help!"

Malik climbed into the van again, anticipating the same attack. He wasn't disappointed. He dodged the kick, then caught Kandace's legs under the knees. He flipped her into the space between the seats. As he sat in the driver's seat again, he pulled out his gun.

"Stop moving or I'll kill you."

Kandace struggled to sit up.

"Bullshit! You gonna kill me no matter what I do! Just like you killed Bryce."

Malik lowered his gun. "I didn't kill Bryce. If I had come to kill you, you'd be dead already."

"How do I know? I don't know who the fuck you are," Kandace spat back.

"I'm a friend. Someone he knew much longer than you," Malik said. "So, what are you to Bryce?" Malik asked.

"A business associate," Kandace said.

"What kind of business?"

Kandace sat up, then grinned. "So, you his boy and you don't know?"

"No," Malik said. "All I know is that whatever it was made him run to Jamaica and get killed."

Kandace's smirk faded. "Bryce was a thief."

Malik sat silent for a moment, letting the words sink in. "What kind of thief?"

"Bryce had this kinda Robin Hood shit going on. He stole from the rich and gave to himself."

"What rich?"

"Drug dealers, mostly."

"So, what part did you play in this?"

"I scoped out his hits. I also kept the gear in shape."

Malik looked puzzled. "What gear?"

Kandace hesitated. Malik raised his gun.

"What gear?"

"It's in the back," she said.

"Show me."

Kandace rolled her eyes. "My goddamn legs are tied."

"Hop," Malik said.

Kandace glared at Malik as she stood, then hopped to the rear of the RV.

"In there," she said, gesturing with her head. "He calls it Ghost."

Malik shoved her to the floor, then opened the door. A grin came to his face as he looked inside the room.

"A stealth suit," he said.

"What you know about that?" Kandace said.

"More than you realize," he answered. The agency was testing prototypes. Apparently, Bryce had figured it out. Which was probably why he was killed.

"So, who killed him?" Kandace said. "I figured one of the drug boys figured things out."

Malik stepped into the room to inspect the suit.

"It wasn't a drug hit," Malik replied. "Too professional. I'll bet money it had something to do with this suit. Bryce had to steal some deep tech to make this. Whoever he stole it from killed him. And now they're looking for you."

"You ain't them?" Kandace said.

Malik came out the room with the suit.

"No. Like I said, Bryce was my friend. I'm going to find out who did this and why."

"And what about me?"

"I don't know."

Malik stepped into the room.

"Don't go anywhere," he said.

"Fuck you," Kandace replied.

Malik closed the door, then took off his clothes. He and Bryce were about the same build, so the suit slipped on easily. There was mesh where his eyes and nose were located, which allowed for easy breathing. He looked into the mirror; the suit's construction reflected light in a way that made him invisible, at least visually. Malik was about to take off the suit when he felt a slick secretion flow between the suit and his skin. It was immediately followed by the sensation of a million tiny needles pricking his skin. He hurriedly unzipped the suit and began taking off. By the time he was done, he was exhausted and bleeding all over. He wiped himself off before dressing, then opened the door.

Kandace grinned.

"You put it on, didn't you?"

Malik nodded.

"Felt like it was eating you?"

Malik shook his head. "Bio-attachment. This is some real advanced tech. I wonder where Bryce got it."

"From work," Kandace said. "He called one day, excited about some modification he wanted to make. Gave me the formulation."

"So, you're a scientist?"

Kandace grinned. "A biologist, to be exact. Master's in microbiology. Don't let all this fool you."

Malik looked over Kandace with new respect. He'd let his prejudices get in the way. He thought at the least, Kandace was Bryce's lookout, at the most, another one of his conquests. However, there were more pertinent questions. Why was Gentech developing this type of tech? Most importantly, who were they developing it for?

"I need to make a call," he said. He took out his phone and dialed Sheryl. To Malik's surprise, she answered him immediately.

"Malik, get off this line. Your friend was in some real deep shit. Get another phone and call Moses."

The line went dead. A tightness formed in Malik's stomach. What he feared was probably true.

He untied Kandace. She immediately tried to hit him; he blocked the blow, then wrapped her in a painful strangle hold.

"Listen to me carefully," he said. "Both of our lives are in extreme danger. If you want to survive, you'll stay with me until I figure this all out. If not, I'll let you go and walk away. Do you understand?"

Kandace nodded. Malik let her go and she rubbed her neck.

"You're not going to kill me?" she asked.

"No," Malik said. "Bryce dragged us both into this in his own selfish way."

"So, what do we do?" Kandace said.

"We follow your plan. We head west until I hear from my contact."

Kandace climbed into the driver's seat. Malik took the passenger's seat, tucking his gun in his holster as he sat. Kandace started the RV, then drove to the I-20 exit. As they entered the highway, Malik tried to understand how this was happening. The life he had planned was now on hold until he could figure out this mystery. He was on assignment now; he blocked Tisha and the girls out of his mind. There was no future now, only the mission. He looked at Kandace.

"So, tell me about Ghost," he said.

To be continued . . .

SPYFUNK DOSSIER

The Agents

John F. Allen

John F. Allen is an American author born in Indianapolis, IN. He is a founding and active member of the Speculative Fiction Guild, and a faculty member of the Indiana Writers Center. John began writing early in his childhood and has pursued various forms of writing throughout his career. He studied Liberal Arts at IUPUI with a focus in Creative Writing. John's best-selling, debut novel, The God Killers was published in 2013, followed by a spin-off novella series titled, Codename: Knight Ranger.

John's short stories have been featured in such acclaimed collections as Thunder on the Battlefield: Sword Volume One, Trajectories and Black Pulp II. Some of which are featured in his best-selling collection, The Best is Yet to Come. He also penned the novelization of respected screenwriter, Demetrius Witherspoon's short film, Submerge: Echo 51.

Eugen Bacon

Eugen Bacon is an African Australian author of several novels and fiction collections, and lives in Melbourne. Her recent books *Ivory's Story*, *Danged Black*

Thing and *Saving Shadows* are finalists in the British Science Fiction Association Awards. Eugen was announced in the honor list of the 2022 Otherwise Fellowships for 'doing exciting work in gender and speculative fiction'. She has won, or been commended in international awards, including the Aurealis Award, Foreword Indies, Bridport Prize, Copyright Agency Prize, Horror Writers Association Diversity Grant, Otherwise, Rhysling, Elgin, Australian Shadows, Ditmar Awards and Nommo Awards for Speculative Fiction by Africans. New books: *Mage of Fools* (novel), *Chasing Whispers* (collection) and *An Earnest Blackness* (collection). Visit her website at eugenbacon.com and Twitter at @EugenBacon

Jeff Carroll

Jeff Carroll is a writer, comic book creator and filmmaker. He is pioneering what he calls Hip Hop horror, Sci/fi, and fantasy. His stories always have lots of action and a social edge. He has written and produced 6 films, several comic books and over 15 science fiction and nonfiction books. His short stories have appeared in The Black Science Fiction Society's anthology and their magazine as well as other anthologies. Jeff produces The Monster Panel a traveling sci-fi panel which features writers of color in a lively discussion of comic books, movies and Black people. His comic book series Horror Streetz features a variety of black horror stories. He has written in novel, film and comic books.

Jeff Carroll social mediaCheck out his
books at https://www.amazon.com/Jeff-Car-
roll/e...
And his comics at http://hhcnf.blog-
spot.com/?m=1
Check out his vlog
https://youtube.com/playlist?list=PLzu38aVm
XV0QJfHFOz-MxGdUXSRz4iWy7
Instagram coachyojeff
Facebook coachyojeff

Milton J. Davis

Milton Davis is an award winning Black
Speculative fiction author and owner of
MVmedia, LLC, a publishing company special-
izing in Science Fiction and Fantasy based
on African/African Diaspora history, culture, and traditions. Milton is the author
of twenty-one novels and short story collections and editor/coeditor of ten anthologies. His short stories have appeared in
several anthologies and magazines, most no-
tably Black Panther: Tales of Wakanda,
Slay: Stories of the Vampire Noire, Obsid-
ian Literature and Arts in the African Diaspora and Tales from the Magician's Skull.
Milton's story 'The Swarm' was nominated
for the 2017 British Science Fiction Association Award for Short Fiction and his
story, Carnival, was nominated for the 2020
British Science Fiction Association Award
for Short Fiction. He is a recipient of the
2022 East Coast Black Age of Comics Convention Pioneer Lifetime Achievement Award.

Keith Gaston

Keith Gaston is an author of thrillers and
speculative fiction novels. His books

include The Friday House, the Tease, Joe
Hooks and Taurus Moon series. He also enjoys collaborating novels such as Blood &
Vengeance and A Bitter Pill to Swallow. Recently Keith Gaston has ventured into writing comics and has published his first
comic book: PANTHEON: Escape. Born and
raised in Detroit he often uses the city as
a backdrop to many of his stories. When not
writing, he can be found watching old action, science fiction or mystery films.

Joe Hilliard

Writer. Luddite. Teller of Tales. Michigan-
der by birth, in the wilds just outside the
World's Largest Walled Prison. Misspent
teenage years in Los Angeles on a diet of
Blue Demon, Chester Himes, Philip K. Dick,
the Circle Jerks, Judge Dredd, and This Island Earth, on the fringe of 80s Hollywood.
Graduate of the University of Michigan,
which only added Kawabata, Tsui Hark, Krazy
Kat, and William S. Burroughs to the mix.
Marks time as a paralegal in sunny California.

His short stories can be found in *DIE-
SELFUNK!* from MVmedia, THE LEGENDS OF NEW
PULP from Airship 27, HARD-BOILED SPORTS,
SHUDDER PULP, JAMES R. TUCK'S HEROES OF
HOLLOW EARTH, and ORIGINS AND ENDINGS VOL-
UME 1 from Pro Se Productions; AUTUMN
PAINTED RED from Asylum Ink; MEAT FOR TEA:
THE VALLEY REVIEW; and BLUE COLLAR REVIEW.
His non-fiction comic book work can be
found in APB: ARTISTS AGAINST POLICE BRU-
TALITY from Rosarium Press and COLONIAL

COMICS VOLUME II: NEW ENGLAND 1750-1776
from Fulcrum Publishing.

William J. Jackson

William J. Jackson is a Black, Nanticoke
Native and white indie author of punk fic-
tion from the rural worlds of Sussex
County, Delaware and Salem County, New Jer-
sey. He typically merges superhumans with
alternate history, and the prejudices such
beings endure, to explore the many dreaded
Isms of real life.
Facebook: @author_wjj
Twitter/Instagram/Tiktok: @railroadcity

Tiara Janté

Tiara Janté is a Locus Award-winning author, journalist, and national bestselling
ghostwriter. She specializes in writing
character-driven stories that weave the
fantasticism of speculative fiction with
the realities of the Black experience. Her
characters reflect the authentic and multi-
layered dimensions of Black people and
their experiences in America. A staunch ad-
vocate for the ownership of Black content,
Tiara is also a co-founder of Black Is The
Standard, a social network that centers
Blackness and promotes freedom of digital
expression for members of the Black community. Follow her on all social media:
@iamtiarajante or visit her websites
at www.tiarajante.net and www.black-
isthestandard.com.

B.J. Jones (Most Secret Spy)

B.J. Jones is an attorney, business con-
sultant, writer, artist, community activist, minister, and mom. She is C.E.O. of
Griot Arts Media. Her books "A Call to
Gather" and "Zion Hill" are available on
Amazon.com. She is a NFT artist, active as
an Administrator in the FB writing, film,
and faith communities. Her short film
script "Right Place. Right Time." won Hon-
orable Mention in the Orlando Urban Film
Festival (2017). The film is forthcoming.
B.J. Jones is a graduate of Georgetown University School of Foreign Service and
Georgetown University Law Center. Online:
GriotArtsMedia.com Bjjonesartist.com FB:
B.J. Jones Twitter: @walkinginpower I.G.:
b.j._jones

Balogun Ojetade

Balogun is Master Instructor and Technical
Director of the *Afrikan Martial Arts Institute* and Co-Chair/Founder of *Blacktasticon*,
the largest gathering of Black science fiction and fantasy creators and fans in the
South.
He is the author of 42 bestselling fiction
and nonfiction books and gamebooks, contributing co-editor of three anthologies: *Ki: Khanga: The
Anthology*, *Steamfunk* and *Dieselfunk* and
contributing editor of the *Rococoa* anthology and *Black Power: The Superhero Anthology*, Director and Fight Choreographer of
the feature film, *A Single Link*, the short
films, *Rite of Passage: Initiation* and *The

Dentist of Westminster; and the music video *Forward Motion* and co-author of the award winning screenplay, *Ngolo;* co-creator of *Ki Khanga: The Sword and Soul Role-Playing Game*, creator of the comic book series *Jagunjagun Lewa* and co-creator of the graphic novel series, *Ngolo*.

Russell A. Smith

A London-born author who writes within multiple universes and genres, some you'll know well, some you won't, Russell is a historian, regular podcast guest, gamer and pop culture enthusiast who still spends far too much time watching videos on cats, wrestling and cars he will never own.
Web: projectshadowlondon.com
Twitter: @RASmithPSL

Guy Sims

Guy Sims has authored two of the earliest publication on the subject of Kwanzaa. The first was the *Kwanzaa Handbook* (1981) and the second; *The Kwanzaa Kids Learn the Seven Principles* (1984). An avid poet and writer of short fiction, Guy has completed a collection of new American Tall Tales, *Rife Powers, and Other Too Tall Tales*, and a critically acclaimed novel *Living Just A Little* (2013).

He is also the head writer for the Brotherman: Dictator of Discipline comic book series and the companion novellas, *The Cold Hard Cases of Duke Denim: #1-Hold'em Close* (2013), *#2-Silver Roses* (2014), *#3-High Notes, Low Blows* (2014), *#4-The*

Troublesome Troupe (2016) #5-Field of Head-stones (2017), #6 Old College Try (2018), and #7 Muttin But The Best (2020).

In 2016, he authored the graphic novel, Brotherman Revelation with his illustrator brother, Dawud Anyabwile. Sims also wrote the graphic novel adaptation of Walter Dean Myers' award-winning youth novel, Monster (Harper-Collins, 2015).

He is the recipient of Best Story for Brotherman: Revelation graphic novel from the East Coast Black Age of Comics Convention

He has also received recognition from the Junior Library Guild Selection for the graphic novel adaptation of Walter Dean Myers' novel, Monster.

Guy A. Sims is a native of and resides in Philadelphia, PA.

Rodney Turner

Rodney Turner is a Baltimore based writer and co-host of the long-running podcast, Microphones of Madness. His weird fiction has appeared in Resonator: New Lovecraftian Tales From Beyond and A Breath From The Sky: Unusual Stories of Possession. Rodney also publishes free-to-read stories at www.microphonesofmadness.com. When not writing or working on the podcast, you can usually find him playing Go, painting toy soldiers, or being a general menace.

Dennis R. Upkins

Dennis R. Upkins is a speculative fiction author, digital artist, model, activist, journalist, and a lifelong comic book herald. His first two YA novels, Hollowstone and West of Sunset, were released through Parker Publishing. Both Upkins and his previous work have been featured in Harvard Political Law, Bitch Media, MTV News, Mental Health Matters, Nerds of Color, Prism Comics, Comicbookdotcom, Geeks OUT, Black Power: The Superhero Anthology, The Connect Magazine, OUTvoices, Yoppvoices, Sniplits, and Spyfunk: Anthology. When he isn't busy working (which is almost never) he enjoys raising money and donating to notable charities such as the St. Jude's Hospital, the Warrior Wounded Project, Black Lives Matter, and Youth PRIDE. A compulsive high performing overachiever, The personal mantra for Upkins can be summed up in four simple words: Be Your Own Superhero.

https://dennisupkins.wordpress.com

Napoleon Wells

Napoleon Wells is a Clinical Psychologist, Professor and author of Black Speculative Fiction. He focuses on stories that center Black lives, mythologies and experiences. His works tend to incorporate the Psychology of Black/African experience across the diaspora as a means of building rich, fully realized frameworks for stories centered on Black heroes, villains and worlds. He believes that the erasure and exclusion of

Black existence from many genres can be directly and necessarily defeated by the stories being brilliantly told by Black Griots and artists. He builds stories based on the magnificent reality of Black futurism which he already sees in daily life. If he isn't busy writing something strange and beautiful, he is likely treating patients, writing a social justice column or watching a rap battle. You can find and follow him on social media at: https://napoleonwellsphd.medium.com, https://www.instagram.com/napoleontheblerdpsychologist, https://twitter.com/napoleonbxsith.